# CELESTIAL FIRE

THE CELESTIAL MARKED SERIES: BOOK TWO

EMMA L. ADAMS

To be notified when Emma L. Adams's next novel is released and get a free prequel short story, *Celestial Hunted*, sign up to her author newsletter.

1

———

Vampires. Creatures of darkness and fear, and also terrible manners, outdated dress sense and a fairly bland taste in decor. Also, zero concept of housekeeping. I crept across the floor of the vampire's lair—or rather, house—trying not to breathe in too much dust. Rachel, the first warlock I'd befriended, had added a stealth option to my gravity-defying shoes, but a dust repellent and a light would be more useful at the moment. Since light would wake the vampires, however, I had to rely on my other senses to find my way around the house. I had reasonable confidence he wasn't in this room, but like any vampire abode during daylight hours, every window and door was sealed to prevent the tiniest speck of sunlight from entering the house. *This wasn't your best idea, Devi.*

I carried a handmade magic detector around my neck, set to vibrate when I got close to my source. A regular demon detector would make too much noise. Somewhere here was a collection of bloodstones infused with demonic magic—a highly illegal magical item, newly on the market thanks to a fire-wielding warlock from another realm who'd decided to recruit the local vampires by giving them blood infused with demon magic. When they infected celestial soldiers with that venom, they'd died. Horribly. And even though I'd destroyed one nest, calls like the one the warlocks had this morning came in every other week.

The smell of blood—fresh and old—filled my nostrils as I re-entered the hall. Ugh. Vampire houses weren't the most hygienic places. My feet found the lower step of a staircase, and I rested my right hand on the banister. I'd checked the entire floor, which meant the source must be upstairs. The solidness of the cuff binding my left wrist—a present from Javos, my sort-of-boss—was a reminder that I couldn't use my celestial powers on this mission. I'd have to rely on stakes and quick reflexes instead.

A floorboard creaked overhead. I stilled, cursing silently. Someone was awake, and switching a light on to see who it was would alert the house's other inhabitants. The tiniest creak on the stairs betrayed movement. *Shit. He moved fast.*

Oh no.

I'd taken one step back when a solid body slammed into me, knocking the breath from my lungs. We crashed into a heap, my elbows scraping the floor. Warm breath tickled my neck, and cold, hard teeth pressed against the skin under my collar.

I might be immune to vampire venom, but that didn't mean I liked the idea of being turned into a pincushion. I slammed my elbow into his side—at least, that's where I aimed for. The pitch darkness didn't abate, but vampires moved by scent as far as their human prey was concerned and even celestials couldn't match them for speed. Freeing my right hand, I grabbed the charm around my neck and hit the switch. The smell of herbs blasted me in the face, and the vampire's grip loosened. Miniature drowsiness spell worked like a charm. It helped that during the day, he'd already be half asleep anyway.

Sliding along the carpeted floor, I wriggled free of the vampire's grip. I might have lost the perks of using the celestials' lab, but I could improvise handmade spells when I wanted to. Saying farewell to my promise not to use torchlight, I used my phone's light to show the path up into the dark landing. As silently as possible, I climbed the stairs. Hopefully our fight hadn't disturbed any more bloodsuckers. Javos had insisted there wouldn't be more than two, and I'd killed a whole room of them on one memorable occasion. But that was when I had my celestial blade. Without it, I felt naked, undefended. *It's definitely not shadow magic I have.* Whatever other magic my demon mark contained remained more dormant than my celestial powers.

I felt my way along the landing. If a vamp was asleep, the door would be locked—I thought. Why that one downstairs had been wandering about, I had no clue. But I needed to search the unlocked rooms first, and only venture into the vampire's lair as a last resort. True bloodstones were energy sources generally used by vampires who didn't have an immediate source of human prey to draw energy from. But the ones I searched for contained a more deadly power. Three novice celestials were currently suspended from action due to the venom produced by the demon-infected vampire's bite, and it would be much worse if more vamps got hold of the demonic bloodstones which someone had apparently hidden in this house.

I tried the first door. Unlocked. Faint light from my torch showed an empty bedroom. I crept in, searched every corner, then backed out. The second room yielded a similar result. Testing all the doors, I found none of them were locked. No more vamps, then. I breathed out, pushing open the last door.

A creaking noise came from downstairs.

I froze, my hand on the doorknob, and turned it the rest of the way. A vampire leered at me from the corner, his mouth stretched open, pointed fangs curling from his lips.

*Screw this game, Javos.*

I gripped my left wrist and yanked at the cuff the warlock boss had put there. White light shone from the arrowhead tattoo on the underside of my wrist, celestial fire designed to burn out evil, and skimmed over the vampire's face.

The vampire didn't turn to ashes. Because he was very, horribly dead.

Blood slicked his neck and covered his chest in jagged stripes. His body had been propped in a sitting position against the wall, but terrible wounds marked his body. Thick red blood soaked into the carpet, its fresh coppery tang permeating the air. *Not a vampire killing. A demon savaged him.*

I swallowed bile and backed away, not daring to switch off the light in case something else jumped at me. Like, for instance, the thing which had decided a vampire would make a good snack. Vampire bite wounds were small punctures that sealed within a minute. This guy had apparently run into a wild animal attack—or a demon.

Another creaking noise came from below. Oh hell. The other vamp plainly wasn't the attacker, but maybe he was in league with them. Why else would he be creeping around the house with his buddy lying dead upstairs? Tensing, I pushed the cuff further down my wrist, white light flooding my hand. I slipped out into the upstairs landing and shone the light down the stairs. The vamp lay slumped where I'd left him—younger than I'd thought, a man of maybe twenty with floppy blond hair. Nobody else was around.

I swiftly climbed down the stairs, one eye on him. "Who else is in here? Show yourself."

My knees buckled under the unexpected weight when

someone crashed into me from behind. A muscular arm wrapped around my waist, pinning me flat. I wriggled, waving my celestial hand. "Get off me."

"I'm disappointed," said a soft voice in my ear. "I really thought you could complete the mission without resorting to using your celestial power."

"Ouch." I pretended to struggle feebly, though relief made my legs go wobbly. "Oi. Nikolas. Let go of me. There's a dead body upstairs."

"Javos told you *not* to stab the vampires."

"Javos is a prick." I freed my hand. "And I mean the vampire's more dead than usual. Someone *ate* him."

Nikolas loosened his hold, allowing me to scramble to my feet. "Seriously?"

"Why do you think it smells like something curled up and died in here?" Nikolas had offered to supervise my training, but he was as much of a stickler for the rules as his boss. Hence the 'no celestial powers' condition that made subduing demons and vamps a royal nuisance.

Nikolas wasn't hard on the eyes, for a warlock. While a lot of them came equipped with horns and fangs, he looked human from a distance—albeit a particularly striking human. Tall and broad, he had dark red hair, golden eyes, and tanned, chiselled features that wouldn't look out of place on DivinityWatch's Warlock of the Week feature. Not that I'd actually told him. I figured guys like him were perfectly aware of how disturbingly attractive humans found them, and stroking a warlock's ego was generally a bad move.

He eyed the man on the floor. "He's not dead."

"No, I caught him first," I said. "I'd peg him as the killer, but I'm pretty sure what savaged the other dude isn't human. Not by a long shot."

"Show me," he said.

I led the way upstairs, and pointed through the open

door, steeling myself to look at the sight of the brutal murder again. Even werewolf kills weren't that messy. "Look at that. Definitely not a human killer."

Nikolas looked through the door with an impassive expression. "I see," he said, prowling into the room, scanning every corner. I switched on the light properly, now there was no need to keep it off. So much blood soaked into the carpet, it seemed impossible that the other vamp had been in the same house and not flown into a blood frenzy. *Damn. We need to get him out.*

"The killer was a demon," he said, "but it wasn't summoned in this room. Check the others."

"Is Javos coming to take away the guy downstairs? Because that spell won't last forever."

"I'll let him know." Nikolas pulled out his phone. "But we need to be certain if the demon was summoned here."

"If that guy did it, I bet he regrets it now." I backed out of the room. Switching on the landing light, I kicked in every door, moving loudly and swiftly to gain control over my jangling nerves. There were dozens of demons who could savage someone, so figuring out who'd done the summoning was the priority before we tried to pinpoint *what* they'd summoned.

Inside one of the bedrooms, I found a pentagram on the floor, smeared with brimstone. Dead. I kicked it just in case, treading on the lines. Several bloodstones lay nearby, but clear-coloured, not dark red or black. They'd been drained. I picked them up anyway and returned to Nikolas.

"I found a small pentagram in there," I told him. "And these. They're dead. All the energy's gone."

"I see." He took the bloodstones from me. "I'll ask Javos to inform the vampires' local sire about the body so it can be removed. I think we're done here."

"And the vampire downstairs?"

"Still unconscious, so we can take him for questioning," he said. "I'd congratulate you on knocking him out without waking the rest of the house, but considering the only other person inside the house is dead…"

I gave him the finger. "Very funny. Nobody else is here? The vampire downstairs… unless he's seriously in a blood rage, I doubt he's the one who ate his friend."

"No," said Nikolas. "I suspect not. We'll question him when he wakes up. This is the third raid this week that's resulted in a botched summoning."

"Might not have been botched," I said. "A lesser demon's capable of taking a bite out of someone."

"I'll report this to the vampires' leader," he said. "She won't be pleased. However, as it's daytime, we can take this man for questioning ourselves."

"I'm up for that," I said. "He knows *something*. You can't walk around in a house with a dead body without knowing how it got there."

"Are you certain there's nothing else here?"

"Positive." Warmth filled my chest at the notion that he trusted my word—and it was a hard-won trust, considering we'd once suspected one another of murder. He thought the celestials were the enemy. I distrusted warlocks who showed up at murder scenes and had terrifyingly powerful shadow magic. With my newly discovered demon mark, and the fact that the celestials had treated me like shit, I'd decided to sign up to work with the warlocks to figure out what magic my mark contained.

The demon mark had only manifested a few weeks ago, but it'd been on me ever since I'd killed a demon in its home dimension and sent a prayer to the Divinities to help me get home. I hadn't expected an answer, much less that the Divinity in question had apparently gone dark in the years after saving me from the car crash which had killed my parents by turning me into a celestial soldier. And in unknowingly making a deal with an arch-demon, I'd ended up wearing its mark.

Unfortunately, I'd seen no signs of the arch-demon in question, so I didn't know which dimension it was from—or which type of magic I'd been given. Aside from my ability to use demonglass, a rare substance from the netherworld dimensions, to transport myself around in a similar manner to the way Nikolas used shadows to move between this dimension and the shadow realm.

Nikolas and I left the house, carrying the unconscious vampire along with us. A shiver of unease slid down my spine, looking at the dead bloodstones. The energy must have gone somewhere, but the vampire upstairs was dead. The unconscious guy might have taken in the power himself, but the way they'd been left beside that pentagram made me certain they'd been fuelling a portal into a nether dimension. *But which?*

Nikolas hauled the vamp into the back of the car, and I slid into the front. We'd settled into a partnership fairly easily, which came as a surprise considering my usual issues with authority figures. In the two years since I'd left the celestials, I'd worked alone on independent cases, generally relating to magical misuse. The celestials dealt exclusively with demon attacks and major infractions, while the preternaturally inclined policed their own. But that left humans vulnerable to magical trickery, and not every rogue preternatural got caught. I could do more good with the warlocks than alone, but if I admitted it, I'd been trying to fill the hole left by the death of Rory, my former team-mate, partner, and friend. Working with Javos caused me no end of frustration, but it was better than drifting.

"You're being unusually quiet," Nikolas said, closing the door as he settled into the driver's seat. His seatbelt snapped into place and the car engine started with a purring noise. "I thought you'd be pleased the killer wasn't lurking in the house."

"Ecstatic," I said. "My life wouldn't be the same without narrow brushes with death. I take it you explained to Javos that I had good reason to remove this stupid cuff?" I wiggled my wrist. He'd fastened the damn thing tight, too much for me to take it off myself.

Nikolas took his hands off the wheel and reached for my left wrist. The engine continued to run, but the trembling in my limbs wasn't down to the car but the sensation of his thumb brushing against my pulse. There was a click, and the clasp loosened.

He paused, his fingers lightly resting against my exposed wrist. Warmth rose to my cheeks. We'd rarely had a moment alone together since I'd started working for the warlocks, and I'd forgotten how good he smelled close up. Power swarmed in his golden eyes, and I longed to cover the inches between us and see if he was as good a kisser as I remembered. He was temptation personified even when he wasn't using his lure ability. And he hadn't used it on me since we'd first met, despite my growing suspicions. Somehow, attraction had happened all on its own.

The vampire snored in the back seat, and Nikolas dropped my hand. "Javos will be wondering where we are."

I got the message. We were partners, and while it wasn't an issue for warlocks to be involved with humans, celestials with questionable demon marks were a different story. I didn't think it bothered Nikolas, but I was also fairly sure he'd only kissed me because he'd thought one or both of us was about to die. He'd shown no signs of interest since, anyway. And there were so many things I didn't know about him. Like who his arch-demon father was, and how he and his brother had come to rule a castle in the shadow realm. You know. The important things.

"Sure," I said. "Wouldn't want our vampire waking up first."

Nikolas moved his hands back to the wheel. "Considering we don't yet know if he's high on demon energy or not, I think it's best to err on the side of caution."

"Wise idea." I settled back in my seat to enjoy the ride back to the warlocks' place.

2

As predicted, Javos was in full-on Grumpy Warlock Chief mode. His office was on the ground floor of the warlocks' designated headquarters, which had been revamped a little since several demons and a vampire had escaped into it a few weeks ago. It was a fairly ordinary-looking red-brick house with no signs that it belonged to the warlocks other than the pair of devil horns Rachel had put on the gates.

Javos himself was a fearsome sight to behold. Huge and muscled, built like a statue of a Greek god, he glowered at the pair of us across the oak wood desk of his office, eyes blazing beneath a pair of sharp-looking horns. I might know his weakness—classical music, of all things—but that didn't mean he wasn't dangerous.

Of course, my history with authority figures was… questionable, to say the least.

"What do you mean, there isn't a single bloodstone remaining?" he asked Nikolas and me. "Where did all that energy end up, then?"

"Possibly inside the beast that bit a chunk out of the vampire," I said. "Hell, maybe even the vamp himself. Being infused with demon energy doesn't mean a demon can't bite them. If anything, it probably makes them more disposed to take stupid risks."

He gave me a disapproving look. "And I notice you're not wearing your cuff. How are you supposed to learn to use your demon power if you insist on whipping out your celestial mark whenever you're faced with a problem?"

"Way to jump to conclusions," I said. "I moved the cuff when I saw the vamp was dead so I wouldn't get jumped by the killer. Also, I don't think being shut in darkness is the key to unlocking my power."

"Neither is being a smart-arse, Miss Devina," he said.

I rolled my eyes. "Maybe it is. We've tried everything else."

He'd been almost amicable the first time we'd met. Then my former bosses at the celestial guild had arrested several of his warlocks and pinned the blame for the demon attacks on their warlock kin. Relations between the two were somewhat strained right now, and with me resting uneasily between the two worlds, just referencing my celestial mark could set him off. It didn't help that he thought the best way to unlock my demon powers was to spring random tests on me and see if my powers kicked in as a response. I'd grown to treat everything he offered me as suspicious. And nothing bloody worked.

"I don't know what my power is," I said. "*Not* from the shadow realm. I know that much. If it was, I would have been more at ease in that creepy house."

"You're uncomfortable with your magic because you haven't used it yet," said Javos. "If you didn't keep fighting it, then you'd find it easier."

"I'm not fighting it," I said. "I can use my demonglass

power just fine. But unless you let me figure out my other abilities in my own time, you're going to end up disappointed."

"Let me guess," he said. "You used your celestial power the first day you got your mark."

"It switched on by itself." I held up my wrist. I had to keep it covered because it lit up around warlocks or other preternaturally inclined people, and I didn't think he'd appreciate it. "Besides, I *have* used the demon mark's power. Even if it turns out all I can do is travel through demonglass, it's still a pretty damn useful power. Why are you both so certain I ended up with more than one type of magic? Even most warlocks have only one."

"Because shifting through realms is generally a secondary ability," said Nikolas.

There was a knock on the door. "Prisoner's awake!" sang Rachel's cheerful voice.

Javos's brow knotted. "We'll talk about this later, Devi. You're to accompany me to the questioning. I'll let the sire know we'll be delivering the vampire's remains later along with the other body from the house."

He strode out of the office, and Nikolas and I followed behind.

"He sure seems convinced he's guilty," I muttered to Nikolas. "Can he do that—kill someone without letting the vamps know he broke the law?"

"Since the vampire attacked you, yes, he can," said Nikolas.

"All right." I didn't really understand how the warlocks policed one another, yet alone their fragile relations with the vampires. "Just checking it won't provoke them."

"The evidence of a demon summoning in that house is proof enough for most vampires. They're trying to distance themselves from the criminals who worked with the demons."

"Let's hope it works."

Rachel sidled up to me as I walked down the corridor. Her hair was dyed bright pink, and she looked like a normal girl in her late teens. But below her human appearance was a fearsome demon.

"Devi!" she said. "How'd the case go? Nice job knocking out that vamp, by the way."

"Weren't you listening in?" I asked, walking alongside her towards the door leading into the back garden. "It was a total no-show. The bloodstones had no power left in them, and whatever was summoned chewed up the other vamp I found there."

"And did you unlock your demon power?"

"No."

She didn't understand why I wanted to keep my celestial power and not rely on the demon side. But I'd trained as a celestial for years. I'd been chosen for it. The demon mark had been an accident, and unlike the celestial guild, there wasn't a Guild of Unfortunately Demon Marked to explain to me how to use its power. Warlocks' magic was instinctive. I'd never met another person with the same mark I had, probably because no arch-demon had set foot in this dimension for thousands of years.

"It'll show up," she said.

"Probably not while walking in the dark." I jerked my head in Nikolas's direction.

He shrugged. "It was worth a try. Beats Javos's other idea of throwing you into the sea."

"The part where you staged a water demon attack on me was bad enough," I said. "I didn't sign up for unexpected near-drownings."

"Technically, they're included in the small print on your contract," Rachel put in.

"Look, you guys are used to fighting with a hundred percent demon power. That's all well and good, but I've known about this mark for all of three weeks, and it's not exactly a substitute for being able to see where I'm going in a vampire nest. Just saying."

"Don't worry," said Nikolas. "Once a test fails, Javos won't try it again."

"You have to keep things unpredictable, huh." I stopped walking as we reached the back door. Javos stood outside the shed where they'd thrown the vampire, the door slightly open.

The vampire slumped at the back, his hands and feet cuffed. Up close, he was even younger than I'd thought, with floppy white-blond hair and a terrified expression. Probably because of Javos—and Nikolas. When we entered, he scrambled into the corner as though hoping a secret door would open and let him out.

"I didn't kill him!" he blurted. "He was like that when I found him. I woke up when I heard him screaming."

"You attacked me in the dark," I said. "Nice try."

"I thought you were the killer," he mumbled. "Who are you, anyway? You're not a warlock."

"Nope," I said. "But it's you who's being questioned. What were you doing in that house? Guarding your sire's treasure?"

I'd gone in expecting to find a single vampire napping near the bloodstones, so he was either backup or a newly turned fledgling not yet strong enough to survive without the blood of his master. Considering his age, I'd guess he was a newbie, but that didn't mean he wasn't complicit.

He shook his head and didn't answer.

Nikolas stepped in. "We already know your name, Alec

Jacobs, and have a report ready to deliver to your next of kin along with your remains, should you fail to cooperate with us. Is that clear?"

He whimpered. "I didn't do anything wrong. I didn't even mean to attack the girl. I thought she was going to kill me." He eyed me pleadingly. "You're a celestial, right? Don't let them kill me."

"I'm reserving judgement," I said. "Maybe I'll be the one to burn you to cinders. If you have a good excuse as to why you were in the same house as a crate of stolen contraband, a pentagram and a dead body, this is your only chance to explain."

He swallowed, eyes darting to the door. "I—I was asleep. I turned a week ago, and my sire wanted to keep me close by to stop me from falling into a blood frenzy. But I woke up when he screamed. I found him—dead. And I panicked. I couldn't go outside, not during the day, or even call anyone. Then she showed up." He jerked his head at me. "That's it. I didn't see what killed him."

"A demon, obviously," I said. "Someone set up the pentagram. And there were demonic ingredients in the house, too. I'm sure you know what it looks like."

"I don't know how to summon a demon!" he said.

"Neither do most humans who try it," Nikolas said, "but that doesn't mean they're incapable of following instructions. Try again."

"I didn't do it," he repeated. "I'm newly turned—I haven't even left the house in a week."

"You look a little too healthy for someone who's apparently too blood-crazed to be outside," said Nikolas.

"He gave me his blood. Not hours before he died." His mouth turned down at the corners.

"You'd still show as blood-crazed," said Nikolas. "Javos,

would you object if I took care of him myself? Or perhaps Devi might like the chance to exercise her celestial—"

"It was a cure!" yelled the vampire. "There's a cure—they're testing it—and I was the subject. The blood cravings have gone. It's only been a day. I don't know if they'll come back."

He slumped back against the wall as though shouting had exhausted him.

Nikolas and Javos exchanged glances. "A cure?" Nikolas said. "There is no cure for vampirism."

"It's true," he said. "It might not be permanent, but it's true. I was a test subject."

"What exactly does that have to do with the demon one of you summoned?" enquired Nikolas.

He shook his head. "That wasn't me. I didn't kill him."

"Did your sire give you this cure?" asked Javos. "Tell me everything about how you came to be in that house."

"I already did," he mumbled. "I was there because I couldn't leave. He gave me the cure yesterday, but didn't let me outside. And like I said—I woke up to him screaming."

"Were there other vampires in the house?" I asked.

"Sometimes." He shrugged. "They don't let fledglings near one another until we've learned control. I don't know how he died, but it wasn't me."

"Your sire was into dark magic, if the pentagram we found was his," Nikolas said. "And the bloodstones. Have you ever seen one of those?"

The vampire licked his lips. "Yes. I was given one yesterday. They use bloodstones to get us used to taking in energy from sources other than our sire's blood."

"What colour was it?" asked Nikolas.

He blinked. "Colour? Red, of course."

*Not the demon energy ones, then.* His eyes didn't show the odd darkness of the vamps infected with demon energy, so that made sense. It was possible he'd just been in the wrong place at the wrong time, but his presence in the same house as a murderer raised all my suspicions.

"And did your sire show any signs of an interest in demon summonings before today?" I asked.

He shook his head. "No. He was only interested in the cure. He wanted to test it on me, first."

"Do you know why we were at the house?" enquired Nikolas.

The vamp hesitated. "To find out who killed him?"

"Oh, we don't give a shit about that," said Javos. "He can rot in the earth for all we care. No—there was a tip-off about illegal items connected with demon summonings, and the house we found you in was listed as one of the store houses. All records mentioned your sire—but your name wasn't listed at all. Were you aware of the nature of the setup? Did he ask you to guard his store of dangerous items?"

"No. I swear—no." He shuffled back, sweat trickling down his pale forehead. "I was there by accident. I didn't know about demons or anything like that."

"I see," said Javos, stepping forwards. The air trembled as though with the promise of an oncoming storm.

"No!" he yelled. "The cure—I can tell you about it. It works on anyone infected with a vampire bite!"

*Anyone.*

"Wait," I said to Javos. "Keep him alive."

He swung his head around to face me, eyes narrowed. "Why? Nobody will miss him."

The vampire flinched.

"We don't have proof he's lying," I said. "And I'm interested to know more about this vampire cure. If it's widespread, it might affect preternatural relations, right?" I addressed Nikolas, who nodded slowly. His piercing gaze told me he'd guessed the real reason I wanted to know about the cure—to help the three victims of infected vampire bites who could no longer fight as celestials.

"Correct," said Nikolas. "There's no reason to let him out of this shed. We can use him as a source of information until we find out where this cure is, and who's making it."

Javos scowled at him, but his magical effects died down a little. "If you prove a hindrance, you're dead," he snarled at the vamp. "Devina, since you apparently have sympathy for bloodsuckers, I'm putting you in charge of keeping this one alive."

"Oh no." I raised my hands. "I didn't sign up to give blood to vampires."

"We have bloodstones," Nikolas said. "I think it's a good idea."

I bristled. "It's not my job to babysit teenage vamps."

"I'm *twenty*," said the vampire in question, looking highly insulted. "And I don't need a babysitter."

"I'll be the judge of that," said Nikolas.

Fuming, I returned my glare to the vampire himself. "I'm looking forward to hearing more about this cure of yours. Are there any samples available?"

I hadn't seen any dubious-looking bottles in the house, but doubtless the people Javos sent to remove the body would thoroughly comb the place. Still, knowing who was developing the cure would help.

He shook his head. "No. I don't know where he got it from, but it's not his. Someone else made it."

"Are you absolutely certain you don't have any more information?" I asked. "Because to be honest, I'm really not keen on being in charge of keeping you alive."

His throat bobbed. "I don't know. I swear. He took the cure, too, before he bit me."

I looked at the others. "If it's true, the dead guy's blood is laced with this so-called cure. Might be worth looking into."

"Agreed," Nikolas said. "If not, I'd be more than happy to extract a blood sample from our guest."

The vamp made an indignant noise, then fell silent. "Don't kill me," he said. "I—I only became a vampire because I didn't want to die. Please—don't." His voice cracked, and bloody tears trailed down his face.

Nikolas glanced at me. "There goes our need for a sample. Devi?"

The vampire yelped. I glared at the two warlocks. "This isn't my job either. My contract didn't mention bottling vampire tears."

"Technically," Rachel said from behind, "the small print—"

"Okay, that's *enough*." I looked back at the vampire. "Trust me, it's better this way."

Five minutes and a lot of screaming later, I stalked out of the shed carrying a bottle of vampire tears. As I'd predicted, the vampire's instincts had kicked in upon me grabbing him and he'd tried to choke me. Javos, the prick, had watched the two of us wrestle with one another without offering a hand to stop me spilling the bloody tears all over myself. The result was that I had more vampire blood on me than in the bottle, but it was done. Javos took the sample without so much as a thank you, and strode off to the house after locking the shed. Rachel skipped after him, leaving Nikolas and me alone. I made to follow her, too.

"Devi." He held up a hand, telling me to wait. "Don't tell the celestial guild about the cure."

"That wasn't my plan," I said. "There's no proof yet that the cure works on demon-infected venom anyway. Never mind searching for vampire cures, you ought to be working on a Chill Pill for Agitated Warlocks."

"I'm not agitated, I'm concerned." He looked at me. "If vampires are finding a new way to disperse their demonic energy in the guise of a cure, for instance, then we're in for a lot of trouble."

"That's your theory?" I frowned. "If anything, it's a new way of hiding the evidence. Give all the demon energy to a new vamp, then use the cure. Of course, if the cure's permanent, it'd render their demonic energy boosters useless, but there's no proof it is."

"I'd suspect not," he said. "The boost of a regular bloodstone only lasts twenty-four hours, but the demonic taint might linger a little longer. Or perhaps not. We've never caught a vampire alive who used it."

"Until now, potentially," I said. "Now do you see why I think we should keep him alive? Not only is he the only living source of the cure—if it exists—he might be proof that we can actually measure how long the effects of that demon-infected venom last. Maybe if it's only twenty-four hours, it explains why all the murders last time took place within such a short time frame."

"Precisely. You do like being proved right, don't you?"

"I like being taken seriously." I glanced at the shed. "And not given pointless tasks. There's no reason why Javos can't order someone else to feed the vampire. I don't even live here."

"Perhaps not, but you're more likely to be able to get answers from him. Assuming he has any more information. If this cure has a time limit, we'll need to periodically check on him."

I smothered a sigh. "All right, I'll take on Project Vampire. Just as long as I can get a look-in at any information you or Javos might find on the cure. This is pretty damn serious if it's true."

"Agreed," he said, "which is why we'll be speaking with the vampires' leader tonight at sundown. Once she wakes, I'll see if I can get us a meeting with her. I'll call you if we do."

I blinked. "Wait, their leader? Like, the ruler of vampires in the city?"

"The very same." He paused. "I don't need to remind you to hold your tongue around her, do I?"

"Obviously not," I said. My phone buzzed in my pocket. "You're the ones who keep feuding with the vamps. Anyway. I need to answer this." Only one person had my number who actually called on a regular basis—my best friend and neighbour Fiona, who'd narrowly escaped being a demigod's prey when he'd kidnapped her and taken her into the demon dimension. Since then, she'd been calling me at least once a day, convinced that demons had broken into her flat.

I picked up the phone and saw it wasn't Fiona calling, but Clover, retired celestial soldier and the only person left in the guild who I considered a friend.

"Hey, Clover."

"Are you with that warlock?"

I frowned. She, out of everyone at the guild, knew about my new position with the warlocks. The others assumed—I hoped—that I'd gone back to working as an independent freelancer. I'd made it quite clear that I didn't want them getting involved in my life any further, and after royally screwing me over, they'd better bloody well respect that.

"Why?" I said, in answer to Clover.

"Just checking. There's been an incident he may want to be aware of."

My heart sank. "What incident?"

*More demon killings?*

"One of the celestials who was bitten by the infected vampires appears to have killed a student."

"What? Seriously?" The victims had been moved to the celestials' academy for new recruits to reduce the risk of their celestial marks accidentally switching on and activating the virus. The academy was one of the most heavily warded places in town. "I thought there weren't any other side effects."

"Either that, or a demon got in. Or a warlock."

I lifted the phone from my ear. "You've got to be kidding me."

3

After leaving the warlocks' place, I didn't, much as I wanted to, go back home to chill out before meeting the vampire queen. Instead, I drove to the celestials' academy.

I was thrilled to bits to have my own car again, even if it was eating most of my earnings from my new job. This model wasn't quite as fancy as the one I'd had as a celestial soldier and I didn't have the luxury of free repairs either, but the freedom was worth it. I blasted the radio and sang along, out of tune, all the way through the traffic in the city centre. Mostly, it was to shut off the whispers in the back of my head telling me this was a monumentally terrible idea. Not only had I sworn not to get involved with the celestials again, they'd want me dead if they had the slightest inkling about the demon mark. Even my former tutors.

Considering the reputation I'd left behind, I expected to find my name on a 'no entry' poster. The academy had taken the brunt of my displeasure and disillusionment at my new unchosen life calling. I'd been sixteen when I'd joined, old enough to get a job if I wanted to, and I didn't appreciate the school's attempts to control my every move. After leaving and becoming a full-fledged celestial soldier, I'd rarely gone back. But the only 'wanted' poster outside was for Faye Carruthers, notorious ex-celestial soldier who'd gone rogue and summoned a demon inside the old guild's headquarters, killing a ton of people in the process. Rory and I had been on assignment at the time so I hadn't seen the wreckage, nor the aftermath. Until recently, it'd been the worst attack on the guild in one of their own cities in the last decade.

Because their former headquarters hadn't been salvageable, the guild had moved to the old academy and the academy itself had relocated here. The plain brick building looked unassuming, but it boasted some intense security measures. Nobody could get in unless someone opened the doors from the inside, and demon-proof spells covered the place. So someone being murdered within its walls was unheard of.

I habitually checked my right wrist was covered and waited outside to be buzzed in. On the other side of the glass doors appeared Mrs Credence, who'd been one of my tutors and one of many long-suffering victims of my various pranks as a rebellious sixteen-year-old.

"Devi," said Mrs Credence, as though I was some horrifying ghost who'd appeared from her career's past to torment her. "What are you doing here?"

"Clover told me what happened," I said. "Who was the killer?"

"Alyson." She pursed her lips. "If you weren't the person responsible for finding the cause of those other deaths, I'd be hard-pressed to find a reason to let you in. Management won't like this."

"Management is the reason I didn't find the killer sooner," I said. "As a matter of fact, I'm in the middle of investigating a potentially related death amongst the vampires." *And the cure.* It'd be cruel to dangle the possibility in front of the remaining celestials who could never fight again, even if one of them was dead, and another possibly a murderer. "But tell me—who was involved?"

Mrs Credence paused before saying, "I'm not sure if you're aware, but we had the three victims staying in the same area of the academy. The two girls—Alyson and Harlow—were roommates. The girls in the room below were woken this morning by screaming from upstairs. We found Alyson crouched over Harlow's body—both were covered in blood. But she had no weapons. Nothing."

"Where is she now?"

"In isolation. We aren't equipped to hold prisoners here, so the main guild are coming to collect her later for a trial. But obviously, she can't be around anything likely to set off her celestial magic…"

"Otherwise she dies." I nodded. "I see. I'd like to speak with her first."

"How exactly is this vampire case you mentioned connected?"

"I don't know yet," I said. "But a vampire who might have had contact with the same virus which infected the celestials was killed."

Two murders in a day both vaguely related to the same vampires certainly *looked* suspicious. Especially as both victims, and the murderer, might have been carrying said venom. Who knew if it had any other side effects which only manifested later?

She sighed and beckoned me forwards. "Come with me, and try not to scare the students."

"I would never."

"Devi, you used to tell gruesome stories *before* you were out in the field."

So I had. Like the guild HQ, the academy was like a cross

between an old-fashioned boarding school and a prison, both in appearance and atmosphere. Only the terminally dull wouldn't have ghost stories on the mind after spending a night in one of the towers.

"I got bored easily."

"The evidence of your boredom is still carved into the guild's walls."

I grinned. "Mr Roth never told me that. You mean they never managed to remove it?"

I hadn't been back to the guild since Mr Roth and I had parted on less than pleasant terms. I'd blamed him for letting Inspector Deacon swoop in and remove me from the murder investigation, not to mention letting Gav get killed on his watch. I sincerely hoped he'd have more sense this time.

"Unfortunately not," she said. "I take it you've found someone new to torment?"

"You wound me. Where's the victim, then?"

"This way."

Poor Mrs Credence. Really, I'd gone easy on her. She was one of those downtrodden department heads on the perpetual brink of a nervous breakdown. I'd only gone out of my way to annoy the most cruel and sarcastic members of staff, the ones who'd picked on other novices or been dicks for no reason. Even I had a limit.

"Why put you in charge of this investigation?" I couldn't help asking as we reached the office, and she unlocked the door with a key.

"There weren't many volunteers, and I'm the girls' head of year."

I grimaced. I could read between the lines. The guild hadn't known what to do with the victims at all, because most celestials either retired at an old age or died in the field. Few did what I had, and left entirely. And because of the dangers of using their celestial magic, the victims had been shoved out of sight to avoid accidentally triggering the spell that had killed the last ones. It couldn't have been pleasant for them. But enough to turn one of them into a killer? I couldn't say.

Alyson sat hunched in the corner of the empty office.

"I didn't kill her." Her mouth looked bloody, and she avoided eye contact with me.

"The room was locked," said Mrs Credence. "You were the only person inside, and you were standing over her body."

Alyson's eyes focused on me and widened. "Devi?"

"That's me," I said. "I'm prepared to give you the benefit of the doubt, which is more than I can say for the guild. So tell me what you know."

"That's just it. I don't remember. I fell asleep, woke up to the sound of her screaming, and I was—I was standing over her body. I don't remember how I got there. I assume I sleep-walked. But I swear, I didn't kill her. I don't even know how she died."

"She was clawed to death," said Mrs Credence, who hovered by the door, looking faintly nauseated.

I could understand why. The girl's fingernails were crusted with blood. As though she'd dug them into something fleshy. Her clothes were splattered, and so was her face. Not to mention the blood between her teeth. She might as well have been a dictionary illustration of the word 'guilty'.

"A demon," said the novice. "It must have been."

"If it was a demon, the security would have gone off," said Mrs Credence.

"Not to mention your celestial light would have activated, killing you," I added.

"You don't know that." Her voice rose, hysterically. "You have to let me out of here. The killer's still out there. I know they are."

"All that blood came from somewhere," I said. "Maybe you communicated with a demon through some other means."

She shook her head. "How can I? I've been watched almost all the time since I came here, in case I accidentally used my celestial magic."

I looked at Mrs Credence for confirmation. "All right. We're going to need to look at the body."

I backed out of the room, leaving the despondent ex-celestial behind.

"Do you believe her?" asked Mrs Credence.

"I don't know," I said. "I think she was the killer, but perhaps she's telling the truth when she says she doesn't remember. It *might* be a demon… or it might be a side effect."

"Of the demon venom?" Scepticism tinged her voice. "She did bring up a good point. Normal vampire venom doesn't affect us, but it usually runs its course within a day or two. If a person is going to change, they'd have been through the process by now."

"Only if they drink their sire's blood," I reminded her. "Which obviously isn't an option here. Anyway, a celestial can't turn into a vampire. Unless… unless she's some kind of demon vampire?"

Just imagining what both the vampires *and* the warlocks would say to that made me shudder. Not to mention Azurial, who'd started all this. He was locked up in another dimension, but if anyone was sneaky enough to implement another plan to attack the celestials in this realm, it was him.

"You want to see the body?" she asked. "It's unpleasant, but I'm sure you knew that."

"Then let's get it over with."

The academy didn't come with a morgue, for obvious reasons, so the body was locked in a spare room. A foul smell wafted out when she opened the door, decay mixed with blood, fresh and otherwise. The girl lay sprawled on a table, blood soaking into her clothes. Horrible wounds crossed her chest and neck. Like a monster had bitten chunks out of her. Bile burned the back of my throat. If I hadn't seen the state of the body, I wouldn't have believed a human could have done it. But maybe the demon mark had caused her to lose her memory of the attack.

"Who was the third person who got bitten?" I asked.

"Damian Greenwood. He was in the boy's dorms, on the opposite corridor, and didn't see the attack. I brought him downstairs anyway. He's in my office."

"I think we should speak to him," I said. "Her story has holes in it, but assuming the demon mark was responsible, it might be that something similar will happen to him. We need to be ready."

"Nobody mentioned a demon's mark," she said. "I thought they were invisible."

Ah. I'd forgotten they knew so much less than I did about how demons operated. It wouldn't do to make them suspect I had up-close-and-personal experience with demon marks— not to mention, it'd make life even more difficult for the last victim.

"I meant the vampire's bite," I said. "Have there been any more reported side effects?"

"No," she said. "That's why we let them stay here. They're too old to retake classes, but if they're unable to return to the field… there are a few other options for them within the guild. Academia, for instance."

I nodded, quelling an unexpected twinge of guilt. I'd spent most of the investigation thinking the deaths were connected to the death of my partner, Rory. I guessed he'd died in the same way, though I'd never found a conclusive answer as to why, when there'd been two years between his death and the more recent murders. And my own demon mark hadn't been the result of a bite.

"He's here, if you want to talk to him," she added, beckoning me towards another office. Unlocking the door, she opened it to reveal a young man with jet black hair and a pale, almost vampire-like complexion.

"Hey," I said.

"Devi Lawson?" Damian raised an eyebrow. "They've got *you* investigating? Didn't they learn their lesson from last time?"

Well, that was nice. "What, when I saved your ungrateful necks?"

"Ungrateful?" he snapped. "I lost everything, while you didn't even bother to come and tell us in person that we can never go out into the field again. You left everything to the guild."

"Because it was *their* fault." The guild hadn't believed me when I'd told them the cause of death, and in any case, he and the others were lucky to have survived. "Besides, you're the one who got bitten by a vampire."

"You never even bothered to ask how it happened," he said.

"I was in the hospital with severe burns from demon magic." I'd always have scars, however much of a miracle warlock healing remedies worked. "Besides, it's not like I even work for the guild. Maybe you should talk to them about your issues. They kicked me off the investigation before I even figured out the vampires did it."

"My life is *over*."

He'd make a great vampire, considering he had the dramatics down already. And the acting skills. His high-pitched whining tone was a little too on point. I wouldn't be fooled. Not like I had the authority to let him out—or the inclination.

"No, it isn't," I said. "Not unless you turn into a blood-thirsty killer, too. I hear the academy's looking for new positions." My gaze fell on an open book on the desk next to him, which looked like it'd come from the library. "Researcher?"

"It's boring as shit."

"Maybe take up a new hobby rather than whining about how awful your life is. You're not the one who got mauled to death."

He threw the book at me. I dodged and caught it in one hand, while Mrs Credence gasped behind me. Rolling my eyes at him, I tossed the book onto the desk and left the office. "What a prick."

"*Devi.*"

"The guild isn't spreading rumours that it's my fault, are they?" I asked suspiciously.

"Of course not," she said. "He's just... not taking his new role well. The girls were, until now. That's why we weren't watching them closely."

"Look, if you have an epidemic of vampire-demon-celestial hybrids, you have a problem," I said. "For that reason, you might want to keep an eye on him. Two eyes, if possible. He's a melodramatic prick, but that might be a cover."

"You know how the guild is," she said. "If we preemptively judge him guilty, it's not a stain that will wash away easily."

"Neither is murder, even by accident," I said.

"I will talk to Mr Roth about the situation. I've already updated him."

"Good." I hoped he wouldn't overreact, unlike a certain inspector. Not only had Inspector Deacon labelled me the villain rather than going after the bad guys, thanks to him, we'd been almost too late to stop the killer. To avoid a repeat of that scenario, I was prepared to involve the warlocks... but the guild's hatred of preternaturals made it impossible to imagine them working together without a fuss. Especially given that they'd recently provoked Javos by arresting several warlocks, and the vampires had been partly responsible for the murders in the first place. But it was nice to imagine some sane, sensible people taking care of the problem in a diplomatic manner. Preferably *before* someone else ended up dead.

Unfortunately, it did look like Alyson was guilty. And unless she was a hell of a lot more vindictive than she'd seemed, the vampire's venom must have been at least partially responsible. But it wasn't like there was an established method for dealing with victims of demon-infected vampire bites. The guild was doing what they did best—hiding their problems from public view and hoping they could sweep everything under the rug.

Like Rory's death.

Nobody had mentioned it since. But I couldn't help wondering if he'd been yet another victim of the same attack. Rory had died in a raid on a demon's nest over in Cornwall two years ago. Nowhere near Haven City. And every time I recalled that mission, I didn't remember either of us getting bitten by anything.

*Put it out of mind,* I told myself. I'd return to the subject once my meeting with the vampire queen was behind me. I'd spent entirely too much of today dwelling on the dead.

## 4

Fiona looked at me across the coffee table, brow furrowed. "I know that one." She pointed at the card I held up, which depicted a demon shaped like a scorpion—except the size of a cow—with a long waving stinger. "Venos demon."

"Right." I put the flashcards down. We sat opposite one another in the living room of my flat, which was half-home-made lab, half shrine to the places I'd visited as a Grade Three celestial soldier. Once you hit the third level, you were qualified to travel the world on all-expenses-paid trips to hunt down demons. I'd improvised the hand-drawn flashcards from a book of demons I'd 'borrowed' from the guild library and never returned. Not very artistic—the pictures looked like child's scribbles—but they got the job done.

"I really don't know about this, Fi," I said. "If you want the nightmares to stop, looking at pictures of ugly demons at night probably isn't doing you any favours."

"I *need* to know," Fiona said insistently. "I have to. They have my scent now. Doesn't that mean they can track me?"

"Azurial's gone," I said. "Also, nobody else was there in the palace, aside from some dead vampires. If anyone targets you, the defences I put on the flat will be more than enough. Besides, I'm here most of the time."

I'd finally got round to properly setting up security around the flat, not to mention I'd given her one of my traps in case anything grabbed her. The unspoken truth was that if a powerful warlock like Azurial got in here again, there was little either of us could do to stop them. I hadn't mentioned that Azurial wasn't technically dead, either. As a demigod—half arch-demon warlock—he had regenerative powers. I had Nikolas's reassurance that he wouldn't escape his prison, but it didn't feel right keeping the truth from her. After all, the last time I'd withheld information, she'd nearly been killed.

"So you're investigating *how* many murders?" she asked.

"Two," I said. "One at the celestials' academy, one vampire. I'm going to meet the vampires' leader tonight, anyway, and hopefully get this vampire case straightened out. The only link is that a demon might have been involved in both murders. But the guild's taken over the other case." Hopefully, they'd handle it better than the last one.

"The guild?" said Fiona. "Aren't they the ones who nearly got you killed?"

"Yep," I said. *And they* did *get Gav killed.* For that reason alone, I'd never go back to working for them, not even if the situation escalated like last time. "I trust the warlocks a damn sight more, but I don't think it's a coincidence that one of the celestials who was bitten died right after it turns out there might be a cure."

She paled. "What? You never mentioned that before. What cure?"

"Apparently the vampire who got killed was testing a cure for vampirism. We caught his minion, but he doesn't seem keen on answering questions. Might be true, might not. But the guild incident was something else entirely. Not really my business, but I'm keeping an eye on it in case we end up blindsided again."

I'd check in with the guild tomorrow, assuming the meeting with the vampires didn't go south. Which, considering my track record, was highly likely.

"Okay," she said. "Well, you'd better warn me of any new developments. Tell me all about the vampires' leader."

"I thought it was a Divinity you wanted to meet."

She wrinkled her nose. "Now I've seen what happens when they go bad, I'm not so keen."

"Trust me, you don't want to meet a vampire on a blood craze, either." Fiona's addiction to DivinityWatch—a website dedicated to usually-false pictures of Divinity sightings—had taken a hit lately. But I'd still caught her checking the site again the other day. Old habits, I guessed. "I'm going to get changed before I head out to meet Nikolas, okay? Text me if you like. I'll be back before midnight."

"Don't let the vampires bite," she said. "Seriously—don't. Isn't their venom… like, super addictive?"

"To humans," I said. "Celestials… it does affect us, to a lesser degree, except when it comes to the demon infection. That's why we're working hard to make sure the vamps can't get hold of any more dodgy bloodstones."

She swallowed nervously. "You're not helping."

"Told you the demon cards were a bad idea."

"I keep thinking they're breaking in."

"The only warlock I know who's been here recently is Nikolas, and he's harmless."

She raised an eyebrow. "Harmless? You wouldn't have a crush on him if he was. You're a danger junkie, Devi."

"I am *not*. And I never said I had a crush on him."

She grinned. "Ha. Knew it. I won't tell him, don't worry. Bet he already knows."

I shrugged. "He's my mentor, sort of. And I'd bet the other warlocks would judge him for dating a human."

Either that or our 'kiss for good luck' was just that. Which really shouldn't have bothered me. I had enough on my mind. Gav's death, the aftermath of Fiona's kidnapping, avoiding any celestials and the continuing worry that they'd find out the real reason I'd left—and, of course, working for the warlocks. And I'd be wearing my anti-preternatural blister attack trap tonight, so no chance of any action. Of the non-violent sort, anyway. I had to admit the chances of getting through a meeting with the vampires' leader without someone losing their temper were fairly low.

"Keep telling yourself that." She pushed to her feet, grinning. "I'll go back home. Wouldn't want them to know you're teaching a human all their secrets."

She'd grasped the warlocks' measure better than I expected, considering I'd spent the last two years trying to keep as much distance between her and the preternatural world as possible. But it was true, unfortunately, that I wasn't supposed to tell her any details of my training. And Nikolas wasn't supposed to tell *me* anything that was above my level. Maybe tonight I'd pry some secrets out of him.

"Just don't tell anyone," I said to her.

"Like I would. My co-workers already think I'm weird." Fiona worked in a call centre, in which the biggest risk was being yelled at by strangers. Getting kidnapped by the son of an arch-demon had shaken her up, to say the least. "All right. See you tomorrow."

Fiona left, while I put the flashcards back on the bookshelf next to my collection of ornaments, cleared away the empty takeout cartons we'd strewn all over the table, and went to change into something suitable for a night out with vampires.

At five-eight, I didn't have much use for heels, though

Nikolas was much taller than I was. I wore dark colours—with vampires involved, getting covered in blood was always a possibility. What with that and my black hair, I looked like I was going to a Goth party. I hadn't got my summer tan yet, and when you added the elbow-length gloves I wore to hide my demon and celestial marks, I'd fit in more with the vamps than the warlocks. I didn't know if the vampire leader knew what I was. Probably not. It was none of her business whether I was a celestial, warlock or plain old human.

Finally, I put the handmade trap around my neck, which reacted whenever anyone touched me without my permission and gave them a hell of a nasty case of blisters. Zadok, Nikolas's brother, had never forgiven me for that one.

Nikolas arrived five minutes early, as I expected by now. I answered the door, heart fluttering in anticipation. Maybe I should have left the trap and risked it. It wasn't like I didn't have four stakes concealed in various places on my person.

He looked me up and down with obvious appreciation. "I like the gloves. You'll fit right in."

"Hope so," I said. "Have you told her about our pet prisoner?"

"Javos felt it best if we left that piece of information out of our discussion, in case she accused us of trying to blackmail her into cooperating by using her own people as leverage."

I raised an eyebrow. "Isn't that exactly what we're doing?"

"Technically, yes, but as of yet, nobody has brought up our little fledgling. It's possible they didn't actually know he existed, since by his own admission, he's been kept locked up since he turned."

"Shit, yeah," I said. "Okay. Just wanted to make sure we aren't pissing off the vampire lady before we even start. I take it Javos is sitting this one out."

"Yes, he is. You haven't said where you went this afternoon."

I figured he'd have noticed. Very little escaped him.

"Yeah, about that," I said. "One of the celestials who got bitten by the infected vamps killed someone today."

His jaw tightened. "Don't tell me you spoke to them."

"All right, I won't." I kept my tone light, not wanting to start an argument. "It's up to you if you want to hear the full story *after* the next demon tries to chew my face off or not."

"For someone who's apparently encountered twice as many dead bodies today as I have, you seem to be in an alarmingly cheerful mood," he said. "I dread to think what will happen in a roomful of vampires. They don't have much of a sense of humour."

"Neither do dead bodies," I said. "Trust me, if I learned anything from the celestials, it's graveyard humour. Anyway, I'm not kidding. Alyson apparently went mad and killed one of the other bite victims but the wounds were more like a wild animal did it. I wouldn't have thought a human was responsible, but she had skin and blood under her nails, and in her mouth."

"Ah," said Nikolas, his forehead pinching.

"Exactly. Now do you see the connection? Two people get torn apart by a cannibalistic killer in the space of a day. I know the city is demon central lately, but I don't think we've ever had a problem with people eating one another before. Not even vampires."

"And was there a demon summoning at the academy?" he asked.

"Nope," I said. "Demons can't get in, or attack from the inside. My theory is that it was the aftereffects of the demon-infected bite. It turned them against one another. Which means I have to get the guild to listen when I say they should keep the third victim isolated in case he turns into a cannibal, too."

"That seems a tall order."

"I've had worse," I said. "Let's go and meet the vampire queen, then."

We walked out into the cool evening air. The sky stayed lighter for longer now it was May, but vamps rose the instant the sun set. We'd given the vampires an hour to prepare for our visit. Hopefully the vampire queen, Madame White, wouldn't flip out if word got to her that we had one of her people held captive for questioning.

Nikolas drove us to the nice part of the city, far away from the night clubs and bars I usually associated with the party-loving vampires. After fifteen minutes or so, we pulled up outside an extravagant townhouse with expansive grounds. Clipped hedges lined the gravel path to the doors. No Halloween decorations here—this place looked like it belonged to someone with a lot of money and expensive taste. And even a doorman—human, by the look of things.

The wide hallway was dimly lit, casting shadows around the gathering of vampires. All of them seemed to be dressed in expensive suits and dresses, not at all like the rowdy gatherings of the younger vamps in the local bars. It felt more like we'd crashed a socialite gathering than a vampire hangout. Most of the vamps I'd met until now were fairly young— which for vampires, meant less than a few centuries old. These ones had been around a while. Long enough to stand in a room full of candles without worrying they'd knock one over and catch on fire, apparently.

Heads tilted in my direction as we walked in. Looks of disapproval followed our path, though I noted hunger in some of their expressions. The weirdest thing was the perfumed air. Most vampires carried the coppery scent of blood wherever they went, while this place smelled like someone had sprayed every corner with perfume. With the dizzying scent, I wouldn't know if they were ensnaring me until their teeth were in my throat. I clenched my hands tight, feeling the reassuring weight of the trap around my neck. Any vamp who touched me would be the first to find out if my anti-warlock defences worked on the undead, too.

The dim candle lights didn't make it easy to see the way forward, so it took me a while to spot Madame White sitting on an elaborately carved wooden chair as though it was a throne. Immortality—specifically, consuming fresh blood—ensured eternal youth, and however old she was, she was no exception. She sat with a male human on either side, a bored expression on her face. She wore a form-fitting black lace dress that clung to every curve. Dark curls cascaded to her shoulders, and her skin was the porcelain pale of someone who hadn't seen the sun in a few decades, if not centuries. Her blood-red lipstick and necklace of rubies stood out starkly against her otherwise black-and-white ensemble.

She rose to her feet lithely, demonstrating with that simple movement that she wasn't simply a pretty face. Like any vampire, she was a predator designed to kill, and her beautiful facade was just that—a mask. She hadn't survived this long by lying down.

"Nikolas Castor." Her gaze passed onto me. "Why did you bring a celestial with you?"

"I'm working with the warlocks on this investigation," I said, as though she'd addressed me. I should have known someone as ancient and clever as she was wouldn't dismiss me on sight as a regular human.

"If this investigation concerns my people, then it's not your job." Her eyes narrowed. "I'd quite like an explanation as to how you ended up involved with my people in the first place."

"Tracking contraband bloodstones infected with demon magic," said Nikolas. "As we've told you. Since you refused to investigate the matter yourself, we took it upon ourselves to remove the illegal goods before they did any more damage."

She raised an eyebrow. "And what, pray tell, would someone want with damaged bloodstones? Demon magic would render their purpose useless, even if it were possible to contain it within an object. Which would be your area, warlock, not mine."

*Play nice,* I thought, resisting the urge to give her a piece of my mind.

Nikolas looked calm, impassive, under the flickering candles. "As I mentioned, an arch-demon's son infected the bloodstones with demon energy, and in this case, the vampires in question were able to spread the demon virus through biting their victims."

"I've seen no evidence of any of this, and I've lived a long time."

"Since the bloodstones were destroyed and the nest purged, we felt that the matter was over," Nikolas said. "Unfortunately, that doesn't seem to be the case. In the last few weeks, we've heard reports of similar bloodstones appearing, in the same place as botched demon summonings. Today, we found a dead vampire in such a position."

"Bloodstones can indeed be used in demon summonings," she said, without so much as a flinch at the idea of one of her own being dead. "If the foolish man wanted to summon a demon, then he deserved whatever fate he met. I've no interest in associating with people who deal with the netherworld."

*Meaning us, then.* So that's why his death didn't bother her. Dealing with demons or even warlocks presumably ostracised vampires from their community. And plainly she didn't believe our story of what'd gone down in Pandemonium. Nikolas and I had been too thorough with taking care of the evidence, leaving little behind to prove that any other vampires were involved in illegal operations.

"Aren't you interested in policing your people?" I asked. "I thought it was your job."

"My job?" She gave me a withering look. "I rule many vampires in this city, and none of my people have reported anything like you claim. If the occasional rogue decides to break our rules, we enact punishment ourselves. Do not presume to trespass into the affairs of the undying."

"Wouldn't dream of it," I said. "Unless it affects us. And the humans, too. I'd say a vampire who can spread a demonic virus by biting people is a cause for concern."

I didn't want to bring up what the infected bites did to the celestials in front of her. She might use the information against us. Unfortunately, that took away a major part of our argument.

"I wanted to propose an allegiance," said Nikolas. "Since we have a common enemy—"

"No, we do not," she said. "I could hardly care less about the fate of anyone who deals with the netherworld, and I won't permit you to push yourself into an undeserved position of authority over my fellow vampires."

"Nobody's questioning your authority," I said. "All we want is to work with you to stop this demonic virus. Can't you figure out where these bloodstones are coming from?"

Her lips pursed. "I've never seen the need for a substitute for fresh blood, but these pitiful new fledglings grow weaker by the day. It's their problem if their methods backfire on them. You're free to involve yourself in whatever capacity you see fit, but if I see you probing into our secrets or putting us in danger, your lives will be forfeit, as will any of my people who aid you."

She spoke every word in a calm, reasonable tone, not at all like she'd slipped a threat or two in there. So her people didn't use bloodstones? I supposed, given the human servants present here, they had no need for them.

"It's everyone's problem if you all get infected with demon viruses," I said.

Nikolas rested a hand on my back, a warning. I shrugged it off and stared the vampire queen out.

"You are dismissed," Madame White said, waving a hand. "Take your netherworld contacts elsewhere."

*It's your people, too, you selfish vampire.* But several heads turned on us, the hint of bared fangs a promise of danger if we disobeyed. Turning around, I left the room with Nikolas at my side.

"She's like that," he said when we were back in the car. "Only cares for her own tribe. If one of her blood-children fell victim, *then* she'd care. Not before."

"Great," I said. "I mean, it's helpful that we're allowed to go it alone, but I hoped we'd get a little direction. So she doesn't use bloodstones. Who started that trend, then? They didn't come out of nowhere. Someone must have worked out it's possible to store human energy inside an object."

He cleared his throat. "Actually… that was the warlocks."

I blinked. "Seriously?"

*You might have mentioned that before.* It wasn't pertinent information, but still pretty relevant. Because a warlock might be behind this, not a demon. Vampires must be getting the demon energy from somewhere, and Nikolas had been downright vague when I'd asked how the whole thing worked.

"Yes. The primary use of energy is in summonings, so they invented a way of storing that energy which didn't involve causing unnecessary damage to the people involved. Certainly not demonic energy, however."

"But that doesn't explain… it's not Azurial's magic in those bloodstones, right? He's a fire demon."

"Correct," he said. "Bloodstones aren't strong enough to hold the power of a demigod—up until recently, I didn't know they could store demonic energy at all. Demons and vampires would have no use for such a thing. It's human energy that holds value for them."

"They don't drink demon blood," I said. "It's poisonous to them. But someone must have come up with the idea of using energy instead. Azurial? I can't think how a fire demon on a realm where celestials don't even exist would have figured out how to kill us in that way."

"I've always suspected he didn't work alone. He never struck me as a revolutionary thinker."

"Well, he apparently started it," I said. "The vamps were just pawns. I'm pretty sure he only got hold of them in the first place because they're his dad's major weakness, and he needed their venom to keep him down. But then again, that might not have been his idea either."

"There must have been another mastermind." He nodded slowly. "The vampires didn't all come from this dimension, either. The demon energy they put into the bloodstones certainly didn't."

"Exactly," I said. "Say it's still happening—the odds are high that it's coming from over there, right? I know the celestials don't have a permit to go to the palace and stop them. I mean, people like us don't even exist in Pandemonium."

The worlds weren't parallel. There weren't another dozen Devis running around. The countless realms diverged at such crucial points—like who won major demon wars—that the very nature of civilisation shifted. When demons won the wars, things never seemed to work out very well for the humans involved.

"I'm not concerned with needing a permit," he said. "But if there's a demon from that dimension, someone here is responsible for summoning it. That's the part which concerns us."

"And—you don't have any idea who it could be?"

He shook his head. "If the answers lie anywhere, it's in the blood of the person who might have taken in the demon energy himself."

"You mean our prisoner," I said. "Has anyone tested his blood?"

"It's not that simple. Vampire blood cancels out most demon viruses—she was right about that part. But as to isolating the demon energy itself... as of yet, even Rachel hasn't managed to do so."

"Seriously?" My heart sank. "I need to talk to her."

"I'm heading to the Harpy's Nest to meet with her and Javos now," Nikolas said. "Want to join me?"

"You don't even need to ask."

But one thing was for certain—if even Nikolas didn't have the answers, we were deep in the shit.

## 5

The Harpy's Nest was a mostly-warlock bar run by a vampire with spiky hair who kept trying to get me to buy blood cocktails. Weirdly, nobody here seemed to mind that I was human, though I kept my celestial mark hidden just in case.

I sipped at a vodka and coke while I filled Rachel in on our unsuccessful meeting with the vampire queen, and Nikolas went in search of Javos.

"I had a feeling she wouldn't cooperate," she said. "She's set in her ways. Doubt she ever thought anyone would find an alternative use for bloodstones."

"Most of us didn't, either," I said. "So she's off the list, which means we have to go back to tracking them the old-fashioned way. Unless you or Nikolas knows anyone who might be an expert in separating the demon venom from our prisoner's bloodstream."

"Was that your idea or Niko's?" Her eyes gleamed. "He didn't tell you. Oh, boy. Well, there *is* one person who might know how the whole demon energy thing works… Niko's brother."

I choked on my drink. "Zadok."

Nikolas's brother lived in the shadow dimension, Babylon. Unlike him and Rachel, they were biological siblings, so their magic was similar. Except while Nikolas could travel between realms, Zadok could lock someone into a shadow trap of his own making, and attack with shadowy clones. He also had a small army of scorpion demons and lived in a demonglass tower adjacent to the castle that belonged to Nikolas. So, not the sort of person you visited without backup. But Nikolas had known the whole time he'd been talking to me that his brother might know something we didn't. If he'd told Rachel, why not trust me with that information, considering what was at stake?

"I'd ask Niko to take you to him," Rachel said. "But Zad's pissed off with you, and Niko will be pissed off with *me* for suggesting it."

"Just what I was afraid of." I rolled my eyes. "What about our prisoner? Nikolas said you couldn't isolate the demon energy."

"That's the other problem," she said. "I tried to get more of the cure from the vamp's blood, and couldn't find anything. I think the regular vampire venom obliterates it. Besides, it's worn off by now."

My eyes widened. "It has? But—doesn't that mean he'll go back into demon mode, if he's still under the effects of the venom?"

A tremendous crash rattled the table, and glasses shattered on the floor. The room trembled as though an earthquake shook the whole pub. I looked for the culprit and spotted a huge horned warlock swinging a smaller human-sized figure by the neck. He hit the table, apparently unconscious or dead.

The horned warlock cast a furious gaze around the bar, and my wrist tingled uncontrollably. *There's a demon. Close by.*

Of course, the mark might well be reacting to the close proximity of a pissed-off warlock.

The door smacked off the wall, and three vampires ran into the bar.

For a moment, everyone stared. Then one of the vamps leaped onto the nearest table, grabbed a fork-tailed demon by the neck, and sank in his fangs.

Panic erupted. Warlocks rose to their feet with furious cries, launching themselves on the enemy. Since the average warlock was twice the size of a vampire, it shouldn't have been an issue—if not for their speed. What with the brawling heaps of claws, tails and wings, it was beyond me to pinpoint the vamps and take them out.

*Fine.* I climbed on the table, pulling off my cuff. Celestial light blazed from my wrist, bouncing off the walls, and drawing the eye of every demon and vampire in the bar. My gaze snagged on a vamp chewing on a young warlock, and I leaped at him. Our bodies collided against the table, sending several glasses shattering on the wooden floor. The vampire's eyes were flat black. *I knew it.*

I waved my celestial light in his eyes, struggling to break free from his iron grip. My free hand found a glass and smashed it on the side of his neck. The vamp screeched but didn't loosen his hold. Rachel yelled, the noise buried beneath the sounds of brawling filling the air. I punched the vamp's already-bleeding neck. This time, his grip slackened enough for me to knee him in the crotch. Sliding out from underneath him, I grabbed a stake and thrust it into his back.

Dropping the blood-soaked glass, I pivoted, trying to see the other two vamps. A pile of warlocks brawled several feet away, accompanied by the sound of ripping and tearing. A bloody-mouthed warlock climbed off the heap, grinning. *I think Vamp #2 might be dead.*

Lightning spiked the air, and I pinpointed Nikolas in

the far corner. The third vamp fell to the floor, having apparently been running away. Maybe he'd rethought his foolish plan to attack a bunch of overpowered warlocks on their own turf. I elbowed my way through to him as the vampire fell to the ground, his neck snapped at Nikolas's hand.

"This is my fucking bar!" yelled the vampire bartender. "I've been here for fifty years. Kill the interlopers."

Whoa. I hadn't thought he was older than me. I shouldn't be so quick to judge vampires.

Problem: all eyes were on me, not the dead vamps.

Nikolas moved forward and grabbed my arm, as the vampire disappeared underneath a heap of writhing bodies. At the same time, shadows closed in around us, and the next second, we stood in a ravine.

"Thanks for asking before you dragged me away," I said, yanking my arm free.

"You know things were about to go off into the deep end." Nikolas shot me an irritated look, like I'd brought the vamps there myself.

"I could have made it to the door," I said. "Now they'll blame both of us."

"Half of them were drunk and won't remember by tomorrow. They'll take their rage out on those dead vampires, and that'll be that."

"No, it won't," I said. "Those vamps were jacked up on demon energy, *and* they attacked a neutral bar. Do you really think there won't be backlash?"

His eyes narrowed. "Don't presume to think I haven't considered the possible outcomes. I think the two of us have caused enough damage."

"Yeah, by killing the vamps trying to attack everyone." I yanked down my cuff. "Some gratitude."

"I never said *I* was ungrateful," he said. "Just that those who do remember tonight will remember you as a celestial who came into their establishment."

"I had an invite from Javos himself. If he's so dead set on converting me over to Team Warlock, he can explain to the others. It's not like they'll listen to me."

"Recruit you?" he echoed. "You signed up of your own accord."

"I signed up for a trial," I corrected. "I'm not an honorary warlock until my magic shows up, which as long as he forbids me from using it properly, isn't likely to happen anytime soon. Besides, I'm bound to the celestials by blood, and that'll never change. He can't undo that."

Neither of them really understood. They'd been born with demon magic. I'd been *re*born from death as a celestial soldier, and it'd been written into my very nature. The demon mark had come along later, and the celestial magic had always taken precedence. Using it to kill demons felt right, and not being able to access it was like cutting off some crucial sense. It was part of me. But that wasn't what was bothering me. *Your brother might know something important, and you lied.*

"We're not trying to take away your celestial mark," he said. "But I think it's worth unlocking your demon magic before someone forces it on you."

"Your boss *is* forcing it on me," I said through gritted teeth. "You know, if I'd used demon magic tonight, I'd be facing a whole different set of questions. It's not a matter of simply switching over from one to the other. I'm both at once. Unless the Divinity or arch-demon who marked me decides to alter my marks, I don't have a choice in the matter."

There was a pause. "You might be correct, but I don't believe the demons who've seen your power are being idle."

"Your brother? What's he up to these days?"

Nikolas had told him in no uncertain terms to leave me alone—and Rachel, for that matter—but warlocks didn't play by the rules, and that particular warlock carried a grudge and a half. Surely Nikolas would have considered asking him for help… though given their ongoing rivalry, maybe not.

"Sulking," Nikolas said. "He tried to overstep his boundaries in the castle, so I was forced to put him under a spell to keep him trapped in his tower with his powers bound until I could arrange alternative accommodation for our other guest."

"I take it he got curious."

"Right," he said. "Who wouldn't? Themedes is ensconced in a different part of the castle, but Zadok's curiosity knows no bounds. And besides, I never did devise an appropriate punishment for what he did to you." Anger flared in his eyes. "No spell can bind him permanently, but I know his weaknesses. He's without his shadow power for a few weeks, at least."

"Damn. Remind me not to get on your bad side," I said, to disguise the irritating rush of warmth that flooded my body at his indignation on my behalf. Annoyance didn't quell my instinctive response to being close to him. On an alien world where I'd nearly died once before. Okay, the spired castle and starry sky were beautiful in their own way, but when it came down to it, most people in this realm wanted me dead.

"You bound him," I said. "Like Azurial. Is there a level I have to reach before you can tell me how to do that?"

"Each warlock is different," he said. "Zadok's prison isn't permanent, but he seems to have a disturbing fascination with you."

"Not going to answer my question, huh," I said, cutting to the chase. I could excuse him not telling me other people's secrets, but on the other hand, my own demon mark was inextricably tied to the nether dimensions. "Rachel said your brother might know which demon's energy is in the blood-stones, and how to isolate the cure."

His mouth thinned. "No. If he does, he wouldn't share that knowledge, not without a price."

"So that's it? You'd put your grudge above people's lives?"

"He won't help us, Devi," he said. "Not because of my grudge, but because of his own. He's far less human than I am. If he gets the slightest clue you're in need of information from him, he'll reel you in with words and shadows until there's nothing left of you."

"Delightful," I said. "He's a real prize. Fine. Can I speak to the arch-demon instead?"

"Not tonight. The path to the castle isn't safe."

"I'm not an untrained human." I blew out a breath. "Tomorrow, then. Otherwise I'm taking on this case alone."

He looked sharply at me. "It's not worth it, Devi. At least one other demon already has a claim on you. The more time you spend in the nether realms, the more they'll try to pull you in before you're ready to handle them."

I swallowed down an angry retort—or several. I didn't want to argue with him, and heaven only knew I'd have a job and a half getting through to Zadok, considering he wanted me dead. But letting that knowledge dangle out of reach while people were dying…

*He might know who killed Gav.*

Going back to the guild had brought all the memories rushing back. The demonic magic the vampires had taken in had corrupted them, but the ones who'd attacked tonight had apparently acted at random. Attacking a bar packed with warlocks was downright foolish, but it hadn't been an accident that they'd targeted a neutral place where warlocks and vampires generally got along just fine. But it'd been suicidal at best. They'd known—or the people who'd sent them had—that they wouldn't make it out of there alive.

As much as I wanted to storm into the castle and question the arch-demon, a mile of wasteland and an impenetrable wall lay between us and the castle, and I had entirely too many questions to answer at home. Maybe it *was* worth looking into the attack in more detail rather than jumping right into questioning arch-demons. Someone in our own realm had sent those vampires with the apparent purpose of sowing chaos, without a care as to whether the vamps in question lived to tell the tale.

I breathed out, willing the clenching sensation inside me to go away, and let Nikolas's shadowy aura envelop my body, taking me back home to Haven City.

6

"What a disaster," Rachel commented when I walked into the warlocks' headquarters early the following morning. I hadn't heard a word from the celestials about any new developments on the bite victims. I'd assumed Javos was dealing with the fallout from last night, because he hadn't contacted me either.

The door on the right lay open, revealing a living room where Nikolas and Rachel sat in front of an old-fashioned TV with a VCR.

"What're you doing?" I asked.

"Watching the CCTV tapes from the pub down the road from the attacks," Rachel said. "To see which direction the vamps came from."

"Has anyone looked at the bodies?"

"There wasn't enough left to examine." Nikolas glanced at me. "The warlocks took them to pieces and burned the remains. If we'd stayed, we'd have been caught in the melee."

"So they destroyed the evidence." I sighed. "Great. No clue who gave them the demon energy? Is Madame White actually taking this seriously now?"

"I haven't spoken to her," said Nikolas. "As for Javos, he's storming around trying to work out which collective those vamps came from. If he can find a pattern, it might be possible to track the source of those bloodstones that way. The real question is what they hoped to accomplish. Why target a warlock bar?"

"To inflame tensions between preternaturals, obviously," I said. "The bites don't affect warlocks, right?"

Nikolas returned his attention to the screen. "For all our sakes, I sincerely hope not."

The camera played the grainy image of people passing by outside the pub. Since more than half the clientele were warlocks, even the black-and-white images made it a little easier to pinpoint any human-sized figures passing by.

"Three people walking that way," I said, squinting at the image. "Looks like they were pretty calm before they started smashing things in the pub. Must be how they avoided attention."

"I imagine so," said Nikolas, in a bored voice. "That's all we've got. No footage from inside the pub itself—most of the people there were swept into the fighting."

"And no bodies, because someone got overexcited and shredded them." I rolled my eyes. "Did Javos want us to spend all day watching pointless videos? Because I have a few other things I'd like to look into instead."

Nikolas eyed me. "Not Babylon."

He'd guessed my plan before I'd begun to fabricate a way to sneak off to the demonglass room. "Got anyone else to question?" I asked. "It's not like I *want* to go back into that castle, but I'm not going to sit back while more people fall victim to these vampire killers. I know I'm not supposed to use my ability except as a last resort, but what if this *is* a last resort? Someone's manufacturing this demon energy. Unless we talk to one of the people who had a hand in it, our information's going to be one-sided."

"I agree," Nikolas said, to my surprise, "but there's no evidence that the current source of demon energy is in the netherworld. We closely watch demon summonings now. This is strictly a vampire issue, and you saw how their queen reacted to my accusations."

"Yes, I did," I said. "But the fact is—we have access to those realms. Through me."

"I'm up for it," Rachel said. "So you can shortcut into anywhere with demonglass, right?"

"Yeah," I said. "Those pillars at the castle, and Zadok's tower. There are probably others I haven't found yet."

Nikolas gave me a sidelong look. "If you *do* wish to speak with the arch-demon, then I can take you there myself. I can't promise my brother will behave himself, and as for the rest of the castle… let's just say they can sense something's wrong. It's not traditional for an arch-demon, even a dying one, to take up shelter in another dimension without causing side effects to the other demons living there."

"I thought the castle was yours," I said. "Doesn't that imply you have at least some control over what goes on there?"

"I do," he said. "It's also daytime, which makes this easier. And by the way, Devi, you know where the easiest place to cross over is."

"The celestial guild." I looked at him. "I didn't know warlocks were such stubborn rule-followers until I met you. It's my neck on the line if he catches me, not yours."

"Then it's up to you if you want to take the risk or not. If we cross outside the castle, we avoid the obvious target spots. There's a hidden entrance into the lower corridors which will enable us to reach Themedes without being spotted."

"Fine," I said. "C'mon, then. If we're going to the guild, then one of us has to drive."

Nikolas ended up drawing the short straw, mostly because I was fairly sure the celestials knew what my car looked like by now. When we passed by the guild, I couldn't help peering out the window to get a clue as to what might be happening inside. Hopefully no more deaths. With tensions mounting between the vamps and the warlocks, the last thing we needed was the inspector coming back to the guild and making trouble for everyone. If we could figure out whether the vampires were coming from a particular collective or not, we could cut off the hydra's head before it infected anyone else.

Once the car was safely parked in the street parallel to the guild, we crossed over into the shadow dimension.

Even during the day, the sky was dark purple, etched with bright constellations. The castle's obsidian towers loomed over us, and a cold breeze blew in. Whatever the seasons were like here, it always seemed to be freezing. I shivered a little, drawing my coat tighter around my shoulders. Stakes brushed against my legs, while two anti-warlock traps were concealed around my neck. I hadn't mentioned them to Nikolas, because whatever the arch-demon said, I had plans to speak to his brother one way or another.

Then again, the dying arch-demon might well be just as dangerous himself.

Nikolas led the way to the castle's side entrance. Hoping there wasn't an army of scorpion demons on the other side, I peered past him at a cold stone corridor and a staircase spiralling upwards. Nikolas led us across the dark flagstones, painted in moonlight-coloured stripes from the overhead windows. I kept one eye out for anything lurking in the shadows, and walked with Rachel. She skipped along, humming, as though we were on a shopping trip rather than an excursion into a dimension which had tried to kill both of us more than once.

Finally, Nikolas halted outside a locked wooden door. "Don't provoke him," he said. "He's a little unhappy at the current arrangement. I felt it wise to keep him separated from his son's prison in Pandemonium, but unfortunately, he hasn't taken to the new arrangements well."

"He's still… losing power, right?" I dropped my voice, figuring that asking if the arch-demon was still dying where he could overhear me wouldn't make Themedes any more inclined to give me information.

"Yes." He frowned. "You're still wearing your trap. Why?"

"You know why. Same reason I brought stakes. There are vampires involved in this. It's best to be prepared."

Nikolas's brow remained furrowed as though scrutinising me, then he looked away. "Just don't pull out any weapons and startle him."

He took a key from his pocket and unlocked the door.

Inside the room, Themedes sat on a battered armchair besides a bed which appeared to be the only other piece of furniture. He was in his human-like guise, except for the wings drooping at his back. Luckily, he was fully clothed this time, wearing ragged trousers and a torn shirt. The smell of brimstone permeated the air.

"Come to have a good laugh, have you?" he growled in the demonic language of High Chthonian, his gaze pinning me to the spot. He didn't have the same burning aura as last time, but my body tensed all the same. His terrifying presence was difficult to forget, even weakened as he was now. Dark burgundy eyes clouded with hate and anger, but not overwhelming power like they had before. The spark had gone out.

"Guys," I said out of the corner of my mouth, "maybe I should talk to him alone. I can handle him."

Nikolas's eyes searched my face, then he nodded, gesturing to Rachel to step back. The arch-demon and I were alone.

"It's better this way, you know," I said to him in his own language, remaining in a defensive stance. "Your son wanted you dead."

"He did," he said. "He wanted to wear my power like a crown, because he had nothing of his own. Now I've moved from one prison to another."

"This isn't—"

"Don't be daft," he growled. "I know a prison when I see one, as much as you think I've lost my wits."

*Yeah, I figured that out the first time you tried to kill me.*

"What do you lot want, then?" he snarled.

"To know how Azurial put his demonic energy into the bloodstones," I said. "If it *was* his, or someone else's. And if any other vamps were left in our realm after he died."

"I've never been to your realm, you idiotic human," he said. "As to the bloodstones, I wasn't aware of their existence until a swarm of vampires took over my palace." His voice rumbled, carrying the echo of the power he'd once unleashed on me. A tempest brewed in his eyes, but they didn't rage with flames as they had before.

Still, I took an involuntary step back. Arch-demon powers were no joke, even if the arch-demon in question was less threatening than a Grade Two demon.

"Azurial was a traitorous bastard to even consider giving any power to the vampires," he growled. "They are our sworn enemies."

"But why can he do it and nobody else can?" I asked.

"If I knew how he'd done it, I might have been able to stop him, human," he said. "As for the vampires, they were recruits of his. I can't say I cared where he found them, only that I hope they suffered a great deal when they expired."

Hmm. I didn't know when Azurial had first contacted our realm, but maybe he hadn't found the vampires there after all. Let's face it, vamps hated demons, and most wouldn't listen if one of them appeared and started whispering promises to them. They'd have to offer a hell of a bargain for vampires to even consider pledging what remained of their souls to a demon.

Something like… a cure.

Careful to keep my expression blank, I said, "Azurial frequently contacted my dimension, apparently. Did you watch him at all?"

"Did I watch him?" he echoed. "He was given everything a demigod could ever want, save for my throne. Only an arch-demon is worthy to rule my great city. Now, it will fall with my passing. And I wish I was there to watch it burn."

"Good for you," I responded, irritation prickling up my spine. No prizes for guessing if he gave a shit about what Azurial had done in my realm. Nope—he was the centre of the universe, and if I was to get anywhere, I'd need to appeal to his ego. Or bruise it. "So he was plotting against you by hiding vampires in the palace," I said. "Surely if I were you, I'd want to know how he sneaked them in."

His aura blazed. "Traitor. He had full access, the spoilt little bastard. I was a fool to take my eyes off him."

"Yes, that was a mistake," I said. "It's a pity he can't die, too."

"Did he tell you that? Or the other warlock?" He laughed harshly. "As though I'd pass on that information to a celestial. Don't think I've forgotten what you are. You might wear our mark, but you're still one of them."

"Maybe I'm not," I said. "Maybe I'm something else."

"He knows what you are," he muttered. "Never thought I'd see the day when I'd be outdone by a warlock. He talks about you a lot, do you know?"

"Er… who?"

"Your shadow-aligned friend."

*Nikolas has been here? More than once?* I'd figured he'd kept in contact, but not that they'd been having conversations about me behind my back.

He gave a coughing laugh. "If he came to any conclusions about the nature of your power, he didn't tell me… but I suppose he didn't give you that information, either. In the end, you're a celestial in their eyes. Until you fall."

"What are you talking about?"

He laughed again, wiping his mouth with his sleeve, which came away red with blood.

"I'm not long for this realm or others, but I'd give anything to see it again… to see them die."

My stomach turned over. "The celestials, right?"

"It's a sham," he rumbled. "They're all the same. They fall, or they die believing themselves righteous. All will fall to the netherworld in the end. The shadowy one knows. He knows."

"Wait. Are you talking about Nikolas, or Zadok?"

"Does it matter?"

*He's changing the subject.* As brutally fascinating as arch-demon politics were, I needed answers on our more immediate problem.

"So you don't know where your son brought the vampires in from?" I asked. "You didn't see him set up his summoning connections with our realm?" But he'd done so through Dienes, a lesser demon. Either he'd asked and found vampires on the other side… or they'd already been there. In his own realm. Which at least explained why we hadn't found their lair yet.

"I've been locked up here too long, and policing the vampires was never my job. You're asking the wrong person."

"You must know something," I said. "Vamps can't skip

through dimensions. Most demons can't, and Azurial's locked up. Unless they were already in our dimension before I killed him." But that didn't explain where the demon-infected bloodstones had come from. Someone was smuggling them in… which meant setting up a portal. They weren't dropping out of the sky.

"There are many moving pieces in this game, Devi. Yours is only a small part of it. A tiny, insignificant human with a mark on her soul." He cough-laughed, flecks of blood appearing around his mouth. "Nothing, in the grand scheme of things. This isn't a game you can win."

"Then why did the fallen Divinity mark me in the first place?"

"There's nothing you can offer me for that information that I have need of, celestial."

Damn him. Sure, there were others who might know… but he'd *been* there, with the other Divinities. He'd been on their side. Until he'd fallen.

"Sounds pretty lonely," I muttered. "You know, you say that everyone will fall, and the celestials are deluded. Sounds like you've had a pretty miserable existence anyway."

"Better to reign in the netherworld, Devi, then allow yourself to be blinded."

Great. Not much I could do with that. Demons might not be outright evil, but the realms they ruled weren't exactly paradise. Look at this place.

"Just one more question," I said, holding out a ragged cloth stained with dried blood. "Can you identify this demon? Its essence was in the vampire's blood." When I'd been cleaning off the blood from the vampire attack last night, I'd managed to get enough of it onto the cloth to make a decent sample.

"Are you mocking me?" he growled.

"No, I really want to know."

He let out a rumbling growl of anger, which reverberated through the floor. Crap. I really hoped Nikolas had accounted for mad arch-demons when he'd built this castle. If he'd been the one to build it. The arch-demon's huge body trembled, then he collapsed into a tremendous coughing fit. The room shook, a sound like crackling flames filling the air. Coughing blood onto the stone floor, the arch-demon straightened, his once-proud wings drooping from his shoulders.

"Leave," he croaked. "Leave, before I smite you. It doesn't matter if you die at my hands, since my time is limited anyway. If your fallen Divinity would seek to punish me for torturing you, I'd be dead before he found you."

I backed away, feeling the echo of his power brush against my skin. My demon mark tingled as though in warning, while my celestial mark burned in unison. With both marks warning me to run, I figured I'd better listen.

The door flew open behind me.

"Calm down," Nikolas said in a loud, steady voice. "We are not your enemies."

I didn't miss his sidelong look that implied he wasn't best pleased with me for provoking the arch-demon. I hadn't thought Themedes would help, but it seemed a bit of an overreaction. Especially considering he hadn't responded at all to me calling him a miserable bastard. Maybe because he knew it was true.

Themedes coughed blood onto the floor again, falling back against the bed.

Nikolas steered me towards the door. I yanked my arm free, glaring at him. "That wasn't necessary. There's more he knows—and he won't tell me."

"He's an arch-demon," he said. "He's baiting you, trying to get you to sign over your soul. It won't lead to anything, Devi."

*Fine. I'll ask your brother instead. Or Azurial.* Nikolas might be trying to protect me, but he kept secrets of his own. Dangerous secrets.

"He can't own my soul if he's dead," I said, not particularly caring if Themedes heard this time.

Nikolas frowned at the scrap of fabric in my hands. "You didn't mention you got hold of the vampire's tainted blood."

"Thought you already had a sample," I said. "I figured he'd know where the demon magic came from. It's better than summoning up demons at random and making risky bargains. I'm not sure it *is* Azurial's power inside the blood-stones. Maybe he was using someone else's. There's no way to tell, unless you can identify it."

"You remember me telling you all demon magic looks the same?" he asked. "The aura is the same colour on all the tainted vampires we've encountered. Few demons have the ability to tell which demon the magic came from."

*Is your brother one of them?* The question lay on the tip of my tongue, but we'd had that argument already. Nikolas clearly wasn't budging on that one, and I was less than certain the two hadn't discussed me behind my back anyway. And the arch-demon, come to that.

"It's up to you, then," I said. "We keep going with the limited knowledge we have in our own dimension, or we look to the netherworld."

"The netherworld offers nothing without a price."

"Heard that one from the arch-demon," I said. "You can't investigate a case like this and not expect some bargaining to come into it. You *are* half demon. You know there's no other way to gain the information."

"You lied," he said. "You didn't plan to come here at all. It was Pandemonium you wanted to target."

"I didn't lie. You said yourself there are all kinds of

monsters over here. I'm not naive enough to think the pretty sky makes up for all that."

"Now you're diverting." His eyes narrowed. "Really, Devi? You think you can take on the fire demon without falling victim to his lies?"

"Technically, I killed him once already." I decided not to contradict him and say it wasn't Azurial I'd planned to question, but someone much closer to home.

"You know what his dimension is like," Nikolas said.

"Look, this isn't an optional thing. If we don't find out what's going on over there, things are gonna look pretty crap for Earth. Besides, I can easily shortcut into the palace without setting foot outside."

"Do you really think the other inhabitants of Pandemonium will have left the palace alone?" he asked. "Azurial might be caged, but the remainder of the city is fair game to anyone who wants power. Besides, not everyone can put their demonic power into an object. It wasn't supposed to be possible at all, actually. I still can't figure out how Azurial did it."

"Hey!" said Rachel, from the corner. "If you two have quite finished bickering, I'm freezing my tits off here. Let's go home."

*This isn't over, Nikolas.* I'd return to the subject later, when we were away from this place. I hadn't intended to start another argument, but Nikolas had ties and obligations to toe the line whatever dimension he was in. I didn't. Shielding me from the truth wouldn't end well for any of us. I'd pry the truth from the demons myself if I had to. It was past time I put my training to good use.

## 7

Once outside the castle, we crossed back into the human realm, to the sight of a pack of celestial soldiers running around the corner. Very luckily, they were headed in the opposite direction to where Nikolas had parked. But sending out a group of them meant only one thing: a demon attack, or another related incident.

I took off after them, not waiting to hear the others' objections.

"Hey!" I said, catching the eye of Lydia, former model academy student and the single most cheerful person ever to set foot in the guild. "What's going on?"

"Devi!" she said, her face lighting up in a smile brighter than my celestial hand. Not a demon attack, then. "We've had a slight issue at the guild…"

"The prisoner got out." Bad Haircut Sammy, my former nemesis, swaggered over. He wasn't worth my attention—and I wouldn't let him forget he'd practically run away screaming the last time I'd seen him. Greasy dark hair flopped into his eyes, and not for the first time, he had his guild-issued weapons strapped on backwards.

"Prisoner?" I arched a brow. "Which one?"

"Damian."

*Should have known.* The guy had been a bad-tempered little shit, but if he got afflicted by the virus, people might die. Of course the guild couldn't do one thing right.

"Yeah," said Lydia, concern flashing across her features. "He shouldn't have been able to get the lock off the door."

"He got bitten by a vampire," I reminded her. "The guild should have figured there'd be side effects. Where's Mrs Credence?"

"Inside." She waved a hand in the direction of the guild headquarters. "We're searching the area. Nobody saw which direction he ran in. They're checking the CCTV footage now, but it doesn't extend any further than this road."

Great. Well, I could follow them and put up with Bad Haircut Sammy, or I could take a quick detour into the guild to see if our escapee had left any evidence behind.

And I'd rarely have a better chance to ensure I got some peace for the next part of my plan.

I returned to Nikolas and Rachel, who waited by the car. "Go on ahead," I told them. "We have a rogue potential murderer on the loose—another one. It might be the guild can handle it, but I have my doubts. Besides, it's all connected. Let me know if I need to come over later."

To my surprise, Nikolas didn't object. He nodded to Rachel. "We need to report in."

*That was easier than expected.* Maybe he'd accepted my remaining ties to the celestials, after all. Now to make this meeting as short as possible.

I found Mrs Credence in conversation with Mr Roth, the guild's new leader, inside Gav's old office. Seeing him in there gave me a familiar jolt—grief and anger, and guilt that I still hadn't figured out who'd been responsible for my former supervisor's death. Mrs Credence held a book in her hands.

"This is all the evidence he left behind," she said.

My gaze went to the book's title *The Beginner's Guide to Poisons and Venoms.* I hadn't looked closely at the title when he'd thrown the book at me at the academy.

"Weird choice of reading material," I commented. "Can I have a look at it?"

She passed it me, ignoring a warning look from Mr Roth.

"Is there something you need, Devina?" he asked.

I accepted the book from her, ignoring the question. "I'm not sure I completely understand what happened here." I used my best *give me answers* voice, which I'd mastered while training annoying novices.

Mrs Credence's expression crumpled. "It's my fault," she said. "I didn't think it'd be suitable to lock him in a jail cell, so I suggested an office. Its security levels aren't as tight."

"Didn't I say keep an eye on him, not lock him up?" I said. "From what I saw of him, he was pretty resentful of the whole thing. Of course he got out."

"Devina—" Mr Roth began.

"Just being honest. Where's this room, then?"

Book in hand, I followed Mrs Credence down the corridor, which had been cordoned off halfway. The wooden office door hung from its hinges, like someone had ripped it clean off. A human couldn't have done it. A celestial, though? He didn't even need demonic vampire powers, if he'd asked a friend to help.

"Did anyone else visit him?" I asked.

"No," she said. "I asked if he wanted me to call anyone, and he said no. He's an orphan, you know… no family. No ties, before here."

*Then it's not a surprise he resents you for treating him like a criminal.* I might not have liked the guy, but the guild had once been all I'd had, too. After my parents' deaths, I'd been effectively adopted into the celestials, though I hadn't thought of them as family in a long time. Not since Rory's death.

I turned the book over in my hands, and a slip of paper fell out.

*I know what you did.*

I stared at it for a moment, then turned the paper over. "Did Damian write this?"

Neither of them answered. Holding the paper, I opened the book onto the page it'd marked. From the jagged edges, several pages had been torn out.

"I can't say for sure it's his handwriting," said Mrs Credence, doubtfully. "But… that's odd."

"No idea who this is directed at?" I held up the message. A chill raced down my back. He'd thrown the book at me before… but it might be a coincidence. Had he torn the pages out, though?

"No," said Mr Roth. "Where did that book come from, anyway?"

"I got it from the library," said Mrs Credence, a touch apologetically. "I let him choose one book, and that was his choice."

"Venom and poison," I said. "He wasn't—looking for a cure, was he?"

They exchanged glances. "Perhaps… but there isn't one," she said uncertainly. "Or so I'm told. Whatever bit him had powers beyond a vampire's."

"Yeah, that's the issue I'm dealing with at the moment," I said. "Can I borrow this?"

I didn't believe in coincidence, but right now I was stumped.

"Never mind the book," said Mr Roth impatiently. "We need to bring him back in. If he bites another celestial… who knows what might happen."

"I'd also be concerned about him running into a demon

and catching on fire in public," I said. "Which he must have considered and then took the risk anyway."

I hadn't cared for him, but unease twisted inside me at the words on the note. The book was labelled with angelic symbols, which meant it'd been salvaged from the old guild after it'd burned down. I turned back to the first page which showed who'd checked the book out... and my heart dropped.

Gav's name was listed as the last person to borrow the book, not two weeks before he'd died.

I swallowed hard. *Coincidence...* or not? Had he known something? No way. It wasn't like I could ask. Even his phone had disappeared after his death. I had a nasty feeling the inspector had removed it himself, so I wouldn't be able to ask any more questions about his death.

My old suspicions about the guild had never truly been buried. The inspector might not be in league with demons, but someone here was up to no good. The demonglass in the west wing had never been recovered. And now...

"Can I talk to Alyson?" I asked. "She's here, right? Please tell me you put her in jail, at least."

"Yes, we did," said Mr Roth. "But she's not taking visitors. I'm going to have to ask you to leave, Devina. I'm expecting a report from the celestials out in the field."

*Worth a try.* "All right. I'll go. Just... tell me if you find him. We've enough to worry about without infected celestials biting people, too."

Worry remained, a nagging doubt in the back of my head. The celestials had never been to another dimension, and there'd been no access to anything demonic in the academy. Like the guild, it was demon-free. But plainly, nobody had bothered to keep a close eye on them. They were pushed aside, to protect the guild's reputation. Might worse than vampire bites have affected the victims? And why had it taken until now for the effects to kick in?

I took the train home to pick up my car and ingredients for a summoning, and then drove around town, finding a nice dark alley away from prying eyes.

When I'd worked for the guild, I'd had a partner in my dealings with the netherworld. Rory and I had interrogated demons of all kinds, summoned them in safe locations, and used their expertise to track down interlopers in this dimension across six continents. Those memories seemed a long way off now I spent all my time hanging around with warlocks, especially now I was well and truly going behind their backs.

I must be losing my mind. But the fact was, all my plans had involved going onto the demons' own territory. That put me at the mercy of the beings who knew more than I did about the forces moving behind the scenes. Drawing them here, however, put me in charge of interrogating those who might know useful information. Such as the traitorous little worm who'd facilitated Azurial's access to our realm, for instance.

Firstly, I used my celestial light to burn the shape of a pentagram onto the bare brick wall. Then I set up an extra layer of defence in the form of various herbs. Finally, I tossed the fabric stained in the vamp's tainted blood into the pentagram and waited.

Dienes's small head appeared, horned and scaled.

"Devi!" he said. "What a nice surpri—"

I grabbed his throat, yanking him forward with my right hand and holding his face next to the pentagram's burning edge. The little demon wailed hysterically. "Stop! Please!"

"You deserve worse," I said. "You traitorous little bastard."

He squealed in pain, cringing away from the bright lights.

"I'll tell you anything!" he wailed. "He gave me no choice. Our city is dying."

"Tell me what Azurial is planning," I snarled. "He's still involved in this, right? He still has his people targeting vampires." The fact that the tainted blood had definitely come from that dimension left me no doubt.

He shook his head. "I haven't seen him since you defeated him."

"But you do admit you worked with him. This is all on you, demon. You deserve the consequences for trying to kill the celestials in my realm, including me."

He began to sob. "I was only the messenger, Devi. I never wanted to see you hurt."

"And the vampires? Just how close were you to them? Did he ever ask you to carry the bloodstones?"

"The what?"

I gave him a shake, and he squealed. "The vampires. You knew he was using them as weapons, with demon energy. Where did he get them from?"

"I don't know, Devi, what—"

"Where did he get the vampires from?" I snarled in his ear. "Tell me the truth or I'll end you. You're no use to anyone alive now."

He shook his head, his body trembling. "I don't know… you'd have to ask the vampires here. They were… with him. With Azurial."

Well. That was something. Of course, there was the slight issue of Pandemonium being a city that was pretty much celestial-proofed. Someone like me was an enemy of all the locals by default—all the more because I'd killed their would-be leader and was also responsible for Themedes taking up residence in another dimension. The first time I'd been there, Nikolas and I had been permitted to enter due to an invitation at the hands of their leader. Otherwise, I'd have to knowingly break the contract I'd signed, which would be far more likely to backfire on me than anything else.

Time to go with Plan B.

*Nikolas is going to kill me.*

I'd never directly said I wouldn't speak to his brother, nor was I forbidden to go into the shadow dimension—I just wasn't allowed to use my demonglass power to do it. Which still left some other options. Ones that would protect me, and put me in the interrogator's chair.

After tossing Dienes back into the pentagram and switching it off, I doubled up on the protections around it before throwing in a handful of dirt I'd picked up near the castle in Babylon yesterday. Normally I wouldn't be able to summon a demigod with a homemade pentagram, but if his powers were as weakened as Nikolas claimed, he'd be powerless to resist.

"Answer me, Zadok."

The demon mark tingled, and foreboding rushed over me.

Then shadows filled in the pentagram, as though an invisible hand spilled ink across its surface. I'd debated stealing the gold-plated pentagram from the guild but after it hadn't worked on Nikolas, there seemed little point in risking it. Besides, if Zadok's powers were really bound, he wouldn't be able to do a thing while I questioned him. Of course, getting him to answer was another story entirely.

"Devina." He arched a dark brow, disconcertingly like his brother. They weren't twins, but had the same visible signs of demon heritage. Dark red hair curled over his tanned forehead, while his eyes were deep burgundy flecked with gold. Attractive, but somehow... cold, in a way his brother's weren't. I didn't know their history, not really, but I couldn't help wondering how one brother had come to live in our realm, and the other in the demons'. I didn't find him attractive either, though unlike his brother, he'd tried to throw me off a bridge. I mean, that was reason enough to put me off someone.

"Hey, Zadok," I said.

He laughed darkly. "You really pulled out all the stops. I can't move, so you succeeded. I'm very curious to know why you didn't bring my brother. Or… does he not know you're speaking to me?"

I shrugged. "He can talk to you any time he likes. I want to speak with you alone."

"You never answered my question," he mused. "That means you're going behind his back. If you'd like to stay allies with him, then you're making an unwise decision. Unless you want to ally with me, instead. With that mark of yours, you can do anything."

"Please." I rolled my eyes. "You tried to kill me multiple times. I wouldn't side with you if it came between me and that dying arch-demon."

A calculating look entered his eyes. "Or me and Azurial?"

"This isn't a quiz, dickhead," I said. "Unless you want to tell me the two of you were BFFs, so I can come over and put you out of your misery the same way I did him."

"I'm no friend of the fire dimension, Devi," he said. "But I'm curious… does my brother give you any guidance about your powers, or does he keep you in the dark? I take it he has you in an important position, rather than a menial one. You're valuable to him… important."

I thought of the vampire in the shed. Maybe he had a point, but Zadok's use of taunting to get me to side with him was so blatant as to be yawn-inducing. I wouldn't be bargaining for information with this guy.

"Yeah, I am," I said. "More so than you, anyway."

"Then I assume there's a good reason you didn't use your power to come and see me in person," he said softly.

"Try again. That'd put me on your turf, and you've tried to kill me on it twice."

"It didn't stop you sneaking in to talk to Niko's little arch-demon pet, did it?"

"Someone has entirely too much free time on his hands," I responded, though I was sure we hadn't been spotted. Nikolas had the same way of disconcertingly knowing things he shouldn't, but evidently Zadok's prison provided more freedom than I'd thought. I shrugged it off, having been prepared for him to screw with me. Since he couldn't physically touch me, his words did the work for him. But—shit. Did that mean he'd overheard our conversation in the castle?

He just grinned in response.

"So," I said. "What do you know about cures for vampirism?"

He blinked. Good. Let him try being the one at the mercy of word games.

"There isn't one," he said.

"I'm disappointed in you," I said. "I heard you were an expert in the effects of all kinds of demon venom on humans or otherwise. Why would vampires be any different?"

"Vampires and demons are not alike," he said. "There's no cure for what we are."

"That's not what I'm hearing," I countered. "Tell me the truth."

"I am." He frowned a little. "This so-called cure does not exist in the shadow realm. If someone in your dimension has found one, then it must be a very recent development. I can't say I'm in contact with anyone there aside from my brother... and you."

He might well be telling the truth. After all, while our dimensions did have things in common, there were startling differences, too. But I'd hoped for some clue that might lead to more information on how the demon-infected bloodstones worked. Wait, did even *they* exist in his dimension? I chewed the inside of my cheek, debating how to phrase the question.

"Your magic," I said slowly. "Is it possible for someone else to use it on your behalf? Like a proxy?"

He subtly moved forwards as though to get a closer look at me. I held myself still, resisting the urge to lean out of the way. At least he'd never used a lure on me, which presumably meant he didn't have that ability. Good job, really, because he was annoying enough as it was. "Mine? Perhaps. Anyone's might be usurped, if the usurper knows what they're doing."

Like Azurial had stolen his father's power. I'd already known some demons could steal one another's magic, if they were strong enough. What I didn't know was how it was possible for a vampire to do the same. But putting that idea into his head wouldn't do me any favours. One dimension of demonic vampires was one too many for me. And if he found out how much damage they could do to celestials, the information would make it halfway to hell by tomorrow. It wasn't worth the risk.

"If you're waiting to ask me the name of the demon who marked you, get on with it," he said. "I expected a scintillating conversation."

"I expected a bunch of demonic mind games, but you're not making your best effort," I said. "You're hardly the only person who thinks they can blackmail me into signing over my soul."

"Now, what would give you that idea? You're the one who summoned me, and if you really wanted to know about vampires, you'd have asked someone like Azurial. Or did my brother forbid you from contacting that dimension?" He sniffed. "Apparently not, judging by the state of this pentagram."

"What makes you think I didn't speak to him?" I said.

"You know perfectly well what went down a few weeks ago, and if not, you've had time enough to speak to the arch-demon. He's in a worse state than you are, if possible."

His eyes lit up with amusement. "I suppose I have… but there are a great many questions I have about the nature of those events. I only heard the demons' side…"

"And you won't get my side."

He tilted his head, his eyes gleaming in the pentagram's light. "Why, were you thinking of seeking out the one who marked you? Because if so, there's little point. When the demons want you, they'll call your name, and you'll be unable to resist. That is what it means to be marked by us."

My phone buzzed. *Crap.*

"Is that my brother?" He laughed quietly. "He has you dancing at his beck and call, doesn't he? He's just like the rest of us, you know… we can't help but think like the demons we truly are. We recruit allies, we plan domination, and we crush those who oppose us. He's always hated that I had the power to challenge him. You're only an ignorant human in his eyes until he needs your magic."

"Are you done babbling?" My phone kept buzzing, and he kept grinning at me as though I'd said something hilarious.

"I know why he chose you," he said. "Your soul has yet to be claimed by either side. Unclaimed, you might side against us in this war. As a demigod, he can't risk making an enemy of you. So he keeps you around, as a lackey… and you let him. You could be more than you are, Devi."

The pentagram's edges shifted, and shadows spilled out into the shape of a man, pushing me backwards. I kicked the pentagram, and the shadows vanished, along with Zadok himself.

*He does have some of his magic left, after all.*

I checked my phone. Of course, it would be Nikolas calling me.

"Hang on," I muttered, switching on my celestial hand and burning through every remaining trace of brimstone in the alley. I'd take no chances. Then I answered the phone. "Yes?"

"You took your time," Nikolas said. "We have a mission. The vampire in the shed escaped."

"Shit, really?"

"It's our job to bring him back in. With force, if necessary. As a bonus, we might find the source of his contacts. Javos beat an address out of someone, but it's on the opposite side of town and he doesn't drive."

"Why doesn't he... you know what, don't answer that."

Javos, being a gigantic warlock with a pair of huge horns, had considerable trouble finding chairs designed for him, let alone vehicles. As for the train...

"I'm on my way," I said.

I was already halfway out the alley, and I ran back to my car, throwing myself behind the wheel. What a mess. To think I'd thought I was risking everything by summoning demon contacts, and none had been any help whatsoever. The shadow realm wasn't linked to our current vampire dilemma, but I was still convinced the roots of the problem lay in Pandemonium. That realm could easily have been ours, if we'd been set on a different path. If the arch-demons had won... or if the Divinities had gone dark.

But I'd worry about fallen Divinities and demon marks later. First, we had a rogue vamp to subdue.

## 8

I picked up Nikolas and Rachel on the main road, following the directions Nikolas relayed to me on the phone. Rachel called shotgun and turned my radio up to max, ignoring a disgruntled look from Nikolas.

"What have you been doing?" he asked. "You smell of brimstone."

"I may have contacted Dienes." I figured there was no harm in telling him, since he'd been my contact to begin with.

He scowled. "The scavenger demon?"

"Yeah. He was Azurial's lackey. But if I'm to believe him, there isn't anyone acting in his place. This new plan must be from someone who stole his ideas about using the bloodstones to spread demon energy."

"Or someone who orchestrated it," Rachel put in. "I never did think Azurial was particularly… bright. I mean, for a fire demon. I got the sense that he'd rather swipe credit for someone else's ideas than come up with his own."

"Hmm," I said. "I didn't know him well, but he struck me as… not exactly stupid, but narrow-minded. He also implied it took a while for him to find out his dad was allergic to vampire venom, too. So maybe someone else clued him in on that."

"Who?" Rachel frowned. "There aren't any other big power players in that city, that I know of. I'd understand if there were, like, two arch-demons or even some demigods doing battle over the city, but it looks like he just decided his dad wasn't a competent leader anymore and took over. Makes sense from an outsider's perspective, but not to anyone who actually knew the guy."

"You knew him?" I frowned.

"Not closely. Niko had more experience with the palace than I did."

Hmm. Rachel was originally from that dimension, but she hadn't yet told me how she'd ended up in this one. I knew virtually nothing of her history, but she was the only shapeshifter warlock I'd met from either dimension. Nikolas, though—I'd never been able to get a conclusive answer as to why he'd been in contact with the arch-demon to begin with. Again—his secret. But how long before one of the secrets we kept from each other backfired?

I tilted my head. "This confidentiality agreement of yours —does it still apply if it turns out that dimension's behind the attacks in this one? Because I'd like to know what we're up against if it's from that side. I know the major demons, but my contact decided not to tell me about Azurial *or* Themedes until it was too late. Any others I should know about?"

"Not in that city," Nikolas said. "Pandemonium is the only city this particular branch of warlocks is in contact with, because of the overlap with this dimension. Similar to your celestials."

"Minus the netherworld part," I added. *Your* celestials? What was that supposed to mean? "Wait," I said slowly. "How do you get there without being summoned, if Themedes isn't there anymore? How do you know Azurial's still imprisoned?"

There was a pause, slightly too long to be comforting. With my eyes on the road, I couldn't see Nikolas's expression.

"So you *have* been in contact," I finally said. "You might have told me. He nearly killed my friend, and he was responsible for murdering three of my former colleagues. I deserved to know, Nikolas. You can't deny that."

"It wasn't my call to make," he said. "I have contacts of my own in that dimension. I felt it wise to keep updated, since none of us can actually travel there and check."

"So you left him unsupervised?"

"No, he's under watch all right," Nikolas said darkly. "Which means if there's another demigod involved, it's one I don't know about. It's entirely possible other demons from outside have flocked in to claim power. That's why we voted to leave them to their own devices. Few of us have ties there —I certainly don't. The person I asked to watch him isn't reliable, but no demons in that dimension are."

Thanks to Dienes, I knew that already. You couldn't trust a demon. And warlocks? I still didn't have a definite answer on that one.

"Hang on," I said. "Did that vampire run away—now? In broad daylight?"

"Apparently," said Nikolas. "I suspect it's to do with this cure. We're almost here, by the way. Turn left. It's that warehouse."

I followed his directions and stopped the car, killing the radio in the process. Rachel bounded out, her bright pink hair gleaming in the rare sunshine beaming down on the drab warehouses and litter blowing past. At least if we chased the vamps outside, they wouldn't survive five seconds.

Nikolas strode towards the few lingering passers-by. He only had to glance at them and they all turned in the opposite direction and walked away. I sometimes forgot about his subtle form of mind-control, probably because I'd only really seen him use it on ordinary humans.

"I should have warned you he's in a mood," Rachel said to me. "The vamp escaped on his watch."

"Doesn't mean he has to chide me for taking the initiative," I muttered. "I've never got anywhere on a demon hunt without talking to someone on the other side. Otherwise, all you're doing is giving them the benefit of surprise *and* knowledge. Even the celestials know that."

I looked sideways at her, wondering if even *Rachel* was playing games with me. Javos had sent her to recruit me in the first place, and she definitely kept her own secrets. Her carefree demeanour might be as much of a mask as her human disguise.

I stopped outside the wide doors of the warehouse. To no surprise, they were barred. Still… was the vamp stupid enough to lead us right to the source? One could only hope so. The padlocks looked easy to break, but there was a faint scent around the place I couldn't identify. Blood, yes, but…

"Wait!" I held up a warning hand. "It's doctored with some kind of spell. I've seen it before. Only someone with knowledge of this particular type of anti-demon defence could know how to undo it."

Like… the celestials.

*No way.* We'd thought they were evil before and turned out to be wrong, but the vampires were a whole other issue. I'd seen how the guild treated the two bite victims: with zero sympathy.

Unease spiked, and I pulled down the cuff on my wrist to direct my celestial light at the padlock. It fell, sheared in two, and I caught it in my free hand. The demon mark tingled like

I'd put it in stinging nettles. Not great. It meant significant anti-demon defences—possibly invisible ones. Like the celestial guild's.

"I think I've got it," I whispered. "Let me lead the way. If something hits me, it probably won't do much damage. But if this is the sort of thing that sets off alarms when there are demons present, then we might have an issue."

"Then go in alone." Nikolas's gaze swept the warehouse, his eyes narrowing. "The defences alone are proof there can't be demons inside the place."

"Do the vamps not count?" asked Rachel.

"Apparently not." I glanced at the others. "Watch out. They might be setting us up."

Nikolas briefly rested a hand on my arm. I jumped, not expecting the contact. "Be careful."

I pushed the door open and held my left hand high, walking into the dark.

My celestial light flared, showing bare concrete floors and metal walls, with a high ceiling disappearing in shadow. My footsteps echoed, and a chill breeze blew in, magnified by the empty space. The darkness made this room a perfect vampire's nest, but who had set the defences up? And how, for that matter, had our prisoner got inside? He carried the essence of a demon inside him, cure or no cure, if he'd used one of those damaged bloodstones. But the celestials' own defences hadn't reacted against the bite victims. Maybe the virus was too subtle to be detected. *Not good.*

I walked carefully, using my light to show every inch of space, and it finally settled on a trapdoor in the corner. Of course they'd be underground.

Gritting my teeth, I wrenched open the trapdoor, holding my celestial light like a torch.

Several people screamed. "Put the light out!" they wailed.

A number of vampires hunched away from the light, all

looking terrified. They ranged from teenagers to twenty-something adults, all with the pointed canines of vampires, their hands raised to shield themselves. No visible weapons.

This wasn't exactly the death trap I'd been expecting to find, but I remained tense, half convinced one of them would jump at me. I kept one hand on the nearest stake at my waist, but these people didn't look threatening at all.

"What in the world is going on here?" I demanded.

"Don't kill us!" yelped an Asian girl with red-tinted eyes. Blood cravings. They all had a similar look—vamps who hadn't fed recently, if at all. And I was a warm-blooded human, for all my celestial powers.

"Give me one good reason not to. You're fugitives, right?"

"It's not illegal for us to be here," said the girl who'd spoken first. "This warehouse isn't inhabited and doesn't belong to anyone."

"I'll be the judge of that," I said. "I'm searching for a runaway vampire who was seen near here."

I spotted his blond head, hidden at the back, and leaned over, grabbing him by the scruff of his neck. Alec yelled and kicked, and I tossed him onto the concrete.

"This guy was in the same house as a demonic summoning and murder," I told the others. "You'd better start talking, fast. Who are you, and what are you doing here?"

"We ran away," the girl said quickly. "We're not part of the vamps' inner circle, and it's downright brutal for us out there now. The warlocks think we're killers."

"There's not much evidence to the contrary," I said. "Especially when you're skulking around an old warehouse covered in anti-demon defences."

"We're all newly turned," mumbled the blond vampire. He avoided eye contact with me. "We stick together. Please don't hurt us. We haven't done anything wrong."

"Then what's with the defence system?" I asked. "That's not something just anyone could learn how to do." I scanned the group again, and saw another familiar figure at the back, leaning casually against the wall of the underground cellar. Damian, the celestial runaway.

"You," I said. "So this is where you've been hanging out? With vampires? You're not one."

But if he'd been affected like Alyson, he might be something else entirely.

"He helped us when nobody else would," said the girl in a defensive tone. "The other celestials didn't want to know."

"That doesn't surprise me," I said. "But someone close to that guy murdered someone in a similar way to the vampires who keep attacking people. Does anyone want to explain?"

The blond vamp attempted to sidle over to the trapdoor again, and I grabbed him, holding him back. "Not so fast."

"We're dying," he whimpered. "The cure—it turns one in five of us, but it's too late once we've taken it." Bloody tears dripped down his face. "So far, none of us have turned yet. When one of us does, they get thrown out."

"You're saying the *cure* is what's turning people into murderers?" I asked. "Just where are you getting it from?" I eyed the group of them. "What about the other celestials who got bitten? They took the cure, too?" My gaze caught the celestial runaway in the corner, who gave me a defiant look.

"Yeah, they did," he said. "Congratulations, O Great Detective. You managed to catch a bunch of innocent people."

"Innocent my arse," I said. I couldn't forget the note that'd fallen out of the book he'd been reading... the book Gav had checked out of the library before his death. What was the link? I didn't want to ask him about the missing pages in front of the other vamps, especially when it seemed insignificant compared to the other crap going on. "I was sent here to find this guy. But the celestials are looking for you, too, Damian."

Damian snorted. "Yeah right. They don't give a shit about us. They're just trying to save face."

"You know the other bite victim murdered someone, don't you?" I said. "The cure. If that was responsible, how did you get hold of it in the first place?"

"We gave it to him," said a couple of the other vamps. "We didn't know—it was all over the market."

He nodded. "The cure's not permanent, but it's the only way to survive. My celestial powers will destroy me otherwise. So don't you act all high and mighty because you never had to make that choice."

Damn. Of course the guild would have offered him nothing. But still, he was a prick. And while his tone was defensive, there was something calculating in his expression which raised my suspicions.

"Are you sure it's the cure that's doing it?" I asked. "Isn't it a cure for general vampirism, not the venom?"

"Both," said the blond vampire. "It's powerful stuff. But once you take it, you can't go back. We really didn't know it'd have permanent side effects."

"It's some zombie apocalypse movie shit," the girl put in. "We lose at least one person every day. The authorities don't care—we sent a group to speak to Madame White, and she kicked us out."

"She's not a fan of bloodstones," I said. "Demon or otherwise."

"What she doesn't get is how hard it is for us to find fresh blood," said the girl. "She has a bunch of human blood slaves. We don't. Attacking random humans… it's a last resort. We didn't know the bloodstones were infected."

"Where'd you get them?" I asked. "The bloodstones?

That's what I was originally sent to track when I found this guy." I indicated Alec.

The girl shrugged. "It's a trade thing. People pass them around in night clubs. Go to any vamp bar and you'll find bloodstones."

"But the demon-infected ones," I said. "If you don't know where they came from, can you at least tell me where you ran into them?"

A dozen people spoke at once. "You'll have to slow down." Wishing I'd brought a pen and paper, I pulled my phone out, typing names and addresses to check later. "All right. And the cure? Who gave you that?"

Similarly, all of them had different answers. Enough, however, to know we were in trouble. Both the cure and the bloodstones had appeared on the market in the last few weeks. Maybe even at the same time, from the same source. But with different distributors, none of which I knew.

The real question was… was the source in this dimension, or Pandemonium?

"All right." I looked up from my phone. "I'm not going to have you arrested for dealing with the situation in any way you could, but I have two angry warlocks waiting outside and a third back at the guild who wants to torch the whole place. Pretty sure the celestials would, too. And the vampire queen is indifferent. I can't promise I can help, but I need some cooperation. You're on the run from the law, and if more people die, then fingers will point right at you. Let me help. Tell me if you learn anything new. And I won't tell anyone about you."

Several nods. I decided not to mention my suspicions about the source. As for letting the blond vampire go… I'd ask Nikolas first. After all, having an insider in this operation might help all of us prevent more murders.

The ex-celestial, though… that's where I got stuck. If I

reported him, the guild would storm this place down, and who knew what they'd do to the other vampires. But if not, he might turn under the cure's influence like Alyson.

Then again, so might anyone here.

"Hang on," I said to Alec. "One second. I want a word with you. I'm not reporting you, don't worry."

He hesitated, then followed me away from the trapdoor.

"The celestial guy was already here, right?" I asked in a low voice.

He nodded. "Yeah. Apparently he and the others were in contact."

*Definitely suspicious.* "Okay. Can you keep an eye on him for me? He's on the guild's wanted list and might potentially draw them to you. It also sounds like he's been involved with vampires for a while, behind the guild's back."

He nodded. "I've not been here long and I don't really get how things work, but sure."

"Give me your number."

I typed it into my phone as he spoke, hoping I wasn't making a mistake in letting them go. Because if I was, it wasn't my own life at stake.

## 9

"There you are," said Rachel. "I was starting to think we'd need to blast the doors down."

"No need." I briefly summarised what I'd found. "The vamps are innocent, but they might be a danger to others," I finished. "I'd put a watch on this place, but our priority should be finding who's distributing the bloodstones *and* the cure. I have a bunch of names and addresses where the vamps were given both of them."

"Then we'll look into it," said Nikolas. "We can't let those vampires go unwatched. They're breaking the humans' laws, not to mention the celestials', if those defences are anything to go by."

"I volunteer," said Rachel. "For some reason, it's hard for me to blend in at vampire establishments, so I'm best off guarding this place instead."

"You can change your appearance to mimic a vampire, right?" I asked.

"Technically, yes," said Rachel. "But everyone always says I'm too cheerful."

"You are," said Nikolas. "Nobody can mimic vampires' speed of attack, anyway."

"But these vampire hubs are open to the public?" I asked. "Or do we have to tail them while they sneakily trade these bloodstones in alleys?"

"Possibly," Nikolas said.

Rachel grinned, then she flickered around the edges, her appearance turning into that of a giant horned warlock.

"You're pretending to be Javos?" I arched a brow. "Seriously?"

"Nobody will question why I'm here. They'll think it's official warlock business."

She had a point. It was just weird to think of Rachel's pink-haired hyperactive nature hidden behind the façade of our grumpy warlock leader. "If you're sure."

I led the way back to my car, waving goodbye to Rachel. "Hope she'll be okay."

"She will," he said. "Bodyguard duty isn't her strong suit, but she came prepared to deal with vampires."

"So did I." I tapped the stake inside my right sleeve. "Several times over. Unfortunately, all I found in there is a bunch of terrified people hiding from warlocks, celestials *and* the rest of the vampires. I have blond vamp dude's number, anyway, so I can keep in contact that way."

He looked at me. "You have his number?"

"Yes," I said. "It's that or tell the celestials their runaway is hiding there, and I don't fancy being in the middle of *that* shitstorm."

Did it bother him that I'd given Alec my number? No way. Vamp dude was over five years younger than me, for a start. And that wasn't the issue. The slightly more significant problem was that he hadn't been forthright with me. If I wanted answers, I needed to channel every ounce of persuasive ability I'd honed while trying to get out of detention back when I'd been a novice celestial. I had no shortage of experience in that area, but getting answers from warlocks was like squeezing—well, blood from a bloodstone.

Once we were on the road, driving back to the warlocks' place, I said, "The cure and the bloodstones—I'm starting to think they have the same source." I risked a glance at Nikolas. His expression was impassive. "What do you think? Seems a weird coincidence that the cure works on the virus as well as vampirism."

"That would depend on the nature of the cure itself," he said. "Which we'll find out in due time."

"Assuming these addresses aren't duds," I added. "Which is possible. They were scared, and besides, this operation seems designed to throw everyone off the trace. Every vamp in there got the bloodstone and cure from a completely different location or person."

"That suggests a collective is involved," he said. "The more people there are, the easier it'll be to track them down. They just need one weak link."

"Unless they're not operating from this dimension." I paused to let my words sink in. "Have you considered that?"

"It's a valid theory, but it has its problems," he said. "For them to get hold of the cure from another dimension implies that a permanent link like a portal is established—which we would have detected by now."

"We haven't found the link yet, but that doesn't mean it isn't there. If the cure *is* manufactured against the demon venom in particular, the person making it would have up close and personal experience with its effects."

"Right." He nodded, still not looking pleased. "If Azurial himself isn't involved, then he must have passed on the information to someone. And in order to travel through into this realm, there must be a portal set up on this side, too. But it takes a powerful warlock or demon to do that, and all of ours are accounted for."

"Are you absolutely certain?" I asked. "Because Azurial managed to get the vamps to set one up fairly easily. Through demonglass. We never did find the piece that went missing at the guild. They denied knowing about it, but someone must have put it there." *Or stolen it.*

No demon had got into the celestial guild, and the glass had gone missing immediately after Azurial's failed attack, along with the evidence—on Gav's phone. Of course, it might just as easily have been the guild covering their tracks, but I had to wonder.

I thought of the girl locked up there, a victim of a force nobody understood. If it'd been the bite that'd turned her, then she was liable to kill again. As was Damian, too, reduced to living with real vampires rather than staying with the celestials.

The guild had failed a lot of people. The most recent victims weren't the half of it.

I slowed as we reached the warlocks' headquarters, pulling into a parking space. "Are we going to Pandemonium, then? Because this might be urgent."

"I can ask," he said, "but I've told you I don't make the rules."

"Except in the shadow realm." The words slipped out before I could stop them, and he raised an eyebrow.

"Where did that come from?" he asked. "What exactly did the arch-demon say to you?"

"I can add two and two. You're probably more powerful than Javos is, yet you do everything he says. You must be getting something out of the deal. But in that realm, anything goes, right?"

"I respect Javos's authority as all warlocks in this city do," he said tightly. "It's a necessity to keep the peace with the celestials, the human authorities, and the other preternaturals. As you rightly said, however, in the shadow realm as any nether realm… anything goes." He leaned over to look me in the eyes, and my breath caught as the scent of brimstone filled my senses, along with a hint of the power he could unleash at will on any opponent. I was no closer to understanding *his* limits than before, nor the shadow realm itself. He and his brother might share similar magic and even the same alluring nature, but his gaze was all heat.

I'd had my fill of danger as a celestial, yet I craved more. Impatience burned in my blood, the desire to explore my demon side—tempered by the memories of Rory's and Gav's deaths, of Fiona's kidnapping, and the chaos the fire dimension had wrought in my life.

I pulled back a little, my hand seeking the door release, and there was a hint of disappointment in his eyes as though I'd failed some kind of test.

"You people get a kick out of being cryptic, don't you?" I said. "Themedes said you'd spoken to him about me, too. I'm not keen on people gossiping behind my back, to be honest."

"That's what's bothering you?" He raised an eyebrow. "I didn't talk about you, or even your magic—no more than he already knew, anyway. I was trying to pry information from him about where your power might have come from. If he'd told me anything useful, I'd have passed on the information."

*Hmm. So either he was trying to turn me on Nikolas—or it actually was Zadok who spoke to him.*

"Themedes can't escape that room," he added. "I'm surprised he's lasted so long without his power, though archdemons tend to be resilient."

"So they all die, eventually?" I asked.

"Some live for longer, others expire." He shrugged. "Their offspring aren't afforded the same extended lifespan. I can't say I know why that is. But regardless, no demigod is to be underestimated, Azurial included. In any case, the vampires are our priority until we have more information."

"Sure. But even if we play by the rules and don't contact that dimension until we have evidence, the enemy doesn't care. Rules don't matter to them. And if we want to outdo them…"

He leaned in close, his breath tickling my neck. "I'd like nothing more than to unleash the limits of my power on those murderous vermin, make no mistake, Devi. And if it comes to it, I'll do exactly that. But not before."

My demon mark tingled at his presence, craving the darkness of his magic. Maybe there was some lust in there, too, but the demon part of me would always be drawn to him for that reason alone.

Nikolas pulled away. "Let's see if these vampires' contacts give us any answers."

*You're not off the hook yet.* Whether his brother knew anything relevant or not, his secrets were all tied up with the demon dimensions. Pandemonium included.

Javos was in the office, yelling orders into the phone to what sounded like three people at once. He barked at Nikolas and me that we were to look into the addresses and names the vampires had given me as though it'd been his idea, not mine, and returned to ordering people around.

As it turned out, most of the addresses were dead ends. Others were public places not frequented by many vampires during the day. As for the names, they'd presumably been aliases. I spent several hours running Internet searches on each name or address, trying to connect them to an actual person. Nikolas hovered behind me, making the occasional comment, and searching his own files. He seemed calm, but I knew that was a front. And if we did find the enemy… why did I get the feeling that they *wanted* us to find them? I mean, flooding the whole market with those bloodstones was bound to attract the wrong kind of attention. Add in the very public attack on the bar yesterday, and all was clear—there was an attention-seeker at the heart of this. Someone who craved the chaos they'd unleashed. Demon, warlock, or human, who knew.

"This one's a real address," I said, leaning against the cushioned back of the office chair. I'd been driving Nikolas mad for the last twenty minutes by wheeling it back and forth from the desk and spinning around between searches, but nothing would solve my boredom more than disrupting a vampire nest.

"Which one?" Nikolas looked up from his phone screen.

"Mather's. Vampire bar. It's a real place. Of course, it'll be closed during the day. These transactions will only take place after sundown."

"Naturally," he said. "Given our current tensions, going in person would be risky business."

"Yeah, well. Going into a demon dimension is risky business." And then some. Considering there might be a demigod or worse involved, the vampire bar seemed a safer bet.

"This vampire place… it strictly vampires only?" he asked.

"Sounds like some of them bring their human blood slaves." I grimaced. It was a common enough practise, and hell, most humans enjoyed the sensation of having their blood drained. Vampire venom was made to be intoxicating in that way.

"Rachel will be able to safely get in, right?" I asked Nikolas. "It's not ideal, but she's the only one of us who can blend in amongst them."

"Not if they hear her heartbeat," Nikolas said. "Their enhanced senses will see through her disguise. The same if you or I went in there. They know one of their own by sight."

"Then can't you do your mind-trick on them? It works on vamps, right?"

"Technically, yes, but keeping a whole room distracted would take all of my focus, preventing me from anticipating a potential attacker."

"Look, we don't actually have to go into to the bar, right?" I asked. "These bloodstone trades might not be blatant. I'd say we wait outside and see if we notice anyone acting suspiciously. Drunken vamps aren't the most subtle of creatures. You can divert passers-by. If all else fails, I can always persuade my little friend in the warehouse to come along as an accessory."

He raised an eyebrow. "Accessory?"

"Well, technically I'd be the accessory," I amended. "Unless you'd like to volunteer."

"No," he said tightly. "You mean to say you'd pretend to be a helpless human? Are you sure you can pull that off?"

"I can try."

He frowned. "If there's a definite link to the bloodstones, we should be going for a more direct approach."

"We've been breaking doors down and trying to arrest people for weeks, while this has been going on right in front of us," I said. "I think it's time to try something more subtle. Believe me, it's not my first choice."

He nodded. "No, I suppose not. If you're convinced you can fool a room of vampires into thinking you're helpless, then we might stand a chance of cornering them. However, if they don't fall for the act—or if they decide to take a bite out of their defenceless human—then we might have an issue."

"You know I have a built-in anti-vamp switch, right?" I waved my left hand. "It'll be fine."

I didn't believe we'd get through this without a conflict, but I was sick of running in circles while demons laughed at us behind the scenes. If the vamps were really working with demons, then they'd get what was coming to them.

## 10

Music pulsed in the air, a drumbeat that pounded through my body as we walked to the bar. With that racket in the background, you wouldn't think vampires would be able to hear my heartbeat, but vamp hearing was apparently weirdly selective. Including the blond vampire hanging onto my arm. I'd worn flats instead of heels and was still taller than him, but since vamps usually looked younger than their actual age, hopefully the others would assume he was actually a century old.

I'd put on full makeup and actually dressed up, in a strappy top and skirt, trying to underplay the fact that I was expecting a fight. Stakes were concealed on my thighs and arms, under my jacket, but I grinned stupidly up at the blond vampire, pretending to be a love-struck lackey. Vampire venom had an intoxicating effect on humans, making them crave more at the expense of safety and common sense. Nikolas and Rachel walked further behind, the former using his mind-control ability on everyone within reach to make them forget seeing him. Rachel was disguised as a young female vampire, but considering Nikolas looked so much more intimidating than she did, he'd never make a convincing human blood slave.

"What are we doing?" Alec muttered in my ear. "Things get pretty heated in there. You don't want me to bite you, right?"

"You can try, but it won't be much fun for either of us. I'm mostly immune to the venom, and I don't think my blood tastes particularly nice." I kept a dopey expression on my face while I spoke. "Just keep it casual. Get in there, find this dealer woman—you know the description—and let me take care of the rest."

The air thumped with music, drowning any other sound. Vamps drank bloody cocktails and lounged on leather sofas. Humans sat amongst them, too, usually two or three per table. They wore skimpy clothing, revealing the bite marks on their necks and collarbones, and had doting expressions. One girl draped herself around a male vampire, neck bared, an expression of ecstasy on her face as he plunged his fangs into her skin. A ruby droplet of blood splashed onto her collarbone. The vampire licked it off. I fought the urge to gag, even knowing what this place was like. The humans held no objections, but a vamp with little self-control could easily accidentally kill one of their pets. The coppery smell of blood in the air drove them into a frenzy, and there was some shoving in the corner, two vamps squaring up over possession of a blood slave. Gritting my teeth, I forced myself to scan the room once, twice, searching for the female vampire from the description.

*There she is.* She had silky black hair, with lipstick the same colour as the humans' blood. And her fangs were buried in a human girl's neck. The girl writhed and moaned against her, completely under her spell. I poked Alec in the arm, but he apparently didn't take a hint.

I subtly pulled Alec behind a group of cocktail-drinking

vamps in suits and leaned in to whisper— "Her attention's on the girl. We can sneak up and see if she has the bloodstones without her even noticing."

He nodded once, his eyes slightly glazed. Like the humans'. Oh hell. The blood scent must be affecting him particularly badly, since he hadn't fed in a while.

"Stay close by," I whispered, and skirted around the crowd again. I dodged a vamp carrying a tray of blood cocktails and kept one eye on the vampire feasting on the poor girl's neck. The vampire lady wore a string purse around her neck. Big enough to hide bloodstones in? I'd say yes. I crept in behind her, avoiding the gaze of her human prey.

Her head swung around. "Want something?" she said lazily, a droplet of blood running off her chin.

I sidled up to her, keeping one hand on the blond vamp's arm. "Heard you had some bloodstones," I said. "He gets desperate when I'm not around, and I want him all to myself."

I elbowed him in the ribs to get him to respond. "She's mine," he said.

Ugh. I shuddered inwardly. He was a terrible actor, but the bad lighting and the dazed expression on my face must have fooled her. She cast a look at the human girl, drawing an arm around her, and dug in her bag with the other.

*Sorry.*

I jabbed the human girl in the spine with the stake.

She yelped, abruptly cut off when my vampire buddy bared his fangs over her exposed neck.

"Give me the bloodstones or I'll drink her dry." His threat came out garbled, but the stake in my hand made it perfectly clear where the threat lay.

"That's not playing fair." Her slightly red eyes widened. "What the hell do you want?"

"Those bloodstones," I said, in a low voice. "We can take this outside if you'd prefer. No need to cause a panic."

"Who are you?" She dropped into a defensive stance, and I dug the stake in harder. Alec's grip on the girl tightened. The vampire took a step back. "Outside. Don't you dare bite her."

"She's not the problem," I said. "You are. C'mon. Play nice and nobody gets hurt."

Shooting me a glare, the vampire moved where I pointed, the human girl stumbling behind. She didn't look capable of fighting back, which gave me a pang of guilt—however the vampires might be involved with the demons, she was an innocent human. Like…

A familiar face flashed across my vision as a group of humans passed by, following two tall male vampires. I stopped, hoping to hell I was mistaken.

I wasn't. Fiona followed the other humans, wearing the same dazed expression as the others. Her head bobbed, her body moving as though under hypnosis.

*Shit. What the hell is she doing here?*

I couldn't stop, not now, but my attention spiralled. Fiona headed to the nearest table, following the vamps—and that was all I saw before we reached the door. I grabbed the back of Alec's coat to stop him from tripping over his own feet—whoever heard of a clumsy vampire?—and shoved both him and the human girl out into the night.

*Dammit, Fiona. I have to get her out of there.* Leaving her to become a human subjugate forever wasn't an option, but neither was letting my captive go. Steering the human girl around the corner into an alley beside the bar, I kept my other eye on the vampire lady.

"Give me the bloodstones," I said to her. "Now. Hurry up."

"All right!" She dug in her bag and shoved two red stones into my hands.

"These aren't the same stones you were trading before." My heart sank. They weren't demon stones, but the regular ones.

"Obviously not," she said. "I don't give the same stones out twice. Let her go—you promised."

The girl moaned. Blood dripped down the back of her neck where Alec's control had apparently slipped.

"I'm looking for a specific type," I said. "You know the sort."

Her eyes widened. "What's it to you? You're no vampire. Your boyfriend won't want you anymore if you take one of those."

I held up the stake. "Tell me exactly where you found those other bloodstones. This isn't optional."

She took in a breath—an involuntary response which must have remained from being human, because vampires didn't need to breathe. She was either a really good actress or innocent.

"Ranger," she muttered. "He distributed them to all of us. He's back in the bar, the huge guy with the whiskers. I only sell the stones. I don't ask questions. Besides, I was only supposed to sell them to serious clients. Not bloodbags, and not—" She broke off. "You said you wouldn't bite her. Let *go!*"

She threw herself at Blond Dude, who latched onto the girl's neck with a ferocity that betrayed his real strength.

"Hey!" I kicked him in the kneecap, but his grip was steel. Fiona was still stuck in the vamp bar, and Alec had successfully screwed up my plan. I was tempted to let them fight it out, but I'd dragged Alec into this myself. I kicked him again, and he made an angry hissing noise.

The female vampire slammed into him, bashing his head on the pavement. I winced at the noise.

"What seems to be the problem here?" Nikolas stepped in,

grabbing the blond vampire. His head lolled, apparently unconscious.

"What the hell—you're a warlock." She spun around, as though wondering if everyone had gone mad.

"That's our cue to leave." Rachel grabbed my arm from behind.

"No." I shook my head. "I just saw Fiona in there. In the bar. I have to get her out."

Rachel's eyes widened. "What—your human friend? She's a blood slave?"

"No clue. Also, the vampire said the person we're looking for is in there. The one selling those bloodstones. Guy called Ranger. He'll be coming after her any second now."

Rachel swore. "You'd better be right."

I put the stake away, turning my back on the others. The vampire yelled at Nikolas, comforting the human girl, while Nikolas irritably threw Alec into the alley. "Leave," I heard him say. "If he doesn't wake up before the sun rises, it's his problem if he gets incinerated. Take the human and get out of here."

The bar swallowed us up, as confusing and loud as ever. The beat pulsed through me, and for all the humans around, there was no longer any sign of Fiona.

I swore quietly. "She was right there. I'd have seen if she'd come out."

"Let me." Rachel swaggered up to a couple of teenage male vamps. "Seen a redheaded human girl?"

A dark-skinned, muscular vamp with a bright silver lip piercing took a long sip of his drink, eying me with interest. "The vamp with the dye job? Over there."

"Not a vampire," I said. "She said, human."

"What's your problem?" He raised an eyebrow at Rachel. "You need to get your blood slave under control."

Rachel hissed under her breath, and I grabbed her by the

arm, pulling her away before she started a fight. The low lighting made it impossible to see people's faces clearly, but Fiona didn't appear to be in here, and neither did the others she'd been with. *Dammit, Fiona. Why did you come here?*

"There's a back entrance," Rachel whispered. "They must have left through there."

We pushed through the crowd, using elbows to gain leverage. One vamp spilled his blood cocktail all over the floor and yelled after us. I ignored the disgruntled shouts, and saw a hulking figure approach the door and slip outside.

Ah, crap. "That's the guy we were supposed to find," I whispered to Rachel. "He sold the bloodstones. Guess we're not the only ones making a quick exit."

"No better chance." She squared her shoulders and approached the back door as it swung shut. Stake in hand, I pushed the door open again and we exited, coming out into the other end of the same alley where we'd left Alec.

Vamp Dude filled the entire space, towering over me. He hadn't appeared quite that large from a distance, but his whiskers made him resemble a lion standing on its hind legs. My stake felt like a useless prop in comparison to those muscles. And his eyes were flat black.

*Shit.*

I gripped the stake, and the next second, he was in front of me, moving with dizzying vampire speed until his mouth was over my neck. I pulled out the stake, inching it backwards, but his hand gripped my arm hard enough to bruise.

"Let go," I warned. "Or I'll be forced to burn this place to the ground."

Rachel made a quiet growling noise. Out of the corner of my eye, I saw that two people held her. Vampires. They'd been waiting out here for us. *I should have known.*

Gritting my teeth against the pain in my left arm, I twisted my right wrist, freeing the stake hidden inside my sleeve. Whirling, I slammed it into his arm. His fangs broke the skin on my neck, but I didn't care about pretending to be human anymore, and I'd rather get a vampire bite than a wound that wouldn't heal. The stake pierced his arm and he let go, blood spilling down his sleeve.

With a snarl, he lunged at me, and I ducked, easing my left sleeve up. I sank the stake into his upper thigh. As his leg gave way, I grabbed his shoulder—and strong hands yanked me away from him. A blade pressed to my neck. *Not* fangs. One of the vamps who'd held Rachel had broken away, and was apparently armed with more than teeth.

The second vampire pressed a knife to Rachel's throat, holding her firmly.

The bleeding whiskered vamp spat at my feet. "You're no human. You're a celestial. Where's your light now, bitch?"

I tugged my sleeve halfway down before they were on me, pulling my arm behind my back. I wriggled, cursing, but the blade kissed the skin of my neck, drawing blood. If I could just get an opening—

The smell of brimstone hit me in the face, followed by an unexpected rush of warmth. The vampires let go, allowing me to breathe. I was supposed to be... doing something with my left sleeve... but it seemed unimportant. A pair of golden eyes swam before me, making everything else go hazy. The vampire's knife clattered to the alley floor, and Rachel disappeared from sight. But all that existed was the person the eyes belonged to, the source of the intoxicating scent. And why was it so hot? My skimpy clothes were too tight, too warm, pressing against my burning skin.

Lightning spiked from Nikolas's hands, piercing the dazed-looking vampire. He fell down, dead at my feet. My senses felt dulled. I should feel shocked, horrified, or at least relieved, but those golden eyes held me captive, and the smell of brimstone infiltrated my mind.

*Lure...* the word drifted through my head, unaccompanied by any context. A snarl came from ahead, from Rachel, and I caught a glimpse of her tearing the vampires to pieces. The night air caressed my bare arms as I pulled my shirt over my head. Much better.

"Devi," said a male voice—a *seductive* male voice. "Stop. Think. Can you remember why you're here?" His strong hand gripped mine, stopping me from undoing my bra. Wait. How had my hand even ended up there? Lowering my hand, his fingertips brushed against my right wrist.

Euphoria rushed through my veins. I gripped his shirt tight with my free hand, craving that sensation again. He was warm, too. Really warm. He took my shirt and attempted to slide it back over my head, but I pressed my body against his, pushing both of us into the alley wall.

Why were we in an alley? We should be in a luxury suite on a four-poster bed, the best the guild's money could buy. Still, at least I had him where I wanted him. He might be one-handedly trying to push my arm through my sleeve, but I could see the heat simmering in his eyes. He wanted me. I wanted him, too. I closed my mouth over his, and he tasted just as good as I remembered. Images exploded behind my eyes of our bodies sliding together, and I moaned against his mouth, one-handedly easing my skirt down. I really should have dressed more appropriately for the occasion. Or at least worn nicer underwear. Not that I'd be needing it...

*What in hell, Devi? Vampires kidnapped your best friend. Wake up!*

That voice in my head was getting really annoying. I deepened the kiss, grazing his bottom lip with my teeth. He growled against my mouth. "Devi. Stop this. Now."

"Why stop," I murmured, my hand dropping to his crotch. "You want me."

He pressed his hands firmly to my shoulders, pushing me

away from him. "This is neither the time nor the place, and you're going to be really pissed off with me when you come to your senses."

"The only reason I'm pissed off with you is because you won't fuck me." I attempted to unclasp my bra again, only for lightning to strike at my feet, stunning me. While I stood frozen, he grabbed my left hand and pushed up my sleeve. White light flared in front of my eyes, and old instincts kicked in.

I jumped back, away from whoever had set off the mark —it never shone like that unless a powerful demon was on top of me. My legs tangled in my skirt, which was halfway to my knees, and I staggered against the alley wall.

*Oh... Divinities.*

Nikolas stood there in a wary position, looking over both our shoulders. I pushed myself upright, my cheeks burning, and yanked my skirt back into position. Divinities above, I'd nearly screwed Nikolas in a public alley, when we were supposed to be—

Far too late, alarm crashed over me. "Fiona."

"I sent Rachel after her. She told me about your predicament."

Predicament. Like being hit in the face with warlock lure. I'd be able to smell it for weeks. Not that it was a bad thing... oh, hell. I shakily fixed my clothes, and sought to get a grip on the situation.

"The guy responsible for selling those bloodstones—he was trying to sneak off," I said. "You killed him." I glanced at his prone body. Even the dead guy looked like he was judging me.

"That's why I used the lure. It'd have been too late for me to get to him before he cut your throat." His mouth tightened. "I knew it'd hit you, too, but there was no way I could aim the lure at the others alone."

"Don't worry about it." How humiliating. A warlock was apologising to me for making me attracted to him. As though I wasn't already, against my better judgement. "Seriously, though. Fiona. At a vampire establishment. We have to go back and get her out."

"There's no need." He pointed at Rachel, who approached at a run—alone.

"I was too late," she said. "They took her round the back road while we were dealing with these bastards."

"Damn." I pushed upright, cursing my shaking legs. "We can ambush them."

Nikolas steadied my arm. "You're in no shape to fight."

"Whose fault is that?" I staggered away, treading on the dead guy's face and not particularly caring. The cramped alley circled around the building to a dimly lit street, and the sound of a car engine roared through the air. I caught a glimpse of Fiona's terrified reflection in the wing mirror as it blew past, leaving the smell of exhaust fumes in its wake.

"Shit." I whirled around, wishing I'd worn Rachel's upgraded shoes—but even they weren't enough for me to outrace a vampire-driven car.

"This way." Nikolas led the way back to where he'd parked. "We can't fight them all, not with Devi incapacitated."

I glared at him. "How long does this take to wear off?"

"Five minutes tops," Rachel said from behind. "I'm really glad *one* of you had some self-control back there. A demon could have materialised behind you and you wouldn't have noticed."

Great. I shoved what I'd almost done out of mind. Rescuing Fiona was more important than explaining myself to Nikolas. If there was even anything to explain.

Nikolas opened the car door. "We'll follow. If there are too many of them, stay in the car."

"No chance." I climbed into the back, pulling my spare clothes from my bag. Nikolas raised an eyebrow at me.

I gave him a look. "What makes you think I didn't pack for the occasion? Not all of us can shape-change or shoot lightning from our fingertips. A girl has to be prepared."

I hadn't been able to pack anything too bulky, but while Nikolas started the car, I slipped out of the skimpy clothes into jeans and a less revealing shirt, pulling my jacket on top. Rachel had returned to her pink-haired self, though her demon side wouldn't be far behind. The car veered around the corner, nearly sending me upside-down, but I managed to wrestle my shoes back on. With no regard for speed limits, Nikolas drove us down the dark streets. Everyone who stopped to stare at us looked away almost instantly, including several police officers. Someone wouldn't be getting a speeding ticket. Apparently the vampires were unconcerned with such things. *Not good.* That meant they were confident they wouldn't be followed.

Rachel leaned out the window when we drove around another corner. "There they are!" she shouted.

"Got them," Nikolas muttered, slowing the car down so abruptly, I nearly fell into his seat. The vamps had parked their own car at an angle in the road, another hint that they didn't care about being found. The door of the building they'd run into—a run-down apartment block that was closed for reconstruction—was open, too.

I adjusted my stakes, pulling one of them out. "I'm ready."

We ran to the door, which Nikolas blasted away with a palm of lightning. Rachel ran behind, while I held my stake in one hand and my celestial light in the other. As we crossed the threshold, it lit up bright, and my demon mark tingled, too.

"There's a demon here," I warned. "I think."

"As well as the vampires?" Rachel cursed quietly. "They must have backup."

"Worse," Nikolas said, glancing sharply to one of the open doors on the left. I did, too, knowing what I'd see.

The vamps didn't need to worry about being followed… because they were no longer in this dimension at all.

A pentagram lay in the room's centre, several bloodstones fixed to the edges. By the dimming light, it'd burn out soon.

Rachel touched the edge, hissing in anger. "It's locked. They left it to taunt you. I might be able to get through—even you, Devi—but Nikolas… the portal isn't strong enough to support a demigod. And we wouldn't be able to get back."

I looked at the edges, my blood burning. As though I'd ever let them get away with taking Fiona. *It's Pandemonium. They're with whoever's behind that bloodstone scheme.* Divinities above, how had *Fiona* got mixed up with them? I'd been careful to keep her away from our latest scheme, but it apparently wasn't enough.

Glass fragments were scattered in the pentagram, shimmering with golden light. I touched one of them, knowing it was demonglass.

I'd travelled through fragments before.

"Devi," Nikolas said.

"Nikolas," I said quietly, "I'm really not in the mood for rational judgements right now. So unless you're volunteering to be a punching bag, back off. This is demonglass. I can get any of us in and out this way. It won't be comfortable, but no interdimensional travel is."

"This isn't a situation we can rush into."

"The vamps took Fiona into Pandemonium," I said. "So not only is our theory correct, that dimension is behind it all. I'm armed. I came here expecting a fight, and so did you."

He cast a furious look at the portal. "How exactly did you expect to get back?"

"I don't know, maybe the gigantic palace made of demon-glass? It's right there." I pointed for emphasis. Even through the piece of glass in my hand, its huge shape loomed over Pandemonium's buildings. Wherever the vampires had taken Fiona was within walking distance of the palace. We wouldn't get another chance.

The palace called like a siren's song, a glittering monument to the demons' power. To a power connected to the demon magic burning in me, in the mark on my wrist which hadn't quieted since it'd touched Nikolas. It longed to touch the glass and connect with the demonic magic on the other side.

"Fine," he said tightly. "We stick together. No other options."

"No rules," I said. "Anything goes. Right?"

I didn't wait for an answer. Golden light flared around me, pulling me into the fire dimension.

## 11

Fire burst into life, flames licking at my skin. Even though they didn't hurt, I clenched my teeth as Rory's terrified screams replayed in my head, like they did in my nightmares. The look of terror on his face—as with the other victims—when their own celestial fire had taken their lives. I recoiled, like I did every time I saw the fire. This realm had visited me in my nightmares more often than I'd care to admit.

In reality, I'd fought back and won, but in dreams, I froze, unable to move as the fire devoured everything in its path.

The demon mark on my wrist itched insistently, bringing me back to reality as solid ground appeared beneath my feet. I inhaled the strong smell of brimstone and coughed uncontrollably. We'd landed in a street lined with stone houses, the colour of sand. I'd seen them from the palace balcony. From this perspective, they seemed endless, a labyrinth in front of the huge forbidding shape of the palace looming overhead.

Nobody appeared to be around. I spun on the spot, looking for the vampires. They couldn't have gone far, but the maze led in four directions from here. Nikolas and

Rachel looked around, both frowning. Beneath our feet were the crushed remains of more demonglass, drenched in the scent of brimstone.

*All right. Time to talk to the locals.*

I pushed up the cuff of my sleeve.

"What are you doing?" asked Rachel. "You can't show your celestial power here. People like you don't exist. You'd get mobbed."

"To be honest, I'm past the point of caring. Didn't you live here?"

"A long time ago. It's not exactly a place that's friendly to tourists." Her mouth pinched.

"I gathered." I looked at Nikolas. "Well? What're you doing?" He'd turned the opposite way, peering down the path between two houses.

"They went that way," he said. "I can sense the demonic magic they used to get through the portal. But it'll fade soon. We'll have to move quickly."

*Not like we have much choice.* Rachel and I ran after him, glancing to either side in case of an ambush. My celestial light hadn't switched on yet, so there weren't demons within close range. It struck me as suspicious, but looking closer at the houses, they seemed to be unoccupied. Empty windows, shattered glass. The city had been hit hard by the loss of their arch-demon, so maybe people had left.

The light on my hand flared up, and I stopped. "Demon. Close by." A rumbling noise sounded not a metre away, behind the house on our right. "That... doesn't sound great."

The ground collapsed, sliding away beneath us. I hit the wall, grabbing it for balance, while Nikolas and Rachel disappeared beneath an avalanche of falling stone as the houses slid apart, too. The demon must have been under our feet the whole time.

My fingers dug into the nearest stone wall, stopping me

from sliding into the rapidly opening pit. I kicked off and jumped over the hole, but a rock-hard hand grabbed my leg, dangling me upside-down. Rotating on the spot, I found myself facing a sandstone hand which appeared to have grown out of the house's wall. It was the same colour, indistinguishable from the row of roofs wheeling around me while I fought to break free. Light flared brighter around my hand, illuminating a huge gaping mouth with razor-like teeth, embedded in the stone.

*The demon was disguised as a house?*

The monster's grip slipped as the beast cringed away from the light in my hand. I fought the dizziness, reaching between realms for my trusty celestial blade. With a golden gleam, the sword appeared in my hands.

At the same time, the beast let go. I fell, slashing at its stone hand, and landed on the edge of the pit. Spinning around, I whipped the blade down. The blade sank into stone, prompting a rattling shout. Teeth snapped, its mouth opening wide enough to devour a person. The blocky stone demon pushed against my blade, sending me staggering back, precariously close to the pit's edge. My limbs trembled under the onslaught. The demon, weird-looking though it might be, was a Grade Three, which meant my celestial blade was the only thing that could kill it.

I slashed diagonally, but barely made a dent in its skin. Several teeth fell out as I gave one last desperate lunge. My celestial blade sank to the hilt through the roof of its mouth. I pushed hard, certain that had to be it. The beast roared and swung, forcing me to let go of the sword and jump out of range.

The blade remained lodged in its mouth—but it still didn't die. *Crap.* I'd lost my weapon, but the burning celestial fire ought to have obliterated the demon.

*Run, Devi. Now.*

I pelted down the path between more stone houses, hoping to hell none of the others came to life and tried to eat me. Where were Nikolas and Rachel? *Tell me they weren't eaten by a demon house.*

My feet pounded against dirt. I veered around a corner and Rachel grabbed my arm, pulling me through a gap in the stone wall. "Devi. Thank the seven hells you're okay."

"Man-eating house incoming." My heart thundered against my ribs, and I peered over the stone fence. The monster hadn't moved, but it clearly wasn't dead either. Celestial light shone faintly from the sword I'd left in its mouth. The blade would disappear within a few seconds without my hand to ground it.

"Nah, it can't move further than its roots. I forgot to warn you about them. Niko, is the coast clear?"

"Clear enough." He climbed through the wall himself, gaze snagging on me. There was an unmistakable hint of relief on his features. "I figured you'd have got out alive, but the ground collapsed."

"Yeah, I saw. I stuck my celestial blade in its mouth, but it still didn't die. What *is* it?"

"A parasite demon which eats through stone and embeds itself in any constructions." Rachel bounded up to the wall. "The good news is, it can't chase you. It's more or less stuck in the same place."

"The bad news is that there are a lot more houses here." I pointed to them. "How do we know which might be demons and which aren't?"

"We don't," she said, helpfully.

"Come on." Nikolas beckoned us through the gap in the wall. "Those beasts don't live close together. We shouldn't run into another one before we reach that bridge."

I climbed warily through the gap, onto the cobbled road. Ahead, the road became a bridge over what I assumed was a river, which was at least free of stone houses. The palace's glass turrets and towers glittered against the pale grey sky, and not far away was a high fence surrounding its clear demonglass structure. Our way back into the sane, normal world where houses didn't try to eat people.

"We can't leave Fiona behind," I said quietly, walking alongside Nikolas. "I know you've probably lost her scent by now, but—"

"I haven't. The vampires came this way. I'm almost certain they were heading for the palace."

I blinked. "But—why not transport themselves directly in there? That place is like a beacon."

"Maybe because they knew they were being followed."

We reached the bridge, which arched over sluggish grey water. On the other side was a large open space of cobbled stone, and the high wall surrounding the palace. A gate made of clear glass waited ahead.

"This is the way in." Rachel tilted her head. "Looks different to before. There used to be guards."

"It's also demonglass." I walked towards the gate. "I can get us to Fiona this way. Directly. No need to search the whole palace. It's entirely made of this stuff."

"You can move to a specific location?" asked Rachel. "Even if you haven't been there before?"

"Technically, yes, but I'd need some idea of what I'm looking for. At least, that's how it worked before." I examined the gate, but there didn't seem to be a lock or any way to easily open it. Considering how far off the ground the upper floors were, it'd take too long to search the whole building. *Then how did the vamps get in?* There must be a secret entrance somewhere. Which meant they knew the place, and this wasn't the first time they'd brought in someone from the human realm.

My demon mark tingled as I raised it to the gate. The

glass flickered, and I conjured Fiona's face into my mental eye. "Okay. You'll have to hang onto me."

Two hands pressed to my back and we stepped forwards, emerging in a familiar wide hall. Pillars extended to the ceiling, made of the same glass I'd just stepped through. Our reflections watched from countless surfaces... along with vampires. Dozens of them.

And no arch-demon sat on the throne this time. A dark figure, masked and wearing a long dark cloak, stood between the pillars flanking the golden throne.

*A vampire.*

Oh... shit. I'd honestly thought most of the vampires in this realm had perished before Azurial had failed in his plan. Or he'd killed them. Several vampires held Fiona between them, pulling her towards the throne. Two others wielding long spears stood on either side of their leader, while the others were scattered around, watching the spectacle. I knew vamps moved fast, but surely they'd taken a shortcut to get here this quickly.

"Get away from her," I said.

All heads turned towards us. I marched forwards, my celestial hand igniting. The pillars reflected its white glow back at me.

Dropping Fiona, the two vamps spun around to meet me. Lightning sparked from Nikolas's hands, shattering the calm, but though his aim was perfect, neither vampire fell. Both looked at me with the same cold, dark gaze as the others who'd taken in the demon energy. *Crap. Every vampire in this room is under the same spell.* And Fiona right in the centre, human and vulnerable.

Keeping one eye on her, I advanced towards the enemy. The light from my blazing hand extended into the long, sharp edge of my celestial blade, and I lunged at one of the vampires who'd held her.

He fell back, snarling in agony as the celestial fire burned him. A blur of movement was my only warning before a second vampire appeared, moving with preternatural speed. I spun around in an arc, but he danced out of the way of my blade, apparently unafraid of the light. Not at all like a regular vamp.

Black-edged lightning flared past as Nikolas struck down another target, while the second vamp leaped at me. I stabbed upwards, missed, and he grabbed my arm with inhuman strength, pulling me backwards. Even Rachel's shoes couldn't stop me from falling, the back of my head hitting the floor. Tasting blood on my tongue, I reached into my sleeve for my spare stake and lunged wildly. The stake sank into his arm, but he didn't stop. Darkness gleamed in his eyes, inhuman, not even vampire-like. Most vamps collapsed after a single blow from a stake—and my celestial light should have made him cringe away.

*Time to end this.*

I reached for my blade once more. The shimmering sword of light pierced his chest, pushing him off me. The vamp finally screeched, his skin catching afire until he turned to ashes.

Jumping to my feet to look for Fiona, I spotted the other vamps backing away from Nikolas's lightning assault. Dark sparks shot from his hands, knocking over every vampire that moved—but none of them died. The dude on the throne —I was fairly sure he was male, anyway, from his wide shoulders and stance—watched the carnage without moving or reacting. Rachel ran amongst them in demon form, jaws snapping, but they moved too quickly. Demonic darkness shone from their eyes, and even Nikolas's lightning had only killed one of them. My sword pierced another, turning him to ashes, but they moved too fast, and without the fear that usually put them on the defensive when faced with a celestial.

Fiona screamed. A vampire held her pinned down, blood oozing from a wound on her head. As the coppery smell of human blood filled the hall, I *felt* the mood change, every vampire's head turning in that direction.

And my sword disappeared.

*What the hell? Come on, celestial fire. Don't go out on me now.*

I leaped towards the vampire holding Fiona, stake in hand. He moved fluidly, holding her in front of him as a shield. I held back at the last second, just avoiding impaling her, and Fiona screamed again. The vampire grinned at me, a red tint to his dark eyes. Demon magic *and* blood frenzy? Crap.

"Play nice and let her go," I warned. "Last chance."

My left hand lit up again, and I shone the light directly into his eyes. He didn't, as I'd hoped, look away. Instead, his fangs came down on Fiona—

*No.*

I slammed into her, knocking both of them backwards. The vampire recovered before he hit the ground, shoving Fiona back at me. I caught her with my celestial hand, using the other to thrust the stake into the vampire's chest.

I'd missed the heart, but no vamp could recover from a wound like that in seconds. He fell back, and I stabbed again. This time, I hit my mark. He writhed and twisted, his body disintegrating to ashes. Fiona clung to my other arm, eyes wide with terror.

"Hang on," I told her. "I'll get you out of here."

I kicked the vampire's body, pulling her with me to the demonglass floor—and someone grabbed my demon-marked hand, twisting it behind my back. I kicked back, but the vampire who'd grabbed me moved out of the way, dragging Fiona with him.

*He knows about my ability.*

If they knew—they must also know I was the only shot any of the others had at getting out of here, which meant if they took me out, the others would be stuck here. And they'd picked Fiona as the weak link. As long as they had her, I couldn't look away long enough to kill the remaining vampires. Including the dickhead on the throne.

I willed the celestial light to set my hand ablaze, and pulled out my sword again. The blade whipped through the air, stabbing the nearest vampire through the eye. As he crumpled into nothingness, Fiona ran forwards out of the way. *Time to get her out.*

The vampire king—if that's what he was—stood, raising his hands.

Shards of dark lightning pierced the air, sending me flying backwards—and Fiona, too. My back slammed into the floor, my ears ringing. Rolling over, I found myself face to face with the vampire king, who still hadn't removed his mask. Except that wasn't vampire power he'd used. It was too similar to Nikolas's magic.

*He's a demon.*

"Fight me, celestial," he said. His voice echoed through the hall. "You're a disappointment. I was told to expect someone worthy to slay a demigod."

"Who the hell even are you?" I reached for my sword, only to find the damn thing had disappeared again. *For Divinity's sake, if any time is a crisis, it's now.*

Lightning flared from his hands, dark and menacing. I dodged, grabbing my celestial sword. My blade was supposed to burn through the dark, but now it felt more like I was about to burn out. The sword wasn't supposed to disappear at the crucial moment, surrounded by adversaries on every side. The side of my blade blocked his lightning attack—but without warning, fiery pain shot from my hip to my neck, along my right side. I fell, gasping in pain, blood soaking through my shirt. *How? Did someone stab me?* Through blurred vision, I saw Rachel and Nikolas running over, Fiona screaming my name.

With the last of my strength, I pressed my right hand to the demonglass floor, landing beside Fiona. Grabbing her, I pulled her with me, this time coming out of the floor underneath Nikolas and Rachel.

Clinging onto consciousness, I yelled hoarsely, "Hang on tight."

The vampires' king roared in fury, but I was already falling through the floor again...

## 12

We landed in a heap on the carpet of the spare room at Warlock HQ. Nikolas wasted no time lifting me into his arms while Rachel shouted for Javos.

Things got a little bit hazy then. Pain lanced up my side like I was being stabbed over and over again. I moaned, hoarsely yelling for someone to put out the fire, then blacked out. Then I woke up to Javos's yelling. Apparently while dealing with a full-blown vampire crisis, it isn't helpful when two warlocks, a human girl and a celestial with a deadly injury materialise in the back room.

Since I was more concerned with not bleeding to death than not pissing off Javos, I tuned out for most of that, only coming to alertness when someone pressed a cool cloth to my forehead. I blinked awake, figuring from the furniture arrangement that someone had moved me onto the living room sofa. Nikolas stood over me, holding the cloth.

"You were lucky," he said. "You're immune to demon poison, so whatever was in that sword had no effect on you. I stemmed the bleeding using a spell, so don't try to move for a bit."

"I didn't even see he had a sword," I mumbled.

"It was one of the others who stabbed you from behind. You have an alarming habit of nearly dying in that palace."

"Since I didn't take the vampires' king down with me, I'll have to go back for an encore." I looked up. "Where's Fiona?"

"Sleeping. Rachel took her to a guest room."

"Good." I closed my eyes, then opened them again. "Is Javos still yelling and breaking the furniture?"

"Rachel calmed him down," he said. "We need to discuss our next move, but later, when you've recovered."

"Nope. They're plotting now," I said. "What the hell *was* that guy? I thought he was a vampire before he attacked me."

"Either a demon or a demigod, and not one I've seen before," he responded. "The magic he used was a demon's, certainly. But he looked human, from what I could tell."

*Guess you're not the only one with lightning magic.* "Azurial's replacement."

"I suspected someone of his power level was in charge of the vampires, but I thought they might be following orders their former boss left behind, not following someone new. Azurial himself is, as far as I know, still imprisoned in the palace's west tower."

"Great." I groaned. "So not only are all the bad guys still alive, there's a new hellion who wants me dead. What was his issue, anyway?"

"If I had to guess, it's that you're an outsider, and a celestial at that," said Nikolas. "And Azurial evidently told him about your friend. Or the vampires did."

I pushed a clump of matted hair from my eyes. I probably looked a wreck, and heaven knew how much blood I'd lost. "So *he's* behind the army of vampires messing with this dimension?"

"So it would seem."

"Well, I didn't see any bloodstones or cures in there, but I'm taking a wild guess that's where they came from. The same people are involved, anyway. But what in hell did they want with Fiona? They didn't know me."

"I think they did," he said. "They took Fiona because they knew you'd come after her. It's likely why they lured her over to their side in the first place. However… she must have had reason to go and see the vampires."

I heard the implied meaning.

"She was already bitten. A while ago." My throat closed up. "It must have happened in the demon dimension the first time around. That's why she was looking for them. But why not *tell* me?"

"She went through a traumatic experience, and I imagine she wanted to forget it."

"But she told me everything else. Why not the fact that she was bitten by an infected vampire? What the hell does it do to a human?"

"I don't know," he said. "But the celestials weren't craving blood, were they? Maybe that's why she didn't know it'd affect her. It's been weeks. If she was going to go full vampire, you'd know."

"Crap." I let my hand fall to my side, my heart sinking. "If the venom can kill a celestial via the same transfer, it'll definitely be in her bloodstream. But I've never seen a regular human get bitten. She went to them… deliberately."

"Rachel said she mentioned the cure. I think someone at that bar promised to give it to her."

"Oh." I nodded, exhaustion washing over me. "That makes sense. What *doesn't* make sense is why Pandemonium has such an interest in us. Azurial… I don't get *why* he picked this dimension to target in the first place."

"Generally, the goal of all demons is in the service of the arch-demons. Acting alone or not, they have a single aim."

"To conquer everything, turn all dimensions dark, and wipe out the celestials." With those vampires at their command, they had all the tools they needed to destroy the celestials in this dimension.

*Maybe even planted amongst them.*

I swallowed hard. I was in no shape to check up on the guild, but… I had a bad feeling they were more involved than they knew.

"Exactly right," he said. "I think that's reason enough. It's not like the arch-demons are unaware of this dimension, even if they lost the war here thousands of years ago."

"You think it's one of *them* behind this?" I stared at him. "I mean, sure, I get they want power, but vampires… it's not exactly an orthodox method of conquering. I thought demons were more direct."

"All direct attempts on this realm in the last few centuries have failed."

*Yeah. They have. Because of us.* Even when the demons had attacked the heart of the celestial guild itself, they'd always lost. That's why it was so damned easy to believe in the guild and their mission. Because they'd won every battle.

But maybe this was one they couldn't survive.

"So we need to find the portals," I said. "There must be more of them, if this has been going on for weeks. The answers are in that dimension."

"I agree," he said. "But we don't have anywhere near enough information."

"Vamps can pass through those portals because they aren't true demons," I said. "Right? It looked that way. It's clever, actually, because homemade pentagrams aren't strong enough for Grade Three or higher demons. Definitely not a demigod. So he has the vamps acting as his lackeys. They bypass most demon detectors, too. The ones in the warehouse didn't even set off their own security."

Nikolas nodded. "Yes. Only an arch-demon can summon a demigod without a significant ability in magic, so there's no way for Azurial or his replacement to directly travel over to this dimension without an anchor."

*Like celestial fire.* A chill raised goosebumps on my arms. I wished I'd permanently killed the bastard. Summoning a demigod wasn't impossible for a non-arch-demon. I'd summoned both Nikolas and Zadok myself, but the former had been drawn into the celestial guild's most powerful pentagram, and the latter had been imprisoned with his magical ability significantly reduced.

"They have a whole palace of demonglass," I said. "That's strong enough to make a portal anywhere, especially when you take those bloodstones into account."

"Not if there isn't an equally strong beacon on this side," he said. "Considering Azurial never came through, he'd need more than a portal. He'd need an anchor. For Azurial, that's fire. For me, it's shadows."

"And for me, it's demonglass," I murmured. "Does the arch-demon with the power get to choose, or is it entirely random?"

"Demonic scholars across the realms have asked that question for generations."

*Like your brother?* "I figured demigods knew *something* about the nature of the arch-demons' magic. Or whichever part I got marked with."

*Damn the guild.* I'd never found anything conclusive in their files about demigods, not at all. Let alone arch-demons. It was the one thing I regretted about leaving them. Javos doubtless knew more—and Nikolas certainly did.

"Your mark is unlike anything we've seen on a human, so at this point, everything is guesswork." His gaze dropped to my right hand, and he reached for it with a questioning look in his eyes. I nodded, my stomach swooping. The mark lay across my wrist, an inverse arrowhead. Like the opposite of my celestial mark, pointing inward instead of out. My breath caught when he traced the mark with his fingertip, remembering all too clearly the grip of his lure, how it'd raced through my veins and stirred my blood. Maybe it was the demon in me who was drawn to him, and his demon side who was fascinated with me.

Maybe part of me didn't care.

He removed his hand from mine, to my disappointment. "What are you thinking?"

"The mark reacts… sometimes," I said. "When I'm close to demons… or warlocks. It's like it's drawn to magic. But not all of it. Just demonglass, and you."

He arched a brow. "Me?"

"I don't know, maybe it likes you." I spoke teasingly, though I didn't miss the heat that inched into his eyes. Encouraged, I added, "I can't tell if it's responding to your magic or not, but maybe it's a similar type. The only other thing it reacts to is demonglass."

"I'd know if you were shadow-aligned," he said. "I'd guess that the mark reacts particularly strongly to demigods. It might explain why my power had such a strong effect on you."

Warmth rose to my cheeks. "Your lure's supposed to make people lose their senses."

"It is, but not to that degree. I'm not an incubus. They use a similar power, but render their victims entirely helpless. My ability is more intended to be used as a distraction."

"As opposed to what, seduction?" I could put the tremor in my hands down to the blood loss, but I had my doubts. I remembered all too clearly the fantasies his power had conjured up in my mind. And I hadn't even been the target.

But the vampires hadn't started stripping naked. Admittedly, he'd hit them with lightning immediately afterwards, but still. Maybe there *was* something up with my demon mark. Simple attraction to him didn't explain it all.

"Correct," he said. "Incubi are masters of seducing their prey."

"Then it's pretty safe to say I don't have that type of magic," I said lightly. "My technique could probably use some work. That alley was filthy."

Amusement flared in his eyes, but there was definitely some heat in there, too. "Yes, it was. I'm rather alarmed at how quickly the effects came on. Normally if I hit a victim at that close range, I'd be a mile away before they realised I'd gone. The first time I used the lure against you, I assumed you were mostly immune."

"Huh?" I frowned. "Good point." The first time he'd hit me with the lure, I'd been dazed, but definitely hadn't started stripping. But my demon mark hadn't been active at the time. Was this yet another price to pay for moving closer to hell? Nikolas might not mean me harm, but if demon magic was several times more effective on me now... it couldn't mean anything good.

"Maybe the mark reacts to different types of magic more than others," he said.

"Perhaps," I said. "It's never reacted to any regular demons, though. Or vampires. Guess I don't get a built-in demon detector."

"Unfortunately, I can only track pure demons and warlocks, not infected vampires, unless they've used strong demonic magic. That would at least help us track down which are hiding amongst the regular ones. Even their auras don't show up as exceptionally different. Perhaps because they're already demonically aligned."

"And some are selling the cure or bloodstones without

taking them," I added. "Like the woman last night. The guy at the bar was a different story, though. He'd taken it, all right."

"The bar has been shut down," he said. "Unfortunately, it's looking like the vampires are keen to push blame for the deaths there onto us."

"Because of Alec the idiotic newbie vampire." I groaned. "Any idea where he wound up?"

"Assuming he woke up from being knocked out before the sun rose, he'll have crawled back to the warehouse by now."

"Wish I'd gone in alone," I muttered. "I should have figured I couldn't trust a vamp to control his blood cravings in a room full of willing victims."

"Your plan might have succeeded if the vampire had been carrying the bloodstones herself. I should have anticipated there'd be backup waiting in case of an attack."

"Well, they're dead," I said. "Hand their bodies over to Madame White, and let her deny there's a problem now."

"She won't deny there's a problem," he said. "However, it's a cross-dimensional matter. According to our rules, we don't interfere unless there's a direct threat to the inhabitants of this one and even then, the rules are shaky."

"Thought there weren't any rules."

He looked at me. "In Pandemonium, there aren't. But you know why we can't go back without a plan."

"Because I'm the only way for any of us to go back into that dimension and kill the vampires' king," I said. "Right?"

"In theory, yes. There's also an entire palace full of vampires infected with unknown demonic powers keen to flood this realm. If you travel through, you risk any of those creatures coming out in your place."

"That's what happened before, right? When you used the demonglass portal in here to go after Azurial?"

He nodded. "I didn't anticipate the effects would be that

strong. It blew out the wards all around the headquarters. If we did that again, it'd draw the attention of every demon in several realms. Not just Pandemonium. There are others that lie directly on top of this city which were affected by the events a few weeks ago."

"Like Babylon."

"Yes, like Babylon. I'd prefer not to bring *that* realm into it."

"You're really never going to tell me about that place, are you?" I asked. "Sometimes I think you get a kick out of keeping secrets from me."

"Sometimes *I* think your penchant for asking the wrong questions will get you into trouble."

"Been there, done that." I frowned. "I'm not human, you know? I won't cause untold chaos by eating from the tree of knowledge."

His gaze dropped to my bandaged side. "You're still mortal, Devi." His voice had the faintest undercurrent, some emotion I couldn't place. "And I never said I thought you were a mere ordinary human."

Warmth filled my chest, but I gave him a mock glare. "Nice job flattering me to distract from not answering my question."

"I told you," he said. "We restrict who we give information to. You already know more than you should for someone of your level, and if the other warlocks find out, they'll think we're passing on our secrets to the celestials."

My blood-loss-addled brain couldn't quite process that. "So you're saying I need to earn Javos's trust, right? Or yours?"

"You have mine. It isn't about that. Warlocks are secretive by nature and share none of our secrets with others, and only your position as an honorary novice keeps the others from kicking up a fuss."

Hardly an answer, especially as my link with the celestials was always going to put a wedge between me and earning the warlocks' respect.

"Wait." I screwed up my forehead. "You're saying you trust me? Seriously? Even after all the rule-breaking and winding up Javos?"

"I'd find your winding up Javos more amusing if he wasn't likely to take your head off for it at some point, but yes. Against my better judgement."

My mouth dropped open a little. "Wow. Am I asking the right questions now?"

"Get your rest." He trailed a hand down my face, sparking a current of warmth in my blood. "We'll talk when you're more awake. It's endearing, but you're drooling all over the sofa."

So I was. Way to go, Devi. "I meant every word."

"I'm sure you did."

I think he smiled, but I was too far gone by then.

13

Next thing I knew, the sound of arguing voices drifted in from the kitchen. I pushed the blanket off me and sat up, looking down at my bandaged side.

My wound seemed to have healed up, so I climbed off the sofa and walked upstairs. I kept spare clothes in the guest room and I was covered in blood and dirt, so it was a relief to have a proper shower. Afterwards, I went looking for Fiona.

I found her in one of the guest rooms, lying asleep in the bed. Guilt twisted inside me. I'd put her weird behaviour down to the trauma of being kidnapped. I hadn't considered the possibility that she'd been bitten during the struggle. After all, vampire wounds healed too quickly to be noticeable after a few hours, and I'd been severely injured at the time.

Her eyelids flickered and she tilted her head to look at me. "I thought I'd have to pretend to be asleep forever. Those guys don't sound happy."

"Javos's speciality is yelling and breaking things," I said. "It's me they're angry with."

Her brow furrowed. "Why?"

"How much do you remember of yesterday?"

Her face clouded. "I'm sorry. It was stupid of me to go to the vamps for help. I was just—I wanted to know if I was going to turn into one of them."

"You could have asked me," I said. "Well. I didn't know—still don't. Was it definitely an infected vamp who bit you?"

She nodded. "I didn't know he'd bitten me at first. And then—I didn't think we'd make it out of that realm alive. Afterwards, I wanted to forget about it. I was having night-mares of that place, but I didn't feel the urge to drink blood, so I figured I couldn't be a regular vampire. But then I heard about the others. How they turned violent and attacked people. I was terrified I'd be the same."

My fists curled at my sides. "That was the cure. I think. The only people who turned into killers were the ones who took the cure. You didn't take any, did you?"

She shook her head. "No. I was spotted in that bar, and you saw… they recognised both of us. I shouldn't have gone there."

"It's not your fault. Just warn me next time."

Her eyes shimmered with tears. "What's going to happen to me?"

*I don't know.* Blood cravings were one thing, but she'd never been bitten by a non-infected vampire. But that didn't mean she was immune to the venom.

"If you were going to turn, you'd have experienced symptoms by now," I said. "So the demon virus must have spread but not the vampire venom."

Which was hardly better. Because we didn't know *what* the demon virus did. But I knew I couldn't risk her getting her hands on the cure. Not after what'd happened to the others.

*I have to ask them.* I didn't know if Alec had made it back to the warehouse, but I did have his number.

"What is this place, anyway?" Fiona mumbled. "Warlock headquarters?"

"Yeah. You're safe here," I said. "Come and find me later. I'll still be here."

I left her room, taking out my phone, and fired off a quick message to Alec. I didn't tell him what we'd found out—any of the other vamps in that hideout might be a spy for the other side, and after the disaster at the vampire bar, I wasn't feeling particularly well-disposed towards him. But I did ask if he'd heard anything new about the cure or the blood-stones, and warned him that some vampires were likely involved with demons.

Now I was more awake, I remembered the fight more clearly. The reason I hadn't been able to hit the vampires' leader was because my celestial blade kept vanishing. Was that his power? Or was my celestial power losing strength because of my demon side? *No way.* I was just a little out of practise. And anyone's power would falter in the face of that sort of magic. There was a reason celestials had died out on that world.

But it was all too clear I couldn't rely on my celestial powers to beat him.

I found Nikolas, Rachel and Javos in the kitchen, seated around the table. Javos's chair was custom-made to fit his huge bulk, and he always yelled if anyone else sat on it. From the way he slammed the dead demon leg he was eating on the table, he hadn't got his temper tantrums out of the way last night.

Sure enough, Javos turned and glared at me. "You really couldn't hold yourself back, could you? Not content to cause havoc in that dimension once, you dragged two of my people over there without knowing the dangers on the other side, and nearly died in the process."

"Rachel and Nikolas volunteered to come with me, and

probably knew more about what was over there than I did. So don't blame me for their decisions." I looked at him defiantly. "Also, isn't the existence of a demigod with an army of vampires a little more important than my disobeying your orders to rescue a friend?"

"Insubordination isn't a virtue, whatever you've heard about us," he growled. "Sometimes I wonder if we made the right decision in allowing you to fight at our side."

Rachel leaned forwards. Nikolas looked positively impassive, one hand wrapped around a mug of coffee, but tension simmered below the surface, and for an instant, I half expected him to throw it at Javos's head. I would have done so, anyway.

Instead, I took in a calming breath and gave Javos a smile. "You should have asked the celestials for my report. Some of them would have been happy to talk at length about how much of a troublemaker I am. Unfortunately, you're stuck with me. Did Nikolas tell you the truth? I'm your ticket to getting that realm straightened out, and I'm not resigning from my post. They want this realm, somehow, and if we ignore them, the problem will only get worse."

"And you succeeded in your fight against the one responsible?" he asked.

My jaw clenched. "I thought he was a vampire. Then he came out with demon power—demigod level." I nodded to Nikolas. "I killed several of his vampires, but he must have an army there."

"What you haven't explained is how you ended up following the vampires there in the first place. What is your friend involved in?"

"The vampires tricked her," I said. "She got bitten by one of the infected ones, and heard about the cure."

"She's not a vampire," he said, picking up the demon leg

and gnawing on the end again. "Wouldn't she have turned by now?"

"She would if she'd been bitten by a regular vampire," I said. "I know she didn't take the cure, though. So she won't turn. But it sure would help to know whose magic it is in the bloodstones."

Nausea swooped through the pit of my stomach, not at all helped by the demon leg dangling from Javos's mouth. Normally demon magic had a damaging effect on humans, but if no symptoms presented themselves, anyone else might have been bitten. But... that meant there might be any number of humans carrying the virus in this realm right now.

"As you brought no evidence back with you, we don't know," Javos said.

"We were a bit preoccupied fighting the vamps," added Rachel. "Don't beat up on Devi. If she hadn't got us out, we'd have died there."

Javos's eyes narrowed. "It's essential to our own security that we let the netherworld dimensions police themselves. Not only did you break that rule several times over, the current leader of that dimension is imprisoned in another one entirely."

"I thought you were fine with Themedes staying out of the way," I said. "Besides, they're sending demon infected vamps into our dimension. That makes it our business."

"Since you conveniently left us to clear up your mess," he said, "I sent a team to investigate the portal the vampires travelled through."

My attention sharpened. "And?"

"It was set up on the other side. The part in this realm collapsed immediately afterwards. It was also too small and low-power to be detected."

"I figured," I said. "If they made a big deal of it, someone would have detected it. Was that address anywhere on your lists?"

"No." He bit off another chunk of demon leg and slapped the remainder down on the table. Fighting a shudder, I looked at Rachel instead. She rested her chin on her hands, her elbows propped up on the table.

"It was in the middle of a typically human-inhabited district," added Nikolas.

"But then—there must be more of them," I said.

"We don't have the authorisation to start searching human areas," said Nikolas. "Nobody can grant us that. We barely have leverage over the vampires, and that's only because some of our own were victims."

"Damn," I said. "Never thought of that. What about the human police? Because if there are portals open in there… are there CCTV cameras in the area?"

"I thought vampires' reflections didn't appear in mirrors." Fiona hovered in the doorway, looking warily at Javos.

"That's a myth," I said. "They just don't like anything light or sparkly in case it burns them."

Her mouth quirked. "That contradicts everything I read on DivinityWatch."

"On what?" asked both Javos and Nikolas at the same time.

I stifled a laugh. "You don't want to know. Fiona, we're discussing vampires. Did you happen to see any of them carrying black bloodstones?"

"What? No." She wrinkled her nose. "I forgot about those creepy things. So that's why they weren't the same as regular vamps?"

I nodded. "Yeah. Listen, I don't know if you want to go home, but I think I'm going to have to stick around here for a while."

"I'll be the judge of that," said Javos. "What you did has

caused me an ungodly amount of paperwork—not to mention the anger of several warlocks who witnessed your last stunt. You won't be able to get away with any more public displays without making enemies, Devi."

Fiona looked alarmed. "What did she do this time?"

"Nothing you have the right to know about, human," growled Javos. "We don't usually allow humans to come here, but you're not to speak a word of this to anyone outside, unless you want to face the wrath of the warlock council."

"Hey!" I moved to her side. "That's enough. Fiona won't tell a soul. And if you've got a problem with me talking to her about it, take it up with the prick who decided to take her into Pandemonium. And the vampire who bit her."

"Does that make me a preternatural now?" she asked. "Because I don't want to hang out with vampires. I can go out in sunshine just fine."

"Tell me if you get any side effects." I glared at Javos. "As for you—"

My phone rang. I picked it up, thinking it was Alec or Clover—but the call came from an unfamiliar number. Except the first two digits. The guild's digits.

"Hello?" I said.

"Devina," said Mrs Credence's voice. "Devi—please come to the guild now. She ran away. Alyson ran away. People are dead."

14

"**W**hat happened this time?" I moved into the hallway, the phone pressed to my ear.

"We had her in isolation with no outside contact," Mrs Credence mumbled. "But she got out. Broke the doors clean off their hinges and killed two celestials. I can't be here anymore. I can't. Devi—please—"

The call cut off, with a sound like sobbing. *Oh shit.* Alyson had broken out, too. To join the other vamps? Maybe. But if she'd killed people... this time, it might not have been an accident.

Or she'd got hold of more of the cure.

I couldn't be in two places at once, but her trail of destruction began at the guild. I needed to make sure she hadn't bitten anyone else.

"Who was that?" asked Javos. "The guild, right? You're still in contact?"

"Not exactly. Their vampire bite victims are causing trouble. One of them took the cure and killed another, and now it looks like she's on the loose."

"It's none of our business," he said. "They can take care of their own problems."

"It's linked to this case," I countered. "She probably ran back to the vampires for shelter, and more of the cure."

"If she's no true vampire, she can run around in the daylight," he said. "She might be anywhere."

"Not if the regular vamps are asleep," I said. "They lock their houses, don't they? She'll either be running around outside, or at—" I cut myself off before I said *the warehouse,* not certain if Javos knew the extent of our discovery. Since he hadn't killed the vamps there yet, I'd guess Nikolas had spared him the details. "Look, we can't go after the demon realm again yet, and I'm not much use to you sitting around here. Plus she's likely to tear people to pieces, and I'd like to spare the humans the trauma."

Javos rose to his feet, the chair and table rattling as he knocked into them. "This is not your decision to make. I've had about enough of you striding around as though you're in charge."

Nikolas moved smoothly to my side, his whole demeanour changing from calmness to anger which sent an electric current through the air. I snapped my head up, suddenly overcome with the urge to take the demon mark and shove the overbearing warlock in the chest with it. *Whoa there. Don't do that.*

Clenching my right fist, I stared Javos out. "Go on. Kick me out, if you're really sure the warlocks won't ask questions if they see an untrained wielder of demon magic walking around the city unsupervised. What would that do to your reputation?"

Classical music blasted from the corner and the giant warlock went still. Beside the radio on top of the fridge, Rachel gave me a grin and a shrug. "Didn't want to see him swipe your head off."

"I wasn't going to hit her," growled Javos. "You can turn that shit off. I'm going to need my magic."

The music stopped. Nikolas didn't move. Neither did I. My demon mark didn't twinge again, but my fist remained clenched. For a wild moment then, it'd been like I was holding a sharp, deadly weapon, and was overcome with the impulse to stab the warlock chief with it. Which was ridiculous. I'd never used the mark as a weapon. Apparently I was still suffering weird aftereffects of the battle. Or whatever had happened when Nikolas touched my demon mark.

"You can't toss me around like one of your other warlocks," I said. "You either have me on your side or not, and it's up to you if you want to make an enemy of me."

Javos's sharp gaze pierced me through. "Go. If I need you for anything, I'll call you. But make no mistake—your soul remains bound to one of us, and when the celestials find out, they won't want you at their side any more than I will. When a mortal challenges an arch-demon, their life comes to a swift and brutal end."

"You're such a charmer." I took a step back. "I'll take that under advisement. Call me if there are any new developments." I looked at Rachel, who remained next to the radio. And Nikolas made no move to follow me as I left.

That settled that, then.

Fiona all but ran from the warlocks' place, and would probably have sprinted down the road if I hadn't pointed out my car. "C'mon, I'll give you a lift."

"And then you're going to the celestials? After what he said?"

"I don't give a shit what he said." I unlocked the car doors. "Sorry you had to see that."

"He nearly bit your head off!" She shuddered, climbing into the car's passenger seat. I got in front of the wheel and sneaked a glance back at the house. So much for Nikolas taking my side.

His brother was right. Javos only kept me around because I was less of a risk as an ally. Given how Nikolas and Rachel had behaved, *they* were on my side... for now. But would they stand with me against the entire warlock community?

I shoved the thoughts out of mind and returned to the equally unpleasant prospect of dealing with a rogue celestial with a taste for murder. After dropping Fiona back at our flat with the promise that she'd call me if anything happened, I drove to the celestial guild.

Nobody waited outside the brick building. I locked my car, walked to the front doors, and stood there for a couple of minutes while the security doors refused to scan my left wrist. I waved my hand around irritably. "Come on, wake up."

Uneasily, I remembered how my celestial blade had vanished at the crucial moment in my fight with the vampires' leader. Was my celestial mark really fading? It didn't look any different, but if my demon side was getting stronger, maybe it meant my celestial powers would disappear. *I really hope not.*

I raised my fist and knocked on the door. "Hey! Your security door's jammed."

The door opened a few moments later, and Bad Haircut Sammy loomed over me. Oh, yay.

"Get out," he said. "We don't want warlocks here."

"I've been invited. Tell G—Mr Roth to fix that door. It's glitching." I'd almost said Gav, and the slip jolted me more than I'd expected. Grief was weird like that. I'd put everything from the guild out of mind, but every time I came back here, it hit me again as though no time had passed at all. And I was definitely not in the mood to deal with Sammy. He was too bland to even be considered a nemesis.

"The inspector's coming back soon," he said. "He's making a plan for dealing with those vampire scum."

"Vamps aren't the guild's business. Get out of my way."

"Devi," said Mr Roth from behind him.

For a moment, I was tempted to turn my back and leave them to clean up the carnage from their escaped celestial myself. Except I was fairly certain that 'those vampire scum' also included the bite victims. In Inspector Deacon's doctrine, they were soulless as regular vamps.

Seven hells.

I shook my head at Sammy. "Go hassle someone else. Mrs Credence called me."

"She's dropped out of the case," Mr Roth said. "Stress. We need another senior celestial to step in, but until then, I'm dealing with all contacts on the issue. Alyson attacked several novices on the way out. Two fatally."

"Mrs Credence told me." I should have checked the warehouse first, but the others had already said they kicked out anyone who turned bad. "Can I come in? How'd she get out?"

"The door was melted."

"*Melted?*" I stared at him.

"Apparently so," he said, taking a step back. Shouts came from the corridor behind, where people ran back and forth. "I need to go and speak to the survivors."

He didn't tell me not to follow him, so I did, ignoring Bad Haircut Sammy's disgruntled look. From his behaviour, he was clearly tailing Mr Roth around like he had the inspector. And Mr Roth was letting him. *Not good at all.*

"Where did Mrs Credence go?"

"Home," he said distractedly. "This is the worst incident inside our walls since the last guild burned down."

He hadn't mentioned any of the recent events, but I had the sneaking suspicion that things might well get worse than a demon attack inside the guild. Armageddon levels of bad.

He stopped by the entrance to the nurse's office. Inside, several novices lay in varying states of injury.

"She ran through here, covered in blood," said Sandra Yun, former partner of the first bite victim. "She'd killed two people before we caught up to her, but she moves *fast*."

"Vampire fast?" I asked.

She nodded. "Yeah, easily."

"We fought back," added a guy I vaguely recognised from novice training. "She bit me."

Shit. If the virus could be passed on—and I'd bet it could—then he might turn the same. Unless it was all on the cure. In which case, we needed to get rid of it. Either way—anyone in this room who'd been bitten might never be able to use their celestial powers again without risking death.

Sandra pressed a cloth to her wounded shoulder, her hands shaking. "I thought—after you killed the demon responsible, I thought it was over," she said quietly.

"Me too, believe me." I swallowed, glancing back at the guild leader. Mr Roth looked almost uneasy. Maybe he'd let me in because I was familiar, the only touchstone between the guild and the horrors happening outside.

"I suppose Mrs Credence told you the current situation," I said to Mr Roth, hoping he knew at least a little about the bloodstones being responsible for passing on the virus.

"She did," he said quietly. "The fact is, though Devi, we're on the brink of another visit from the inspector. In fact, he was due to arrive tomorrow."

My heart sank. "Seriously? Didn't last time put him off?"

"People have died," he said seriously. "The inspector has powers the rest of us don't—"

"And the temper of a rampaging bull." I'd almost said *warlock*. "He'll probably get more people killed if he comes in here. What'll he do to the other bite victims?"

He shook his head, pushing the door open into the corridor. "I don't know. But you've been looking into this case for the vampires, too, right? I do hope you're telling me everything, Devi."

*Er... no.*

I couldn't exactly tell him I was almost certain an army of vampires wanted to flood this dimension from Pandemonium. Because I'd have to say I'd *been* there, or at the very least skirt around the subject.

"I'm trying to track down the vampires responsible," I said instead, "but so far all I know is that they have a lot of contacts and multiple hideouts and aliases. Everything I find is inconclusive."

"If there is evidence that a significant percentage of the vampires are caught up in this, then the inspector will have no choice but to order a purge of the whole city."

My mouth fell open. "What? Madame White—I've met her. She definitely isn't involved."

"Not her. I imagine she wants to be rid of the problem as much as we do," he said. "If this doesn't stop, the Grade Fours will have to be brought in from the capital."

My heart sank. Even when things got really bad, it generally took only a few Grade Two or Three celestial soldiers to bring down the usual demons we dealt with. Not the Grade Fours—a whole team of people with the highest rank of celestial powers, and the inspector's implicit permission to play judge, jury and executioner. Like Grade Threes, they worked in teams on independent missions, but in certain cases, to prevent war with the netherworld, they were allowed to do things no normal celestial would ever do.

Like purge an entire city of vampires, for instance.

The vampire queen, if she knew, might even encourage them. Or at least step out of the guild's way. But all they had to do was expand the definition of 'vampire' to cover 'anyone who got bitten', and Fiona would be on their list as well.

I'd walk into hell before I let that happen.

"Are you dense?" I snapped at Mr Roth. "This is probably the demons' endgame. Who needs to attack if they can just turn us against one another? And you're encouraging them."

"Devi!" he said, in a shocked voice. "If you continue to use that tone with me, I'll have to ask you to leave."

"You're being ridiculous," I said. "I'd expect this level of crap from the inspector, but I thought at least one person here had some sense. Do you really think starting a war with the warlocks and vampires won't draw the demons right here? They *want* this. They're scheming against you right now, I'll bet, and apparently they don't even need to make the effort to attack you. You're doing their work for them."

"Nobody has made a decision yet," he said. "I have to stress that it's a last resort, and not one I support. But if quarantine doesn't work—"

"You'll kill them."

"To stop the infection. Imagine if every celestial was infected."

"Might be a damn sight better than whatever's infected *you*," I said. "And for that matter, I'm not going to be a part of this."

I left before he could reply, seething. It wasn't my job to stop the inspector—Mr Roth and the celestials' higher council were supposed to keep the bastard in check. But innocent lives might end, and for all that, the real culprit was still out there, infecting more victims.

I stormed through the entryway, and ran smack into Clover outside the doors.

"Ow!" I caught my balance. "You like to do that on purpose, don't you? I know you saw me coming."

"I thought you needed some sense knocking into you." Her face was heavily scarred from a demon attack, which made her sudden appearance that more alarming. "You said you wouldn't come back here."

"Seven hells, Clover," I said. "Where have you been?"

"Looking for you." Her expression was grave. For someone with a chunk missing from her face, it wasn't exactly a difficult achievement.

"Why? I thought you'd gone on holiday. You haven't called in ages." Unless you counted our brief phone call before the news that Alyson had killed someone, I hadn't heard from her in weeks.

"I've been somewhat preoccupied. As have you, from what I've heard."

"You might say that," I said. "Demon-infected vampires running amok, infected celestials attacking one another, and now the bloody inspector's on his way back—"

"I should have known," she said. "Please tell me you haven't told Mr Roth that you know more than he does."

"Obviously not. But how do *you* know that?"

"I know *you*, Devi. The warlocks are bound to have contacts in places the guild doesn't. But it still might not be enough."

"You know something?"

She shook her head. "Not exactly. More of a hunch. Whenever something bad happens at the guild, all the evidence disappears alarmingly swiftly."

"You don't mean…?" *The demonglass? Or—Gav. That book.*

"I've been here a long time, Devi," she said. "Do you remember when the old guild was destroyed?"

I shrugged. "Not exactly, since I wasn't here. I remember the aftermath. Inspector in town, man hunts for the people who summoned the demons, heightened security…"

It'd been pretty major. One of the other inspectors had been killed, for one thing, and others had gone missing in the confusing aftermath of the demon attack. But I didn't see the connection. No vampires had been involved—just a botched demon summoning by one of our own. Of course, the attack was the reason our city had only one designated Inspector. The one who'd got killed had actually been pretty reasonable compared to his partner, from what I remembered.

"Before these recent events, Gav confided in me that he thought there was more to the attack than met the eye," she said. "He never showed me his research, and his office was cleared after his death. But I always suspected he knew something."

"Something like what?" I asked. "That was four years ago. Faye Carruthers… she was the summoner, right?"

She shook her head. "There never was any proof. She was accused, certainly, and disappeared… as does anyone else who gets on the guild's bad side."

"All right," I said. "The guild's shady. There's probably someone in there communicating with demons. But we knew that already. Nothing connects it with this particular case. Vampires didn't destroy the old guild."

Except Gav had also been looking into demon venoms, more recently. Right before someone died as a result of a similar attack. Had he seen it coming? How was it even possible?

"These are no ordinary vampires," she said. "They walk in the day, and don't need to feed on blood… nothing exists in the guild's records that points to what they are."

I twisted to look at her. "The archives?" I asked. "You're saying there might be answers there? Or Gav has them?"

"If he did, I couldn't find them."

"His phone disappeared," I said. "Someone removed it."

Just like someone else had removed several pages from that book.

*There was an insider.*

I paused. "Do you know who Damian Greenwood is? I mean, did you ever speak to him?"

"No, I didn't," she said. "He was bitten, right?"

"Yeah, he was," I said. "He also had a book Gav checked out the library before he died. A book about demon venoms."

A dark look passed over her features. "Then he might be the one. I thought the girl was—or both of them."

"Damian? He was a dick to me, but he had reason to be pissed off at being forced into early retirement."

Except that note. *I know what you did.* What grudge could he possibly have against me? We didn't even know one another.

But I did know where he was. The warehouse.

*All right. Time to see what our celestial vamp has to say for himself.*

"Be careful, Devi," she said softly. "Others have paid for making the wrong step with their lives."

On that ominous note, she turned back to head into the guild's corridor, presumably with the intention of standing in corners and scaring novices. She'd long since retired from the field. Fixing this crap was up to me.

I drove to the warehouse, hands clenched on the wheel, radio turned up to drown out the clamour of my own thoughts. So much for feeling sympathy for the demons. I didn't think a Grade Four celestial-run purge would help matters much, either, but if I'd let the killer get away…

*Hellfire and ash.* I slowed the car, swearing at the dashboard. The warehouse door was open, and the vampires had gone.

## 15

Rachel answered the phone when I rang the warlocks. "Hey, Devi. Found your rogue yet?"

"The bloody vampires have gone," I snarled into the phone. "Wasn't anyone watching the warehouse?"

"Not since we got back from the demon realm, no. Someone had to stop Javos from breaking a few spines. Didn't they leave any clues behind?

"No, and I've no idea where our rogue vampire celestial disappeared to," I said. "And that isn't the half of it. I need to talk to Nikolas in person. Where is he?"

"He went into the shadow realm for some emergency or other," Rachel said. "I think the arch-demon's finally packing it in."

"What—he's dying? Now?" Not that I'd liked the guy, but his timing might be better. And I never had managed to wrangle any clues about the current shit show in demonland out of him.

Screw rules and consequences. Some things were more important. And I was past standing in the shadows while people got hurt.

I drove back to the warlocks' place as quickly as I could. Rachel let me inside with raised eyebrows. "You're seriously going to an arch-demon's deathbed?"

"Themedes knows more about what's going on in Pandemonium," I said. "I know he does. No way does he rule a whole demonic city and not have a clue who wants to usurp his position. Aside from his own son, that is."

"He didn't know about the vampires, right?" she asked.

"Nope. Apparently. They were his weakness, remember?"

"And you don't trust Nikolas to tell you?" She raised an eyebrow. "You two looked pretty close yesterday."

"I don't have time to wait until I qualify to access the right information. The guild's archives have nothing on vampires. He's our only link."

Aside from making a deal with the almost-literal devil.

Rachel pursed her lips, then grinned. "Well, he won't be happy if you materialise on top of him while he's dealing with our big ugly prisoner, but it's your risk."

"Yep." I entered the hall, turning down the corridor to the one that led to the demonglass room.

"Don't forget the shoes," Rachel said.

I had forgotten. It wasn't like they'd have helped in any situations lately, except perhaps the palace. But Rachel's gravity-defying shoes had saved my life once before. After running to my room to fetch the shoes and grab some spare weapons, I made my way to the warlocks' storeroom.

The door was open, even though Nikolas wouldn't have needed to use the demonglass to travel into the shadow realm. The glass itself wasn't hooked up to a source of energy to make a portal, but it didn't need to be. Not for me.

I approached the glass. Its surface shimmered and my demon mark sprang to attention, itching uncontrollably, demanding I press it to the glass. I could control where I went, somewhat, by imagining somewhere I'd seen before—though I still didn't know all the rules.

A familiar image appeared in the glass—a spire-like tower separated from the huge castle by a bridge over crashing waters. Zadok's tower. My demon mark tingled, inviting me to step through, and I had to clench my fist again. *Wrong target.*

But I knew where else to go. I vividly remembered fighting an army of scorpion demons in a corridor filled with glass pillars. Conjuring the image to mind, I raised my hand.

Zadok's grinning face filled the glass and I jerked back, too late. My demon mark struck the glass and I fell through, toppling onto a plush carpet in a room which was definitely *not* the one I needed. A circular room with walls of stone, and Zadok smirking at me not ten feet away.

"Well now," he said, with a lazy smile. "I wondered when you'd show up to ask for my help."

"I'm not here to see you," I spat at him, staggering away from the glass, which was in a long sheet against the back wall. Why had Nikolas trapped him in the same room as this demonglass?

Wait. He wasn't trapped at all. Whichever room had been his prison, this wasn't it. Shadows crowded around his body, and his eyes shone with power.

Ah, shit. He'd broken the boundaries, and now I'd somehow managed to land in the same room as him. *You traitorous little worm,* I thought at the demon mark. Either Zadok had drawn me here, or the mark's magic had. But the bastard was loose, and Nikolas didn't know. A gleam in his eyes told me enough—he'd orchestrated this. He'd known I was coming. This was revenge for the way I'd humiliated and then snubbed him.

"That was rude of you," he said. "I hear insubordination is

a speciality with you, so I won't get *too* offended... though I imagine your warlock boss is less pleased with you."

"You're free to imagine all you like." I stepped backwards towards the glass, reaching for it—but the glass had disappeared into shadow. A solid shadow in the shape of a person. One of Zadok's shadow clones.

I spun around with an impatient hiss, only to find he'd vanished, too.

"Oh, for fuck's sake." I rolled my eyes. "We've been through this. Can we skip to the part where I kick your sorry arse into the seven hells, so I can get back to more important things?"

"Don't you want to know why your mark brought you here?" The shadows fell away, revealing him standing next to a wall covered in symbols. At its foot lay a small pentagram made out of some kind of luminous metal I'd never seen before. "It took me a while to put this together, but it's a beacon. It can draw any demon. Apparently that includes you."

"What does that have to do with anything?"

Too late, I realised that the room was a lab of sorts, filled with various tools and piles of demonic equipment. I wore my anti-warlock defence, so I wasn't too worried about fighting him—but Themedes was dying right this moment, potentially taking important secrets to his grave. That was more important than Nikolas's brother's eternal grudge or whatever he was brewing up here in his lab.

Zadok casually bent down and picked up the pentagram, tossing it from one hand to the other. "If you wanted to fight someone who's inconveniently ensconced in another dimension, for instance," he said—the pentagram arced high, its luminous gleam reflecting in the demonglass behind him— "this device can draw them to a location of your choosing. I'd wager your friends wouldn't like it if you died next time, would they?"

*How does he even know that?* I'd bet my right hand Nikolas wouldn't have told him. "Look, you're supposed to be imprisoned in here. Not prancing around your mad scientist's lab trying to tempt me into giving up my soul."

"No souls will be involved in the arrangement," he said, tossing the pentagram into the air again. Its luminous spinning light was starting to give me a headache. "That would taint the deal. Though I have to admit, I've never seen one quite like yours."

"You can't see souls. Don't be absurd."

"Your aura tells me what your soul looks like, Devi. And yours is split. I wonder…" He trailed off suggestively, spinning the pentagram on his fingertip. "I've compiled a number of theories on the nature of your power, none of which your delightful warlock mentor in the mundane world would deign to share with you. But I would." His eyes gleamed, reflecting the pentagram's shifting shades of pinkish-gold. "Let me help you unlock your potential."

"The only thing I'd like you to unlock is the door."

Except there wasn't one, that I could see. How in hell did he get in, then? Warlocks.

He laughed softly. "You'll remain stubborn to the grave, won't you?"

"You threw me off a bridge," I said. "Even if we were strangers, you're creeping me the hell out with this weird obsession with me."

He gave me a pitying look. "Humans have no interest for me. The same can't be said for my brother, since he was raised amongst your kind… but if you have more than a business arrangement, it'd be a shame if you elected to keep your celestial status." He flipped the pentagram over and caught it one-handed. "And even more of a shame if you decided to go behind his back."

"It's a shame *you* can't keep your nose out of other people's businesses," I said. "If you're going to waste my time playing the villain, at least make the effort to come up with a more convincing argument."

"You think *I'm* the villain?" He arched a brow. "Devi, my dear clueless human, all demons and warlocks alike are classified as villainous by nature, but I thought you had more sense than to follow the celestials' narrow-minded doctrine. Especially given their fate here."

I looked at him sharply. "What? The celestials don't exist here."

A smile sprang to his lips. "He didn't tell you."

I swore and stepped back towards the glass, willing my celestial mark to respond. "If you don't mind, I have places to be."

My celestial mark burned white-hot—and at the same time, the pentagram in his hand flashed white-gold. I bit my lip and raised the mark up, but nothing happened.

Zadok raised an eyebrow. "Well? Where's your light show?"

I turned my hand around and flipped him off. *Come on. Switch on, light.* But his shadow stood between me and the way out.

*Fine.* Reaching for a stake instead, I froze when a shadowy hand gripped my demon marked wrist. The mark itched uncontrollably, and I twisted my hand, trying to free myself. A second shadow grabbed my other wrist, locking it behind my back.

"I wouldn't do anything hasty," he said. "I rather think you were lucky to escape alive last time."

"What the hell do you want with me? If you're too scared

to fight your brother in person, stop dragging me into your stupid power games."

"The game isn't between my brother and me." His eyes gleamed, as luminous as the pentagram. "It's between the Divinities and the arch-demons. Do you really think you were marked by accident? You are a crucial puzzle piece, Devi, and I for one am curious to know why a celestial was chosen. The gods alone know what games the Divinities play, and all of us are mere pawns to them… if we allow ourselves to be."

I shrugged, with difficulty. "So what? The only person who gets to figure this shit out is me."

"You don't have access to the right information," he said. "The celestials kept it from you, scared you'd run when you found out the truth of the war you fought… but I think you've known it was hopeless from the moment you stepped into the demon's realm, haven't you? Since your friend's tragic death in that saphor demon nest."

My mouth formed a retort about his stupid cryptic responses, but then my brain caught up with me. I'd strayed away from thinking back to that last, awful mission if I could help it, and the only part I recalled in any detail was the desperate battle with the demon in its home dimension, and the horrific sight of Rory dying I'd come back to in the cave. I'd filed the only report, and the inspector had flat-out dismissed it. But there was one slight detail I'd forgotten— before our foray into the demonic dimension, Rory and I had crawled through a nest which had formerly belonged to saphor demons. They hadn't been the worst of what we'd faced down there, but saphor demons… I was almost certain they were parasite demons.

I'd need to check the files again to be sure, but had Zadok just handed me the name of the demon responsible for the virus?

"Nothing to say to that?" He smiled. "I take it you're aware that the warlocks did the very same to you, despite whatever they promised you when you signed up. Because if you were allowed to choose which path to take, and your decision didn't line up with their plans for you, they'd be forced to exterminate you."

*Keep talking.* While he spouted off, I'd managed to wriggle my right hand enough to reach my stake.

To keep his eyes on my face, I said, "They're my business partners. If I wanted access to information, I'd go and find it myself. What do you think I'm here for?"

"The old arch-demon won't tell you a thing," he said. "He lost his power long ago, and clung to his crumbling kingdom until his own son tried to usurp him. Pity. I think a new demon overlord is the only way that realm will survive."

My stake touched the glass, and I slid my fingertips down to the tip and pushed.

Zadok lunged, but I'd already fallen through, toppling out of the tower onto the bridge. Not my first choice of landing, but it'd do. Cold air whipped at me, and I turned towards the castle. A sheer drop on either side reminded me of my close call the last time I'd been here. Rachel's boots kept my footsteps steady, preventing the cold breeze from blowing me too close to the edge.

Of course, that's when the first scorpion demon appeared.

I threw a stake at it without breaking stride. I hadn't wanted to lose my weapons, but with my celestial light malfunctioning, I didn't have much choice. The stake sank into the scorpion's side and it screeched, stinger lunging at me. I ducked and stabbed with a knife this time, my boots giving me leverage. The venos demon toppled off the bridge, and I kept running. My mind whirled with the new information. Demon parasites. Whether he'd given me the information deliberately or not—I knew exactly what to look for.

As long as he hadn't expected me to offer my soul in trade.

A crackling roar erupted before me, and smoke poured out of the side of the wall as I ran towards it. Alarm blared through my mind. Nikolas's castle… it'd caught on fire.

## 16

Flames licked the side of the castle, a dramatic contrast to the violet, star-studded sky. I was almost certain they came from where the arch-demon was imprisoned.

I picked up speed, my heart swooping. Fear for Nikolas burned deep in my chest, and I kept running across the bridge towards the stone tower opposite. I hoped I remembered the route, because if not, I was screwed.

A venos demon ran out in front of me. I called my sword and this time it appeared. I didn't even get the chance to feel relief, just fury. Severing the demon's stinger, I dealt the killing blow without slowing down. Bat demons circled above, but didn't appear to want to get too close to the flames. A wooden door, luckily unlocked, led inside. I wrenched it open and pelted down the stone corridor within.

No burning smells or screaming assailed me, but a strange crackling noise, one I knew from when I'd witnessed the arch-demon's magic before. Had he attacked Nikolas? I'd thought he was dead. Or dying. But having seen what his magic could do… shit. I needed to be sure he was okay.

I veered into the pillared corridor of demonglass I'd been in before, not stopping. The smell of brimstone burned strong but the whole place had the faint trace of nether-world smells around it anyway. The crackling noise, however, told me where to run. And the light burning in the corridor ahead of me told me I'd reached the arch-demon's tower. Despite the light and the noise, the fire left no other signs of its presence—a definite sign that it wasn't normal flames.

I ran into the corridor, and stopped. The door to Themedes's prison was open, and energy poured out, bright and fiery. The arch-demon's aura flared bright enough to smother my celestial light, and the echoing power made my teeth rattle in my skull.

"Nikolas!" I yelled.

Silence followed. I ran to the door, which hung off its hinges, edges blackened to cinders. And inside the room, fire burned in vibrant spirals, surrounding a winged figure suspended in the air. He made no sound, but power continued to radiate off his body.

My demon mark tingled, then my hand rose of its own accord. Fire swirled around me… and Nikolas. He was pressed against the wall as though pushed by the sheer force of the arch-demon's power.

"Devi!" he yelled. "Get out of here!"

"What the hell is happening?"

"It's the last of his power—" he broke off. Blood dripped from his nose, and the way he held himself suggested worse injuries.

The arch-demon floated, wings splayed, a fallen angel surrounded by a dark halo. How the hell did you switch off a dying demon's magic? I remembered all too clearly the damage it'd done when I'd touched him before. I might not survive it this time.

But Nikolas was hurt. Fire engulfed his left arm, filling the room with the smell of burning and brimstone. He swore loudly in some demon tongue, and yelled at me to step back.

The demon power held me still, my teeth chattering as though coldness and not heat assailed me. My demon mark burned white-hot, like I'd pressed it to an open flame—yet it felt more like an itch than pain. Waves of sensation passed over my mark to my fingertips in tandem with the roaring flames surrounding the dying arch-demon.

Themedes's eyes looked into mine, and all the power rushed over to me.

I gasped. My demon mark ignited and power surged through my bones, too bright. Too much. This time, my skin would burn straight off. I'd die if I took on all that magic—but I couldn't stop it from rushing towards my demon mark any more than I could stop a hurricane by standing in its path.

The arch-demon dropped like a stone, the last of his magic slamming into my palm, sending me staggering back.

At the same time, Nikolas pushed me out of the way. I caught my balance, turning to him in alarm—but the flames had died the instant he'd pushed me out of the line of fire.

Nikolas himself hadn't been so lucky. One of his hands had burned away to the bone, and I gagged at the smell of burning flesh.

"Shit," I said. "Shit, shit, shit." On anyone else, I'd have said they were dead for sure. But he had regenerative magic—if it worked on injuries that serious.

"You shouldn't have done that," he said through clenched teeth.

"How?" I croaked. "Fucking hell, Nikolas, your hand's—"

"It'll regenerate soon." Sooty ashes covered his face, but

his gaze was surprisingly steady, considering *half his freaking hand was missing.*

"If someone knocked your head off, would it grow back?" I asked instead of vomiting all over the arch-demon's ashes like I wanted to.

He gave me an amused look, flecked with pain. "I'd rather not find out. What were you thinking?"

"I wasn't. Apparently the demon mark took the wheel." I glanced down at my own hand to avoid looking at his. Sooty blackness outlined the arrowhead symbol. "Anyone want to clue me in on what just happened?"

"I have no idea." He staggered forwards. "Themedes is dead, though."

He crouched down and reached out with his uninjured hand. The arch-demon's winged form lay still, and the instant Nikolas touched it, it crumbled into ashes. Shadows surged from his fingertips over the ashes, filling the room. I backed away, the shadows looking all too close to Zadok's own powers.

"Whoa," I said. "What are you doing?"

"Removing all traces of Themedes. He hasn't left this room, so no traces of his home dimension can get out."

"And if Zadok got in?"

The shadows disappeared. "The room was bound. If he managed to get *in,* there's no chance he could have taken anything *out.* I know how his magic works." He pushed to his feet, swore, and leaned against the wall. A quick glance at his hand confirmed that the flesh and skin had grown back as though it'd never been gone. "Are you going to explain why you came here and walked in front of a dying demon's fire? I take it you didn't use a normal portal."

A twisting sensation seized my chest. I'd broken the warlocks' law for real this time. No disputing it. Sure, I'd never exactly been great at following rules, but working for the warlocks—with Nikolas—had given me a sense of purpose that almost made up for the constant annoyance I felt at not being able to use my powers. Yet here—and fighting in the fire dimension—was the most alive I'd felt in a long time.

I looked Nikolas in the eyes. "Just tell me if I'm out of the warlocks' guild. Go on. I'll survive it."

"I don't doubt you will." He took one step closer. "But surviving isn't enough, for you or for anyone. If you can't decide what drives you, the demons will step in. Mere recklessness for the sake of it is a weakness in their eyes. Why do you fight?"

I hadn't expected the question, but I clenched my left fist, the usual answers on my tongue—because I was reborn to this. I was made for it. But was I, really? That was my old goal.

Maybe I had to let something else take its place.

"Because the alternative isn't acceptable to me," I said. "Letting the demons win isn't acceptable. And I don't rush into dangerous situations for the sake of it. If I did, I'd have ended up in the fire realm much earlier than I did."

His eyes searched my face, and he nodded. Like I'd passed a test. Why did I get the feeling his analysis of me had nothing to do with Javos's orders, and more to do with some personal curiosity of his?

"Do I get a prize for being too reckless for the warlocks?" I asked. "I didn't ask my demon mark to drag me into the line of fire." I flipped my wrist over again. "Any clues? It sounded like Themedes hit me with his own magic. But the mark isn't his. I'm not connected to that dimension." But I wasn't connected to this one either, and Nikolas's lure had affected me intensely.

"You aren't," he said. "Which means he must have felt your magic answered to his in some other way. The demonglass first linked you to his dimension before any others. I've never heard of an arch-demon passing anything on to a human." His forehead pinched. "You really do seem to exist to push buttons."

"That's my best talent. Pushing buttons. Pissing off authority figures. You knew that when I signed up. Nobody is spared. Celestials and bad-tempered warlocks included."

"Am I included in the latter?" he asked. "I'd wager most would find you more endearing if you weren't so dead set on getting yourself killed."

"You nearly lost a hand. I don't care if you can regenerate, you're still as mortal as any of us. And you can't blame it on a rogue demon mark."

"I don't believe the mark has a mind of its own," he said. "Even though you said it liked me."

His hand closed around my wrist, thumb stroking over the mark. Heat sparked low in the pit of my stomach, rising as his gaze slid up my body. His thumb brushed my wrist again, his other hand rising to move a strand of hair from my face. No lure, no hint of his demon power, but the mere thought of it conjured up the fantasies I thought had been the result of his demon magic screwing with my head. I moaned involuntarily as his thumb circled the demon mark again.

He leaned close to me, his lips hovering over mine. "I have a number of buttons I'd like to push myself, as it happens."

I closed the distance between us.

Kissing him was even better without the dazed effect of his lure. I gripped his waist with my free hand as he deepened the kiss, an explosion of sensation rising in my blood. Heat raced through my veins, painless and invigorating, like demon fire. The fire contained in my right hand, which longed to touch the shadowy magic inside him—

I broke the kiss with a gasp. *What in hell was that?* Smoke poured from my right hand, and I yanked it back. "I should probably keep this thing shut away until whatever Themedes did wears off. I don't want you to lose another hand."

"That would be unfortunate," Nikolas said. His eyes were molten gold, inviting me in… but there was something I hadn't told him yet. As much as the fire of his touch had sparked things I'd never thought I'd feel again, much less in the company of a warlock with a dead arch-demon's ashes blowing around us—the annoying, cold voice of reason rose to quench the fire inside me.

I took in a breath. "I should probably mention your brother got out. Did you know?"

His eyes widened a little, the heat dying down. "What?"

"Yep. My demon mark decided to take me into his lab." I dropped my arm to my side, hoping the damn thing would stop itching—and more to the point, stop lighting on fire whenever I was around Nikolas. If I wanted to use it in a fight, I needed to maintain some semblance of control over the damn thing, not give into temptation at every turn. Even though, being a demon mark, it was probably *made* of temptation. No wonder my celestial power was fading.

Nikolas scowled. "He must have got out today."

"You don't think *he* might have killed Themedes?"

"No. I'd know. His killing methods have a distinctive edge. Besides, he's clearly been busy. I destroyed all his equipment several times this year already."

"So how much power does he have?"

"Less than he thinks, and less than he'd like to have. This dimension is a dead zone. You can't summon anything here. You only managed to do what you did because you used the demonglass. It's one of the reasons I didn't want him to work out the nature of your ability… people in this realm would exploit you for it."

"Yeah, well, he doesn't want me dead anymore," I said. "Instead, he offered to help me. I said no, and I managed to get out before he retaliated. Your brother has a pentagram which can apparently draw the demon in Pandemonium anywhere we like. We could get the vampires' leader out of the palace and strike him down."

His hands hovered near mine, but he didn't touch me this time. "That won't stop the vampire army. It wouldn't surprise me if that demigod wasn't working alone. We know nothing about him."

"I don't think we should forget Zadok. Look what he gets up to when we're not around. Are you sure he's not involved with that realm?"

"No," he said. "He's a loose cannon, to put it mildly. What did he say to you?"

"He didn't know about the vampires. But he hinted that he knows about this battle between heaven and hell that's connected to whatever's going on in both realms."

His brow furrowed. "He might have been posturing, but Babylon is still a netherworld realm. He's unpredictable and known to be a liar."

"I don't know, he didn't try to kill me this time. Next thing you know, we'll be best friends. I'm joking," I added. "I know he's a snake. But he sounded so damned convincing, I dread to think what else he can do. And it sounds like if anyone here summons a demon from Pandemonium—that's where it'll end up. Inside his tower. It's like a beacon."

"Luckily, as far as I know, nobody on this realm has the same ability you do. But I'll take care of him later. An arch-demon dead… shockwaves will have passed far beyond this realm."

"Then let me take us back," I said. "It's the quickest way."

"So it is."

For all that Zadok had brought up some good points,

Nikolas *did* trust me. Maybe not with everything, but who was I to talk? The important thing was getting back home, and dragging up the guild's records of that mission two years ago. The records I'd written myself. Because if Zadok was right—I'd had the name of the demon responsible for the virus in front of me the whole time.

But none of that explained why the demon which had killed Rory had resurfaced now, much less the vampires' involvement. For all the trouble I'd caused—and dragged Rory into—I'd never caught the kind of attention which would bring the wrath of a king in a netherworld dimension after me. I think I'd remember if I'd pissed off someone like him.

Unless it was all tied up in the war between heaven and hell, Divinities and arch-demons. Maybe those I loved were doomed to be targeted purely because I was marked.

## 17

Nikolas and I returned to the castle's corridor, found the nearest demonglass pillar and stepped through, landing in the warlocks' storeroom. Luckily, nobody waited on the other side.

I pulled my phone out. "I need to look something up and make a few calls."

"Fiona?"

"Yeah," I said. "Also, our little vampire friend ran away. All of them, in fact." What with our brush with the arch-demon, not to mention Zadok, I'd totally forgotten my renewed suspicions about the celestial vampire and his involvement in what was going on. And Alec still hadn't replied to my message. *That's a bad sign.*

"They all ran away?" he asked. "No traces or anything?"

"None," I said. "The other bite victim ran away from the guild, too. She might have joined them, might not. Point is, one of the two celestials knows something, for sure. The book Damian was reading—about demon venom—was checked out by Gav, two weeks before he died."

His brow furrowed. "So Gavin knew… what, exactly?"

"That's what I'm going to find out." I walked down the corridor, listening out for any signs of warlock presence. Hearing nothing, I loaded up the celestials' old files on my phone, the ones I'd temporarily regained access to when I'd returned to the guild. Then I ran a search on saphor demons. "I think we've been looking in the wrong place."

"What do you mean?" asked Nikolas.

I skimmed through the file list. "I think we were wrong to assume it's a powerful demon doing the energy transfer. And I had that information in my files—the celestials did, anyway. Rory died after we crawled through a nest of saphor demons."

He frowned. "You never mentioned that before."

"That's because we never actually ran into any," I said. "There were a few nastier demons in there instead. We killed them with no problems, but then the big guy showed up…"

"There you are," said Rachel from the other side of the office door. "All right, Devi, do you want the good news or the bad news?"

I looked up from my phone. "Isn't it all bad news?"

She cracked a smile. "Nope. The good news is that we have a sample of the vampire cure."

"What?" I glanced at Nikolas. "Seriously?"

"We isolated the cure from that vamp's blood," she said. "Or I did anyway. Since you two were off gallivanting around Babylon."

"Damn. Nice work."

She grinned and darted back into the office, and Nikolas and I followed her.

"So how did you manage it?" I asked, settling into the desk chair.

"Well, that's the bad news," she said. "The reason we had so much trouble is because the cure's the same as the demon venom. It's the same blood. We had it right in front of us the whole time."

A horrified rush of understanding passed over me. In order to fully turn into a vampire, the fledgling had to consume the blood of their sire. Otherwise they remained human, and addicted to the intoxicating presence of the venom in their veins. But… that meant Fiona was a fledgling, if not in the usual vampire sense, and so were the other bite victims. And the ones who'd taken the cure had fully turned into demonic vampires.

It was no cure at all, but the next step in the transformation sequence.

"Shit," I said, glancing down at my phone. I'd pulled up the files on saphor demons—and the picture of their eggs looked awfully familiar. "Oh—*fuck.*"

"What?" asked Rachel and Nikolas at the same time.

"Has anyone ever got a close look at the infected bloodstones?" I asked. "Really close up? Can you know for sure it's the same material as the regular bloodstones?"

"No…" Rachel gave Nikolas a quizzical look.

"It's the saphor demons' eggs." I flipped my phone around and showed them the picture. "They're the exact same size and shape as bloodstones. And they're demonic parasites. I'm almost certain that's what Rory handled right before he died. It got inside him somehow—we both got injured during the fight, and if it got in his bloodstream, it might have had the same effect as being bitten."

Guilt swirled inside me, and I lowered the phone, swallowing back the rush of emotion. I hadn't known—but of course I hadn't. Nobody had, and no one at the guild had even guessed.

"And that's the deal with the vampires?" said Rachel. "Really? They're playing host to demonic parasites?"

"And it alters their blood," Nikolas said, nodding slowly.

"So much that when they bite someone else, the virus passes on, too. And as celestials' powers are the antithesis to demonic ones—"

"It reacts, killing them." I swallowed. "So Gav knew, for sure. He was reading that book. I'm almost certain that's what's on the pages that went missing. But why did he suddenly get the impulse to check the book out before the first murder even happened?"

"Hang on," said Rachel. "What book?"

I quickly explained. Her eyes widened with each word. "So you're saying this *celestial* is possibly complicit with demons? And the others know?"

"No clue," I said. "I'm not getting a response from our vampire friend, anyway. And I'm at a loss as to whether Gav's researching the demon eggs was a coincidence, or..." *Or if he had a hunch, and someone wanted him out of the way.*

And where did that leave Rory? I thought back to the grief-fogged weeks following his death... to the last time I'd been to the guild, when nobody had believed my report about how he'd died. They hadn't known. But someone might have read the report and put two and two together anyway.

And now a demonic parasite lay in Fiona's head, waiting to tear her to pieces, too.

I took a step back. "I need to check on Fiona. If she takes that cure—it's all over for her."

Once I was outside the room, I called her. Fiona picked up right away.

"How do you feel?" I asked her, gripping the phone tightly.

"Fine. I think. *You* don't sound fine, though. What's up?"

"Too much to tell you over the phone," I said. "Just—if anyone offers you the cure, anyone at all, please don't take it. The cure's fake, and... it's a lot worse than we thought. It'll kill you. It's the real reason people are turning into murderers."

"Wait, really? This cure? So... so what will happen to me?"

"Hopefully nothing," I said. "You haven't taken the cure, and as far as I know, the killers all had. Otherwise... just make sure you don't go near anyone who *has* taken it, even if they claim to be fine. Sorry to go all parental on you," I added, "but keep the defences on the flat and text me every few hours. If you need me to get anything for you, let me know. And if things go downhill, you might have to come back to the warlocks' place again. Unfortunately, all our other potential safe houses aren't so safe."

"If you say so," she said. "How long will this crap take? Because honestly, I don't think my boss will take 'possessed by a demon' as an excuse not to show up next week. I took today off, but I don't want to get fired on top of everything else."

"You're not possessed," I said. "I'll do my best to sort this, okay? Just hang tight."

"Will do," she said.

After I'd hung up, I rang Clover. To my intense surprise, she picked up.

"You shouldn't have called."

"It's saphor demons, Clover," I said. "Demon eggs. The venom's in there. They look exactly like bloodstones, and the people who take the cure fully turn, like vampires. The guild needs to know."

There was a long pause. "Are you certain?"

"Positive." I briefly ran through what I'd learned. "And that means Gav knew, but I've no idea how *he* came to that conclusion. They're pretty common demons. And even he— even he dismissed the reports of mine and Rory's last mission."

"He didn't," she said quietly. "The report was removed

from office before I had the chance to read it. I always wondered—but you never brought up the subject."

"Because I didn't know what I'd missed," I said quietly. "And I didn't. If I hadn't seen a picture of what those demon eggs looked like—I'm positive Rory and I crawled through a bunch of them in the caves while we were hunting the demons. They look exactly like the contraband bloodstones."

"I believe you, but the guild might not. They're preoccupied trying to find their runaways—unless you've seen any signs of them?"

So she'd guessed I'd been looking. "Nope," I said. "Believe me, I wish I had. One of the so-called victims is involved with demons. Maybe all of them."

She exhaled. "Devi, I'd advise you to avoid the guild at the present moment. They've ceased sending out communications, which can't be good. This time, they haven't called me in again, which suggests they really are going ahead with their plan to bring in an outside army."

*Crap.* "Okay. Tell Mr Roth, at least. Someone higher up needs to know, and not the inspector." I wouldn't shed a tear if *he* got infected, but the guild needed to act before the demons did. Because hell was a hundred steps ahead of them.

"If *he* finds out, heaven help us all."

I looked at my phone screen after she'd hung up, unable to get the image of those demon eggs out of my head. I'd left the guild so soon after Rory's death, I hadn't considered that they'd wiped the mission reports off the database before anyone else had even had the chance to read them. It seemed a weird overreaction at the time, but now I had to wonder who else *had* got hold of the information.

"What are you doing?" Nikolas asked.

"Talking to Clover," I said. "She knows—for what it's worth. But the guild's gone off grid. I told her about the demon eggs anyway... I can't believe nobody guessed."

"Maybe they did," he said. "The guild hides information, don't they?"

"Sure, but that's just… odd. Even Rory's death—I didn't witness it, so my report wasn't good enough for them. They dismissed it." My throat closed up. "Apparently they removed all the reports. Or someone did. But word must have got out somehow. And now one traitor celestial vampire—maybe two—is at large with inside information on the guild itself, including how to bring them down from the inside."

I didn't know how to feel at all, knowing how it had all gone down, and how we'd all made mistakes in the end. Gav included. Even Clover hadn't seen this coming. Part of me, like it or not, was still connected to the celestials. I'd be bound to them as long as I lived… unless my demon mark took over entirely. And I hadn't had space in my head to worry about what demonic power Themedes might have passed onto me with his death, and if *that* would affect my celestial mark.

"It's the guild's problem, not yours," Nikolas said. "You did the right thing even if they didn't."

"But—Fiona," I mumbled. "She… she's halfway through turning into one of those vamps. At best she'll be a day-walking vampire who has to keep drinking the cure to survive. At worst, she'll lose her mind like the others."

"It might be that the process can reversed," said Nikolas, a gentle undercurrent to his voice. "If the demonic parasite is a separate entity… this isn't something I've had reason to look into before. Maybe one of the vampires would volunteer to help us investigate."

"Sure would help if we could find our runaways," I said. "I think now's the time to report them to the vampire queen. Maybe she's seen them."

"No need." Rachel looked up from her phone, her expression unusually sombre. "I think I know where our rogue celestial vamp is."

The phone screen showed DivinityWatch, of all things. And headlines filled the page—*Breaking News: Attack at Haven City Shopping Centre.* Along with a picture of Alyson.

"Oh, seven hells."

18

I clung to the side of the car as Nikolas drove at breakneck pace. At the same time, Rachel shouted down the phone at Javos, who'd never get there fast enough. Which left it up to us to take care of this shit show. *Dammit, DivinityWatch.* They just had to panic everyone—though admittedly, from what I saw as I skimmed the news-feed on my phone, the local media hadn't got hold of the story yet, and the more people stayed away from the crime scene, the better. An attack on a public place—on *humans*—wasn't something even the guild could sweep under the carpet.

As we careened around a corner, a blurred figure ran in front of the car. Nikolas hit the brakes, and the car tilted sideways then slammed down, damn near flipping over.

"Did we hit a vamp?" Rachel pushed her door open, while I did the same, my heart still thumping from our hair-raising ride.

"No human moves that fast." I jumped out onto the road.

The guy we'd hit was already on his feet. A male vamp

with flat black eyes. Dark blood ran from the corner of his mouth, but his glazed expression didn't change.

A scream echoed from the shopping centre.

"I'll take him," Rachel said.

I ran for the stone steps leading to the glass-fronted building, which were smeared with blood. Nikolas was one step behind me. Inside, people ran every which way, a chaotic blur of activity which made it impossible to tell at a distance who was attacking whom. I grabbed a stake with my right hand and my gaze fell on an elderly human man trying to beat off a vampire with the same dark eyes as the other, and no apparent aversion to the glaring shopping centre lights at all.

"Hey!" I ran up to him, brandishing the stake. The vampire turned his back on his human prey, and my heart lurched. I knew him. He was the vampire who'd tried to chat me up in a pub not so long ago. No life remained in his gaze now. He was entirely a demon's host.

I staked him in the heart and ran further into the crowd.

Black lightning streaked through the air, hitting two vamps at once. With his magic, Nikolas could fight from a distance, but my stakes were designed for close-quarters combat. Also, I couldn't tell which people were vampires and which were humans panicking and trying to fight their way out. Nikolas must be able to see their auras, of course, and I wished I'd had the foresight to use a potion to let myself do the same. Not that I'd had anywhere near enough warning.

Celestial light sprang to my palm, reflecting off the shattered fragments of glass from a shop window. Dismantled mannequins lay amongst the wreckage, along with the bloody remains of several shoppers. I ran into the fray again, spotting a vamp chewing on the neck of a woman who'd tried to hide behind a shop display.

"Hey!" I yelled to grab his attention, though it looked like it was already too late for his victim.

Running to meet the vamp, I beat him over the head with a stake, and shone the celestial rays directly into his eyes. He choked, but didn't burn like he should have done. The demons' magic stopped them burning in any light. It might be a parasite, but they were far more powerful than vampires had the right to be. Staking him in the chest, I let the vampire's body crumble. At least staking, stabbing and my celestial blade worked on the bastards. *But for how much longer?*

Nikolas's lightning struck down two more vamps. Using his magic, he isolated the vampires and knocked them away from their human prey, and I leapt in to finish them off. But there were too many of them. Far too many. This was a coordinated attack. Some vamps appeared to move on autopilot, as though not particularly bothered what they did as long as it involved hurting someone. They'd been given orders—but who was the mastermind?

As the last vamp fell, I turned to Nikolas. "The report said they appeared out of nowhere. You know what that means."

He nodded. "There's a portal here somewhere."

"Not this floor. It's too quiet." Not to mention one of us would have sensed it.

I skirted around the shell-shocked-looking surviving shoppers and began to run for the escalators, Nikolas at my side.

Two vamps jumped down from the balconies of the floor above, landing in front of us. Nikolas blasted them flat onto their backs without breaking stride, and I ran and staked both of them.

We'd cleared this floor, but faint screaming from above. Bodies littered the floor—not killed by vamps, but people who'd obviously jumped off the balconies to get away from them. Rage ignited in my chest. One glance at the lift told me the vamps had ambushed anyone who'd tried to get out that way, while the way up the escalators was blocked with bodies.

*You're going to burn for this.*

"The celestials will mete out justice for this crime, vampires!" boomed a voice. I stopped, momentarily convinced I'd somehow imagined it, but Nikolas stiffened, looking up.

A line of grey-clad figures in armoured gear ran alongside the balconies above, celestial lights blazing from their hands.

*Shit. The guild really did bring in an army.*

With innocent people still at risk, I didn't dare hesitate. I continued my path up the escalator to the first floor, where the vampires stopped their attack, swivelling to face the soldiers. I staked two of them while their attention was on the new arrivals. As another vamp swung to face me, I grabbed his face in my left hand. The celestial light burned his skin, but he grinned even in death.

"Your time's coming, celestial… all will burn…"

"Nice try." I let him fall, and a light shone across my own face. I jumped to my feet, freezing when the coldness of a celestial blade pressed to my neck. "Hey! I'm one of you, idiot."

The celestial soldier didn't lower his sword. "Who are you?"

"Celestial Devina Lawson." I backed up, my hand still glowing. "What the hell is the matter with you? There's a dozen vampires for you to kill."

"What's wrong with your aura?"

Oh no. Grade Four soldiers had many gifts, but the one that had totally slipped my mind was aura vision. Every one of them could see the demonic taint covering half my aura. Seven hells.

"I ran into demon blood," I improvised. "Someone summoned one on this floor, using a portal. If you don't mind, I was on my way to close it."

A vampire leapt at the celestial from behind, but he moved faster. His blade whipped out, decapitating the vampire in a second, and he turned back to me. "Stay where you are, Devina Lawson. You'll come for questioning later."

Not bloody likely.

When another vampire ran past, I took my chance to run for it. Tackling the vamp with a flying leap, I staked him and jumped to my feet. Then I sprinted through the carnage, searching for any signs of the portal. It'd definitely been this floor, but the cowering shoppers and shattered storefronts blocked every corner, and the presence of the celestials' blazing lights reflecting off every surface didn't help. The demonic portal might be right in front of me and I'd never pick up on it with all the light flaring around. I staked another vampire, while the celestials wielded their blades with the skill of those chosen to advance to the highest level. The vamps should by rights have been fleeing in terror. Anyone else would.

If I'd stayed, I might have been one of them. The Grade Fours didn't just kill demons. They were the celestials' arbiters of justice against preternaturals and humans, as well as other celestials, and they took their jobs very seriously. I was a dead woman if I stuck around and they worked out where my demonic aura really came from.

A scream drew my attention to a shattered shop window, where a human child hid beneath a clothes rack. I advanced one step and then froze, my gaze catching on his glowing red eyes. "Nice try, demon," I said.

The human child crawled out, transforming into a huge gangly figure with pincers. A splitter demon—lovely. I summoned my celestial blade and dodged its attack, cutting upwards into its chest. The beast fell into two sides, and then each side stood up, sprouting a new pair of legs. Ack.

I'd fought this kind of demon before, and was ready for its attack. I cut from left to right, taking down both sides of the demon in one shot. My celestial blade flickered, and then the beast reformed into four copies. I grimaced. Most of them could only do the multiplying trick once. Not good.

My blade flickered again, then vanished.

"Damn." I leaped high, using Rachel's boots for leverage, and the demon clones collided on the spot where I'd been standing, pincers snapping. *Bloody sword.* Grabbing a stake, I thrust it into one creature's back. Not as effective as a blade on a non-vampire, but it did the job. As the beast collapsed, I deflected a blow from the second, my stake impaling its pincer. With my other hand, I hurled a knife at the third beast as it attempted to ambush me from behind. It went down, and the fourth dropped from the ceiling like a bat, landing on top of me. Twisting onto my back, I drove the stake across its neck, severing its head.

Kicking its body aside and stabbing the two which lay twitching on the floor, I backed into the shop. Nobody seemed to be alive in here, but the portal must be close. With my celestial light gone, I couldn't extinguish the portal myself. Which meant I'd have to swallow my pride and go to the celestials.

They'd certainly done a good job of beating down the vampires. Bodies lay everywhere on the floor. No sign of Nikolas—he must have figured they were as likely to try to mow him down as the enemy, which wouldn't end well for anyone involved. The celestial who'd cornered me looked in my direction. His mask lowered, revealing someone I knew. Farrell, a Grade Four soldier who'd never particularly liked me. His severely buzzed hair gleamed blond under the celestial light, while his silver celestial badge marked him as leader of his particular faction of celestials. One step below the inspector.

"Celestial Lawson!" he shouted.

I raised my left hand. "There's a demon portal here somewhere. Get rid of that before you start yelling at me."

"There's no portal."

"Explain that." I pointed at the dead demon. "It sure as hell didn't come here on the train."

"Your attitude clearly hasn't changed," said Farrell. "And you wear the mark of hell on your aura."

Several celestials turned to watch me, hands on their weapons. Great.

"I got bitten," I told them. "You've heard what happens to the other celestials who get bitten by one of those vamps?"

"They die," he said. "I saw you use your power."

"They don't all die," I said—well, it was technically true. "Some of us get lucky. I reckon I'm immune to whatever virus they're spreading. But maybe it's messed up my aura. I wouldn't know, I can't see it. Will you stop pointing that thing at me?"

He didn't lower his hand. Farrell was one of the pricks who'd taken it upon himself to try to humiliate me in training exercises when I'd been a novice. I'd thought he'd permanently relocated to Shanghai. Imagine an older Bad Haircut Sammy with better personal hygiene and the authority to murder people on command, and you get the picture.

"What's she done?" asked a female celestial with dreadlocks.

"Got here before you did and killed a bunch of vampires." My heart sank when Farrell's gaze dropped to my hands, like he could see the demon mark beneath my sleeve. Then his gaze continued to my feet.

"Just what kind of shoes are those?"

"Magic ones." I smiled innocently. "You remember those lab experiments I used to do?"

"I think everyone remembers, Devi," he said. "How exactly did you know to come here before we did?"

"It's all over the Internet." I threw up my hands. "I think I should be asking why *you* didn't get here in time. And you should be thanking me for helping out."

"We've got one!" someone shouted. "This one's wanted by the guild for murder."

I spun around and saw Alyson—pinned beneath three celestials and surrounded by bright lights. She spat out a mouthful of blood, looking terrified.

"Don't!" I said. "When she turned human, she lost all memory of the attack. At least let her speak before—"

"We must eradicate them before they do the same to us." Farrell turned casually. I made to grab his arm, but two celestials seized my shoulders, pulling me back. A blade of light appeared in Farrell's hands, slicing down.

Alyson was dead before the sword took off her head, as the cold hand of divine justice ripped her soul out.

Fury ignited and my demon mark burned again. *Calm it.* I buried my hand in my pocket to avoid decking him in the face with it, and wrenched my arms free. "You bastard," I growled. "You didn't even give her a chance to explain herself. It's not your job to play executioner."

His celestial blade touched my chest, and to my alarm, my skin burned at the contact. "I think you'll find that *is* my job, Devina," he said.

I took a step back away from the blade. The whole shopping centre seemed to hold its breath. No way would any of these people defend me over him. And if they knew the truth, I'd be next. These people would be my killers.

"You should know what happened to the inspector when

he tried to take authority that wasn't his," I told him. "He regretted it. So will you."

"It's on his orders that we're here," he said. "He was convicted on a minor offence, not because he was wrong about the threat these preternatural scum pose to our realm."

"She was one of you," I spat. "You just killed one of your own. There's no law in your book that allows you to slaughter someone who acted under the influence of a demon, except in self-defence. She was surrendering." I looked around at the crowd, but saw no expressions of support or even remorse. They didn't care if she was innocent or not. And the real demonic threat went undetected.

If I told them, I'd likely get arrested, not to mention get the others into trouble beyond belief. If I didn't, the demons would have an open shot at this realm without anyone knowing the true threat until it was too late to prepare. But the world was black and white to these people. Attempting to get the truth into their thick skulls was like getting a straight answer out of a Chthonian lizard. The absolute best case scenario was that they stayed the hell out of my way when everything went to shit.

I took in a deep breath and looked at Farrell. Then I drew back my left hand and punched him in the face. It was a magnificent punch, even without the celestial side effects. His head snapped back, and before he could retaliate, I shoved my way past him towards the escalator. Footsteps and shouts pursued me, but I didn't pause, leaping over fallen vampires, my trusty shoes allowing me to jump several steps at a time without falling. Once on the ground floor again, I pelted out the open doors, right into Nikolas. His timing was perfect. The instant I slammed into his chest, shadows closed around the pair of us.

"You might have shown up sooner," I panted, looking around at the shadowy canyon we'd landed in. "Thanks."

"I decided it was best if I didn't have to kill any of them."

"They murdered Alyson." My fists clenched. "I know she was under the demons' influence, but of all the people the demons manipulated, she was the one who probably never volunteered for it. And they didn't ask questions—no trial, nothing. They'll do the same to me if they spotted us vanish."

"None of them saw," he said. "So they'll assume we got away on foot."

"We need to get Fiona." I breathed in and out, my heart thudding against my ribcage. "The celestials will go after her next if the demons don't, and I'm done letting her get hurt on my watch."

He nodded. "We're a little far from the castle."

Babylon's castle was a dark shape in the distance etched against the night-like sky. Too far to walk.

"Great." I glared at it. "My celestial power's still faulty. And the celestials—they can see auras. They all have that ability. Mine's a dead giveaway. I told them I got bitten, but they'll work out the truth eventually."

And then? I'd be dead. Or I'd end up having to spend an eternity in this demonic realm, which to be honest, was starting to look like a more appealing option. I looked at Nikolas, who frowned. "They can't prove you're guilty of a crime you never committed. Besides, they have a more pressing problem."

"They do. But they'll kill anyone they think is infected. Vampires or not. They just straight-up murdered a fellow celestial soldier. They knew her. They trained her. It's so fucked up."

But their approach, unfortunately, might be the only way to stop the virus from spreading to anyone else. The humans, though—they hadn't been fully infected yet. They might not even know they'd been bitten. As for the vampires—what did that make them? Unwilling hosts for demonic parasites?

No… willing ones. They must have been made an offer they couldn't turn down. That demons could tempt even immortal blood-drinkers wasn't particularly surprising, but that didn't make the unfortunate humans they'd bitten guilty of the same crime.

Fear crawled up my throat. One way or another, innocent people would die if the demons weren't dealt with. If the Grade Four celestials were unleashed, I doubted they'd check their target was actually possessed before attacking them. Anyone might get caught in the crossfire. And meanwhile, the vampires' king stood behind the scenes, no doubt laughing at the carnage.

I turned to Nikolas. "We have to find a decent place to cross over. I take it there isn't any demonglass out here in the middle of nowhere?"

"No," he said. "Aside from the tower and parts of the castle, there isn't any. We'll have to use my power to cross over, but not here."

He began to walk away, and I hurried after him. On either side of us, the sides of the canyon loomed high, the castle a solid shape in the distance. "Tell me," I panted. "Please, Nikolas—if you know who marked me, tell me. This is life and death."

"I already told you I don't," he said. "What brought this on?"

"The arch-demon who marked me was originally a Divinity," I said. "*The* Divinity who gave me the other mark. One's replacing the other, I think, and that's why my power keeps going out. But the only way it can be reacting to fire magic is if it's some relation of Themedes. Right?"

"Perhaps. We'll work it out. But we need to leave."

"No shit." I only hoped that after what the celestials had done, we had a home to go back to.

## 19

We crossed over, landing on an unfamiliar road, at which point it hit me—"We left the car at the shopping centre."

"Rachel will have moved it," Nikolas said, typing into his phone. "When the celestials showed up, certainly."

"Good. Because the last thing we want is them finding us. Actually, the last thing we want is Armageddon, but you know. Complications."

Nikolas put his phone away. "I've asked her to pick up your friend."

"What—Fiona? Damn, you're quick."

"She'll meet us at Pine Street."

We were far enough from the shopping centre not to be followed, but I still walked quickly. I had to, to keep up with Nikolas's warlock speed. Within five minutes, Rachel drove up alongside us. "Hop in," she said.

Fiona waved dismally from the back with her free hand, the other one in a white-knuckled grip on the back of the seat in front. "Devi!" she half said, half screamed. "She doesn't even have a driving licence!"

"I don't just have one licence, I have *five.*" Rachel scrambled over the seat into the back, allowing Nikolas to take over the wheel.

"Fake ones," he said, unnecessarily. "Several of her aliases have outstanding fines."

"I'm not surprised," whimpered Fiona.

Nikolas took over the wheel, while I got in the back with Fiona.

"Are you going to explain why you yanked me out of my home?" she said accusingly.

"Yep. Celestial top tier soldiers running amok and killing anyone who's infected," I said. "You haven't taken the cure so you're probably fine, but between that and the demons, I figured you'd be safer with us."

"No kidding," she said faintly. "I—top tier soldiers? Weren't you one of those?"

"Nope, I only got to Grade Three," I said. "I could have qualified for Grade Four, but I kept skipping important meetings and I doubt I'd have got a recommendation. They get extra perks, like the ability to see auras, but they also have longer working hours and are at the mercy of the guild's orders twenty-four/seven. And they directly serve under the inspectors. So nope."

"Ugh." She shuddered. "They—they're really killing people?"

"They have a warrant," I said. "All vampires are potential enemies, and all infected humans are potential collateral damage. But they don't know what's really going on."

"To be honest, neither do I," said Fiona.

"It's a lot to keep up with. What're they saying on DivinityWatch?" I asked. "I can't believe they picked up on the attack at the shopping centre before the guild did."

"What in hell is DivinityWatch?" Rachel wanted to know.

"The website the attack was reported on. It's run by humans claiming they've seen Divinities," I explained. "They also post any celestial-related stuff, or weird demon sightings. Most of it's fake, but news of the shopping centre attack spread fast."

"That's because all eyes are on this city," said Fiona. "But seriously—they're *killing* everyone the vampires bit?"

"The celestial girl had killed people," I said, figuring it was best to be honest. "But she was surrendering. There are some real pricks in their higher order, and they have the authority to play executioner. Not on members of the public," I added. "But they'll certainly kill any vampires they think are acting under the influence of the demon."

"They *think?*" she echoed. "How do they plan to do that—raid the vampires' places? They're not allowed, right?"

"No," I said. "But they're from the branch who like to make up their own rules if it's an emergency. Which it is. Worse, we've figured the people behind this portal business are operating from somewhere in a human district, hidden away. So innocent lives are at stake if the celestials wage open war. That's what we're up against. And we never did find the portal they entered the shopping centre through. They *must* have done it that way."

"If there's evidence, the celestials will find it," Nikolas said.

"Doubt they'd walk into Pandemonium to take care of our problem," I said. "Sure would help, though."

"But might they be following us?" Fiona asked. "I know I'm the least of their problems, but... they threatened you, Devi."

"I expected it," I said. "They know there's something off about my aura. So *we're* off the grid. Those celestials don't know where the warlocks' headquarters is, and there are rules against them coming into Javos's place. I'm not sure just how many they're planning to break by the end of it. So I guess we're fugitives."

"That's bonkers," she said. "I have a job. A family back in Ireland. How the hell am I supposed to explain this to them? They don't even know I got kidnapped the first time. I said I was jumped by a mugger."

"If it's on the international news, they'll know something big's happening. Nobody can hide this."

Nikolas glanced sideways at me. "The guild *must* have planned for such a scenario. Their entire purpose is to defend this realm against demons from the nether realms. Is there an emergency plan for an attack on this scale?"

I looked out the window, tension gripping my spine. "Yep. Evacuation, and burning the entire affected area to the ground. They've had to do it before. But obviously, they don't know *where* in the city the vamps are spawning from yet. And with the vampire king—I don't know why I keep calling him that, it's not like he's actually a vampire—he apparently has free rein to send his army wherever he likes."

"To keep opening portals, there needs to be a sufficient power source on this side," he said. "The guild and the warlocks control most of the materials necessary. So removing all the bloodstones from the market would, in theory, stop the spread of the demonic infection and deal with the portal issue in one go."

"Not if they already have an unlimited supply," I said. "They can even bring them through from that dimension. It's like an endless loop."

"Not forever," he said. "It's a good question, actually… there's no limit on the number of portals a person can create, but more than a standard portal is required to bring through such a large number of vampires. They must have done that initially, at least."

Now I got it. "Demonglass?"

"There's only one piece in the city that's unaccounted for."

"Then I'll have to find it," I said.

It was a fair plan. Javos, however, had other ideas. When Nikolas unlocked the door of the warlocks' place, it was to find him waiting in the hall in a manner similar to a parent confronting their wayward teenage offspring after coming home late from a night out.

"Just what do you think you're playing at?" Javos growled at me. "Making a scene?"

"Saving lives?" I moved closer to Fiona.

"You should have left it to your celestials," said Javos. "Not brought us to their attention."

"They *killed* someone," I said. "One of their own. I don't think they're done, either."

His gaze went to Fiona. "*And* you brought a human here?"

"I'll go," she said quickly.

"Javos, don't be a dick," Rachel said. "The celestials, vamps *and* netherworld demons are out to get anyone close to Devi, and Fiona got bitten. So—"

"So did other humans," he said. "Is she volunteering as a lab rat to help us stop the virus?"

"No," I said, before anyone else could cut in. "Absolutely not."

"Why not?" asked Fiona. "You need someone to what, test a cure on?"

"You're not taking the cure," I said firmly. "That's what's turning the people who get bitten into rabid monsters. It's basically… you know how a person has to drink a vampire's blood to turn into a full vamp after being bitten? That."

Fiona paled. "Oh. Shit. But… they can walk in the day, right?"

"Yes," said Nikolas and I at the same time. "That's how they've been sneaking around," I added. "Maybe it's enough of a trade-off that some of them don't care about the murderous side effects." *And having a demonic parasite living inside them.*

Javos swore. "Just how did they get into that shopping centre without being seen?"

"I think they went in via Pandemonium," I said. "But I never found the portal."

Somehow, despite Javos's grumbling, we got the story out. Fiona kept looking at him nervously, but she must know we didn't have much choice but to stay here. Which meant keeping on the warlocks' good side. Too bad I'd just caused a public display. If we'd known the celestials would be there... *they'd have killed that girl anyway. Maybe more.*

With them in the picture, stopping the vampires was paramount. Now they could walk in the day... all our usual plans for dealing with them went out the window.

"They couldn't always do that, could they?" asked Rachel, when I said something along those lines. "I'm confused, to be honest. Is it the cure that lets them walk in daylight without catching on fire?"

"Probably," I said. "They're like a new species, almost, and they can be created from humans like regular vamps. That gives them a potentially infinite army, unless we get rid of both the fake bloodstones *and* everyone who's fully turned. Starting with whoever owns the main portal. The demonglass."

I was almost certain I knew who it was. Grabbing my phone, I sent another urgent message to Alec.

"Unfortunately, you're right," said Javos. "If not for the circumstances, all of you would face consequences for your actions in the last few days. But the fact is—these vampires already made a bold attack in broad daylight. They're no longer held back by the weaknesses of their kind."

"Yeah," I said. Javos could be genuinely reasonable and intelligent when he wasn't blowing up at everyone. "So… what are they planning? Aside from more of the same? We never found the portal, but it *must* be near the shopping centre if not inside it. Can't anyone track it? I'd make a demon tracker if I could go near the place without the celestials finding me."

"I can disguise myself and look," Rachel said. "But it's possible it was a temporary thing, like last time. Niko or I would have picked up on it if there'd been actual demonglass there."

"They used bloodstones. Real ones, because I doubt they'd leave the fakes lying around." I frowned. "I guess they're interchangeable, to some extent, but I still can't work out where they made the switch without being detected. Surely someone involved in trading those bloodstones would have noticed they aren't the same."

"Hang on," said Fiona. "The bloodstones… you mentioned them before. What's the deal with them?"

Right. I hadn't told her about the saphor demon eggs. If it was me, I'd want to know the truth, but I was trained to handle traumatic situations. Fiona wasn't, and she'd been through enough crap already.

"Does it have to do with what happened at the vampire bar?" she added. "Because I heard the vampires who kidnapped me talking about them, too."

"Shit, really? What did they say?"

"I didn't catch all of it. I was trying to escape their car at the time." She grimaced. "But when they parked, they shouted something about using only regular bloodstones for the portal. The one they took me through. Something about… a limited supply."

"Their demon egg stores are running low," Rachel said.

"That must be why they have their vamps biting people instead."

"Did you say demon eggs?" asked Fiona.

"It's where the demonic energy infecting people comes from," I admitted. "But it can also be passed on through biting. And I guess—they're not like regular bloodstones, because you can't recharge a living thing. Once the energy from the demon egg is gone, that's it." Real bloodstones, on the other hand, were more like rechargeable batteries. "If that's true, then… then if we take out all the infected vamps, we might have a chance in hell of stopping the virus spreading."

"Exactly," said Rachel, bouncing on the balls of her feet.

"I'm not getting the urge to bite people, if it helps," Fiona said. "But does that mean—*what* kind of demon's magic do I have?"

"Maggot demons," said Rachel. I shot her a warning look.

"We don't know," I added. "This is all speculation."

"One thing's for certain," Javos cut in. "Those bloodstones need to go. I think we have a solid enough case to argue for yanking every one of them off the market. Then we'd know for sure where the fake ones came from."

"True," Nikolas acknowledged, "but there'd be riots if we took away the vampires' entire supply of bloodstones, and if the ones working with demons really do have a more permanent portal somewhere, there's nothing to stop them continuing to bring in supplies from Pandemonium."

"Exactly," I said. "This isn't good enough. We need a cure—an *actual* cure." I looked at Fiona, then at the others. "The virus isn't really a virus. It's a demonic parasite. Because it's part demon, celestial light can destroy it. But I don't think Fiona wants me to cut her head open and shine a light into it."

"Not really," Fiona said, shuddering. "I did say I was

willing to help, but not to die for it. This thing… it's in my head?"

"Unfortunately," I said. "The good news is that it's probably dormant. Humans who get bitten by a vampire can carry the virus around for years without going full vamp. But most of them can't resist the call of their blood."

A chill ran down my back. Demonic power was hard to resist, too. She needed to stay here while I tracked the demonglass down. And there was one sure-fire way to do that.

"I'm going to look into the glass," I said. "If I can track where the other piece is, we can make a plan."

"You can really do that?" asked Rachel.

"Sometimes," I told her. "I don't really understand how it works. It might be tied to my demon mark, might not."

None of the others said anything, but Javos and Nikolas exchanged an unreadable look.

"Just a look," Javos said, with emphasis. "You're a wanted woman, from what I gather. And you know what happened the last time you threw yourself through that glass without knowing what was on the other side."

*Yeah.* And he didn't even know about Zadok. *Or* what Themedes had done, unless Nikolas had told him. But urgency pressed on me. An attack on humans was bad enough, but the culprit must suspect I was onto him by now. He'd left more than enough clues.

*Now you'll pay for it.*

The others followed me to the demonglass room, even Fiona. I hadn't lied when I'd said I wasn't sure what controlled where the glass drew me to, but other than when Zadok had dragged me into his lair, every other time I'd reached a place I wanted to had been because I'd believed I could get there. Just like when I used my celestial power to reach into the space between the worlds and find my weapon.

I approached the glass warily, not trusting my demon mark not to try to drag me somewhere unwanted. Like Zadok's tower, for instance. Crouching down, I peered into the glass, imagining the other side showing the pillars in Nikolas's castle. It was the only relatively harmless place I could think of—if there weren't demons roaming around.

A familiar scene came into focus... but not the one I needed. A pillar climbed up to a high ceiling. Pandemonium's palace throne room.

"What is it?" Javos asked sharply.

"I can see the throne room," I said. "But not the vampires' leader. Maybe he's not there."

"Tell the mirror to focus on him," Javos said.

"I can't turn the ability on and off by demand," I said. "Or choose where to focus it."

"Most magic has a control element," he said. "You're untrained, but you've managed to control it before."

"In the heat of battle," I said. "And if I touch it, I might fall through. Most magic doesn't come with that sort of risk."

"You're one of a kind. Isn't it exciting?" Rachel grinned.

"Apparently the warlocks need a special Rules for Devi's Magic Division." I leaned closer, and my demon mark twinged. "Oh hell." I took a step back. "My mark wants to touch it. If it does, I get dragged through. I don't know how to make it switch over to wherever the demonglass is hidden in this realm." I leaned closer again, willing the glass to respond. *I can do this. I have to.*

My demon marked hand reached out, and this time, I let it brush against the glass. Faintly. Like when Nikolas ran his thumb over the mark, stirring it to life. The glass's surface shimmered, showing a familiar warehouse.

I jerked back, my heart sinking. "The bastard. He left it in the warehouse. Recently."

"Who?" asked Rachel and Javos, at the same time.

"I know who's behind this." I stepped back from the glass, adrenaline surging through my veins. *I knew it.*

"The other celestial—Damian?" Nikolas put in.

"Thanks for stealing the moment." I dropped my hand to my side, thinking hard. "Doesn't look like he's there in person, but given the defences on the place last time—he knows magic. Powerful magic."

"I'm lost," Fiona said. "A celestial who?"

"The only surviving bite victim," I said. "Only I don't think he was ever a victim. He's the one who stored the demonglass in the guild. It fits."

"Yes, it does," Nikolas said, taking a step towards the glass. "No spells can permanently harm me. I'll go through—"

"If he's turned it into a portal, you might get eaten on the way through." I pulled out my phone again, messaging Clover. *"Tell the guild there's a demon planning to attack this realm. There'll be a huge summoning at a warehouse on Blythe Street."*

Sliding my phone into my pocket, I turned my back on the glass. "I'm getting more weapons. Anyone who wants to come with me is welcome to."

Javos shouted after me, but I sprinted down the corridor without looking back. I'd lost my best silver stakes in the battle at the shopping centre, but I had more than enough backups. And if Javos stopped me going through the glass, I'd mow him down, too.

"Devil!" said Fiona, in semi-hysterical tones, as I veered into the lab, grabbing any reachable weapons. "If you go through that glass—can anything come through this way?"

"Yes," growled Javos from behind her. I tensed, ready to

argue, but he said, "I'm calling the other warlocks here. I'll get your friend out the way."

I stared at him. He turned his back without letting me respond and guided her into the office. I mouthed *stay hidden,* and ran back to the demonglass room.

The others were waiting. I didn't even need to ask. With Rachel on one side and Nikolas on the other, I dived through the glass.

20

The fall lasted barely a second. Then the warehouse appeared, and so did a dozen venos demons, tails swinging.

I summoned my celestial blade, slicing down. The nearest demon's head fell, trailing blood, and I moved onto the next target. Nikolas's lightning streaked past, knocking demons into one another and blasting holes in their bodies, while Rachel barrelled past and tore into necks and ankles. Heat blasted me in the back without warning, sending me flying forward several metres. I flipped over in the air and managed to land on my feet.

Behind us, the demonglass was a swirling tempest of fire. Bloodstones surrounded it on all sides, fuelling its power. This was a setup, all right. Maybe Damian had been carrying all the bloodstones on him the whole time. But how was I supposed to shut the damn thing off, with demons pouring out at every second and Pandemonium waiting on the other side?

I brought my celestial blade down, severing a demon's arm and bringing me closer to the portal. I swung the sword down at the nearest bloodstone, willing the celestial light to extinguish the pulsing energy. The stone barely moved. They were tied together in a circle, each fuelling the others, and even my celestial fire wasn't enough to break the circle. It'd keep going until it burned out, and with the amount of power pouring from the stones, it might take hours.

My blade flickered and went out. I cursed, grabbing a stake instead, but a venos demon's tail smacked me in the face, sending me alarmingly close to falling into the portal. Catching my balance, I punched it with my demon-marked hand. The mark burned, and the demon yelled, fire flickering across its face.

*What the hell?* Since when could I set demons on fire?

I waved my demon marked hand around, grabbing a stake and stabbing anything that moved. Maybe my demon mark could burn out the bloodstones. I'd taken in demon energy before—from an arch-demon, no less.

*Crap. Maybe it's Themedes's fire.* But did that make *me* a fire demon?

I dove underneath the nearest demon's feet, slamming my demon marked hand onto his ankle. The beast fell, squealing in pain, fire engulfing him. Holy crap. Maybe I really had taken on the arch-demon's power.

Nikolas had disappeared behind a wall of attacking demons, flashes of lightning the only indication that he was still fighting. And Rachel had gone, too. Fear sliced through me. We were far outnumbered, and the enemy had an infinite supply. More to the point—where in hell had the person who'd set up the portal gone? Was he laughing at us from a distance… or was he planning something else while we were distracted? Fending off demons, I let their movements propel me towards the trapdoor. It lay open, and there was no sign of anyone, vampire or human. Just enough demons to fill the lower levels of hell.

Despite my best efforts, we were driven back towards the warehouse door. Shutting the demons inside wouldn't hold them back. I needed to break the portal, but even collapsing the whole warehouse on top of it wouldn't help, because it'd give the demons free range to break out into the world outside. I'd bet those demon-proof defences weren't here now—

*Wait.*

Either Damian had another plan, or he'd entirely removed the evidence. But he and I hadn't known one another. He didn't know, for instance, that I knew how to reset a demon-proof barrier.

Wielding the blade one-handed, I found the door with my other hand, running my hand over the surface. The demon-proof button had been built into the door, and someone hadn't entirely cleaned it up. I swiped my left hand over it, feeling its answering tremor beneath my palm. Celestial light shone from my hand, and the light snapped on over the door, sending a rippling curtain of energy over its surface. Encouraged, I lowered my left hand and walked alongside the door, burning a line along my path. Seeing the light, the demons fled, tripping over one another in an effort to avoid the celestial flames. Lesser demons would turn to ashes if they touched it. As long as nothing bigger broke through.

Like there was any chance of avoiding *that* happening.

"You know that's not permanent, right?" said Rachel, tossing a venos demon's head over her shoulder. Her serrated teeth were stained black with demon blood.

"It doesn't need to be." I took in a breath. "I called them… the celestials will be on their way here. We need to find the person who set up the portal in the first place. He's not in here."

"The celestials can't take out that portal," said Nikolas, appearing behind her covered in demon blood. "From the look of those flames, there's a more powerful source on the other side. Too powerful."

The doors flew open behind me. Dazzling light poured in, causing the demons to run shrieking back towards the portal. A dozen celestial warriors followed. Grade Fours. *About bloody time.*

They descended on the demons, blades slashing, with no apparent concern for whoever stood in their way. Beckoning to Rachel and Nikolas to follow, I shoved my way towards the door again. My phone buzzed in my pocket. *Dammit.* Either Alec was sending me a warning, too late, or something had happened to Fiona. My demon mark prickled as I got close to the celestial light I'd etched into the floor, but presumably it recognised me, because it let me pass, elbowing the door open.

I pulled out my phone, and damn near dropped it. Gav's number was calling me.

My heart dropped somewhere below the earth.

*He had it all along.*

I ran from the warehouse, ignoring the crackle of the portal and the others' shouts. "So, it was you," I growled into the phone.

"Believe me, when you hear my story, it'll make sense," said Damian. "Can we meet in person?"

"It'd better be a fucking good story. You set up a demon portal here. You know people will die, don't you?"

Silence answered, along with the crackle of flames. So he *was* nearby. There was no good reason for him to have betrayed the celestials. The glass had been at the guild long before he'd got bitten. *He's been planning this for longer than a week.*

I hung up, then rang him back. The shrill sound of a phone ringing drew me in the right direction, around the warehouse's side. I spotted him standing at a safe distance away, hands stuffed casually in his pockets. He turned on me, his face expressionless.

"So the demonglass was yours?" I asked. "Before all this happened, even? Just how long?"

He shrugged. "A while. The guild—there's so much they didn't tell us. It's not right."

"You know what else isn't right? Stealing, working behind the guild's back—oh yeah, and killing a shit-ton of people. Celestials included. You'll get the death penalty from this if you survive, but I'll see to it that you won't."

My hand tingled, demanding I use the demon mark against him, but I needed to find out how much he knew. And if he really did have a hand in Gav's death—or Rory's.

"It's too late," he said, jerking his head towards the warehouse. "I stopped believing in divine judgement a long time ago, so whatever they do to me is inconsequential. I'm just glad to be on the winning team."

"There is no 'team'," I said. "You're working for that pretender of a vampire king, aren't you? Did you even get bitten at all? Or had you already volunteered yourself, and hid yourself amongst the victims so nobody would realise you were already a vampire?" A *celestial* vampire. And unlike Alyson, he appeared to be entirely in control of his mind and actions.

"The guild is astonishingly unobservant when they want to be," he said. "You remember four years ago, right? When the guild burned down? This isn't the first time they've been betrayed. They don't learn from their mistakes, especially the inspector. They had plenty of opportunities to catch me, but they didn't want to see what was right in front of them. You and I know that about them, Devi."

"Stop trying to pretend we're anything alike," I snarled. "You killed Gav, or someone on your orders did."

"Not me," he said. "As for your friend, that was a freak

accident… but it's not my fault the guild disbelieved your reports and left them lying around. I have you to thank for that, Devi. And I'd have believed you."

The world spun. The guild—they'd outright denied my reports on Rory's death. And it *had* been an accident. But by refusing to investigate, they'd left the case information wide open for someone to steal, and thanks to their negligence, Damian—and whoever he worked with—had been able to figure out how to bring the guild down from the inside.

"Devi, you can join me," he said. "You hate the guild like I do. We're the same."

"We're definitely *not* the same. You killed innocent people."

"The guild's made us all into killers," he said, shaking his head. "Besides, I think you're meant to play a role in this. That's the only reason I left you alone until now."

"And now you want me to join your team," I said. "Who exactly is in charge? Who's the vampires' king? The demigod?"

"He's not a demigod," said Damian. "And you'll answer to him if you join me."

*So he's* not *a demon?* Crap. I'd been thinking it was another Azurial calling the shots.

"Not a chance in hell."

I punched him as hard as I could in the neck. He fell back, gasping for breath, and I kicked him in the crotch for good measure. He yelled, the noise swallowed up in the racket coming from the warehouse. The sound of crackling flames grew to an inferno, followed by a series of crashes. Nikolas and Rachel were still in there, along with the Grade Four celestials.

"What advantage does this give you?" I spat in his face. "You die if you stop taking the cure, don't you? Your celestial power backfires on you. It'd be a pity if we cut off your supply line, wouldn't it?"

A scraping noise came from behind me. The warehouse roof had slid down, and smoke had begun to pour from inside. Worse, two demons clawed their way out of the top, and one of them leaped down, gaze trained on the houses in the distance.

*No you don't.*

I ran, grabbing my celestial blade, but Damian tackled me from behind. I managed to tilt my head so I didn't smack my face off the pavement, but hot blood trickled down my neck where I'd scraped the side of my ear. As I shoved at him, a huge chunk of the warehouse roof flew past.

"It's going to blow up!" he yelled in my ear.

"Shouldn't have opened a portal, then, should you?" I yelled back, my ears filled with the sound of crackling flames. "I don't suppose it has an off switch? Or does it keep going until the whole city is in flames? You'll burn the same as the rest of us when it does. You're no immortal."

"It's contained," he said, but he didn't sound certain.

I jabbed my elbows into his ribs, shoving him off me, and sprinted to the warehouse. *Nikolas. Rachel.* The portal had expanded to fill the entire space, though from the dazed-looking celestials running around the wreckage, they'd called a retreat in time to get out of the way.

Not the others, though. Not my friends. The flames soared, climbing higher, and the vortex containing the portal continued to burn.

Again, I'd lost people I cared about to the fire.

*No.* I refused to believe they were dead. And the fire didn't scare me as it had before. The demon mark tingled, drawn towards the orange light. I had nothing more to lose.

With my fists clenched at my sides, I walked into the flames.

## 21

Demon fire had burned me before, but this felt different. More like when I'd got close to the dying arch-demon, as he'd given me some of his power. Maybe that *was* my power. Infernal fire, instead of celestial fire.

The power I'd feared. Always. But what choice did I have, let them die? One thing was certain: either Azurial was involved, or the person who'd set up the portal was drawing on his power to fuel it from the other side. It was definitely his fire—the same power he'd inherited from his arch-demon father. No wonder it no longer hurt me.

If he *was* involved, killing him would be no problem this time.

Through the flames, the shape of the portal began to appear, a rectangle of demonglass surrounded by dark stones. The portal would close the instant they burned out. Demons crawled out of the wreckage, bearing horrible injuries. My stomach twisted, but I didn't see Rachel or Nikolas amongst the dead.

The vibrating bloodstones surrounding the demonglass

flickered with flames. I walked through the wreckage, over dead demons and pieces of the fallen warehouse ceiling, certain the vampires' king would rise from the portal as I approached it... but he didn't. *What's the issue? I thought this was about him finding a way into this realm.*

Unless it was a test. A way to draw out the high-ranked celestials. They'd barely got away from the explosion in one piece. And the others were back at the guild, too far away to come and help if anything worse got loose.

I kept walking. The flames didn't hurt me, at all, and this time, I didn't even hear Rory's screaming.

*Nikolas and Rachel are alive. They have to be.*

My feet finally touched the edge of the portal. In the next instant, the palace of Pandemonium appeared around me. Pillars climbing high to the ceiling, reflecting a steel grey sky —and the huge winged shape of Azurial, a man made of flames. Chains wrapped around his muscular arms and legs, binding him to a pillar beside the throne that he'd once briefly claimed.

"I should have known it was you," he said, in a slurred voice. His wings drooped behind him. "You should be dead."

"I'm hard to kill." I willed my celestial blade to appear, and it did. Continuing to walk, I approached him. Killing him would give the portal one huge burst of power, which wasn't ideal, but it'd last only a few seconds. Then it'd burn out on this side, and die off altogether.

The path was clear. Too easy. But Azurial was right there. Live bait, and half-dead already. Thick chains bound his ankles to the demonglass pillar. The whole portal would be fuelled by his magic, and the demonglass gave it a focal point. Pity I couldn't destroy *that*.

But something wasn't right. "Where are the demons?" I asked. "Was that the last of them? What was the point in exploding the warehouse and killing half of them in the process?"

I stopped walking, squinting closer at the chains. *Nice try.* Magic flickered from his feet, burning fire. He wasn't trapped at all.

Except he couldn't have known I was immune to his flames.

I looked at him calmly. He frowned back, apparently expecting more of a reaction. Then I dropped through the demonglass floor and reappeared out of the pillar directly behind him, sword aimed at the back of his neck.

He swung around. The chains rose and came down, slamming over my head. I leapt through the pillar again at the last second, the chains whispering against the back of my neck. *Close call.* I could avoid the fire, but not the chains. Grabbing a stake, I jumped through the floor and emerged directly underneath him, stabbing his leg. He yelled in anger, kicking out, but I jumped down, out of range again. Using my ability to leap in and out of the floor, I stabbed him twice more, but his regenerative abilities made inflicting minor wounds a futile effort. With the chains protecting his body, it was a waste of time trying to deal a fatal blow. Nikolas and Rachel were my priorities.

"Pleasure seeing you again, but I have other places to be." I threw myself through the nearest pillar, demon mark flaring, willing it to carry me to them—

And landed in a circle of vampires. None of them looked surprised in the slightest to see me. Blackness shimmered in their eyes.

"Nice of you to drop in," Rachel said from behind the vamps. She was chained up… and so was Nikolas.

Behind them was the vampires' king, cloaked as he'd been before, and with a dozen vampires at his side.

Visceral horror struck me. I'd never seen Nikolas

subdued before. *How?* The vampires' king couldn't be that powerful. But then Rachel shifted, and I saw her face was badly burned on one side. She didn't have regenerative abilities like Nikolas did, and from the state of his clothes, he must have shielded her from the fire when they'd come through the portal. *So that's how they got him.*

My hands balled into fists. Doubtless he was scheming a plan, but I didn't have one, short of killing the vampires' leader and ending his scheme to infect the people of Haven City. And now I knew for sure he was a demigod, not a vampire. That meant he had a weakness.

I pulled out my celestial sword, but the vampires moved first, closing in around me. All carried sabre-like blades, their eyes gleaming like dark glass. I'd take them on—were it not for the others. Several knives pressed to Rachel's neck, hard enough to draw blood. Even the infected vamps didn't appear to want to get too close to Nikolas, but with his adopted sibling in danger and the chains binding him, he didn't move.

I lowered my blade. "Let them go," I growled.

"What's the fun in that?" said the vampires' king quietly. His voice was oddly muffled, as though disguised.

"No offence, but who the hell even are you?" I asked. Most of my adversaries who fitted his description were dead. He was human, or at least half human. It'd taken me until now to realise he'd been speaking to me in English the whole time, not High Chthonian like Azurial and Themedes had. "What's your issue with me?"

"Nothing, Devina," he said. "Your friends, on the other hand, have an irritating habit of getting under my feet."

"Yeah, we do," said Rachel. "What's the deal with the mask, anyway? Demons always show their faces. What you are is nothing more than a human coward."

"I'm far more than human," he said. "Devi… I'm surprised you haven't guessed."

I shook my head. "You all blur together, to be honest. Bad guys aren't made like they used to be. I'm disappointed you're no demon, and you're not even a proper vampire either. Go on. Get on with it."

He removed his hood. I blinked at the unfamiliar white-haired man underneath. Nobody I knew well… but definitely someone whose face I'd seen.

For instance, in memorials at the celestial guild, of those killed when the old headquarters had burned down. Inspector Kenneth Angler.

Maybe he'd expected more of a reaction than he'd got. But all I could think about was Inspector Deacon. His former partner. If he knew what the guy he'd assumed dead was doing here… I bit the inside of my cheek, seized with the bizarre desire to laugh at the weirdness of the whole setup.

"You were raised from the dead as a demigod?" I asked. "I'm completely lost. I don't think we've ever spoken, for a start. If you wanted more of a response, you should have appeared dancing in the pentagram in front of the Grade Fours."

"Stories of your defiance of authority reached even me, Devina," said Inspector—ex-Inspector—Angler. "And I wasn't raised from the dead. My former partner saw fit to put me in harm's way to further his own ambitions."

I gaped at him a little. "The inspector? To be honest, I thought *he* was the villain."

"Of course you did." His mouth twitched. "He's never been good at hiding his true nature, and it tends to come out in times of crisis. I'd have forgiven him for what he did if I hadn't survived the attack, only to end up in a demon's realm. Imagine my shock when I fought my way out, only to be told there was no place at the guild for me anymore. The guild isn't good at accepting its outcasts. They haven't changed."

No kidding. But I hadn't even known this demon realm had been involved in the attack on the guild's former head-quarters. The story—documented with witnesses—was that Faye Carruthers, former celestial, had summoned a brutal demon and set it loose in the guild. Many had died, this guy included.

Except not only was he not dead, he'd now joined forces with the demons who'd attacked the guild.

"Vampires weren't involved in that attack," I said.

"No," Inspector Angler said. "They came along later, thanks to the information provided by my contact inside the guild. The vampires in this realm are harder to find than the ones in yours, but they're very adaptable, and were helpful in aiding Azurial in his coup."

"You and him? You want to share power with an arch-demon's child?"

"Power? No. But I'm curious to know how you survived that fire. I have my guesses, but... I'd like to hear it from you directly."

I reached for my sword instead, and an explosion of noise hit my ears. Bits of chain flew outwards from where Nikolas was tied up—or had been tied up. A pair of dark shadowy wings sprouted from his shoulders, and he whirled around, black lightning arcing across the room and striking the former inspector in the chest. He staggered but didn't fall, and I took my chance to grab my celestial blade again.

Rachel dropped to her knees as Nikolas stabbed the two vampires who'd held her, then launched himself at the enemy. The two collided in a deafening crash that shook the whole room. Lightning appeared and flared out, making my hair stand on end with static. I might be able to walk through demonic fire, but demonic lightning would fry my skin off.

Both fought with handfuls of dark-edged lightning, eerily similar-looking. But the vampire king—Inspector Angler—wasn't shadow-aligned, and even demigods couldn't use more than one type of magic at once. *How did he get that magic?*

Then fire burst from his hands, aimed directly at Nikolas. He dodged, his wings carrying him out of range. *That was Azurial's fire.* The exact same. But he'd used Nikolas's lightning before. Could he steal magic? Was that his ability?

Nikolas's wings beat, and he landed at my side. If not for the anger, the rage and the fear, I'd have taken more than a second to admire his true demigod form—a fallen angel with shadowy wings, etched in glowing light like the lightning he wielded.

"I can't get a handle on him at all," he growled at me. "He's drawing on power—from everywhere."

"He uses other people's magic," I said. "Other demons. He's using Azurial's—and yours. Can't you stop him?"

"No, I can't. I don't know if he has a weakness. He's no demon."

"Then how can he use your power at all?"

Azurial appeared in a beat of wings and a flash of fire.

"That wasn't part of the deal," he said to the former inspector. "I *need* that power."

"Too bad for you," responded Inspector Angler, conjuring lightning to his hands. "It takes a demigod's power to beat another demigod. As for the girl—"

"She has a name," I cut in. "What did you do with the portal? Why go to all that trouble just to blow up your own demons?"

"Those two weren't meant to survive." He jerked his head at Nikolas, then he laughed. "Looks like your little pink-haired demon girl ran away."

*Rachel.* Had she come up with a plan? It wasn't like any of us could match the magic of two individuals with demigod-like power single-handedly. Nikolas would certainly try, but with the enemy able to draw on his power and Azurial's at the same time, how could we hope to overcome both of them at once?

"You never should have broken your chains," Nikolas said to Azurial. "This time you'll be buried in a more permanent manner."

"Damn right." I ran at him, but the former inspector appeared in front of me, black lightning surging over my head.

"Are you incapable of coming up with your own magic?" I yelled at him, summoning my sword. "Or is everything you do stolen from other people? I don't even believe this was all your idea. You're a hack. Explains why you and Azurial get along so well."

He blasted me with fire again. I dodged, though the heat didn't burn me. Lightning followed, sizzling the ground at my feet. More powerful than any non-demon had the right to wield. I dodged his attacks and retaliated with a vicious swipe from my celestial blade, only to slam into a fiery shield. Another trick he'd stolen from Azurial. I'd never met a demon who could mimic another's magic, but it sure as hell didn't come from a weak parasite. This guy had another demon's magic entirely.

There was only one type of magic that was stronger than mine and Nikolas's.

*An arch-demon's.*

Had he taken in some of Themedes's magic, too? Azurial had initially drawn on it to fuel his own power, but his defeat at my hands would have long since dispersed that energy, and Themedes hadn't been near the palace since. Not to mention stealing Nikolas's power wasn't part of Themedes's skill set.

Which left one conclusion… he must be demon marked. Like me. He carried the power of one of the fallen Divinities.

*But that means our demon marks are equal.* The problem was, of course, that he knew how to use his magic. I didn't. Unless… unless it was the same one.

He'd stolen Nikolas's powers. I'd never done anything like that—but Themedes's power was definitely inside my mark, somehow. Was that why? Had he somehow known what my ability was all along? *Of course—the former inspector's been here a while.* Themedes must have seen him… but of course the tight-lipped bastard had gone to his grave without telling me a damn thing. But he *had* given me some of his magic, in the moment of his death. And it'd saved my life.

Inspector Angler's palms splayed, and lightning surged towards me. I jumped through the demonglass floor and emerged out of range, raising my demon marked hand. As though it'd been waiting for my permission, it lit up, power crackling inside it. Lightning rippled up my arm, more of a pleasant tingle than a painful one, and exploded from the end, bouncing off the floor. I'd missed—but I'd really done it.

Now to do some damage.

When the enemy fired at me again, I shot lightning back. Black-edged bolts of light sizzled against one another, extinguishing one another.

He laughed. "You finally worked it out? I'm disappointed it took this long, Devi."

Instead of an answer, lightning spiralled in twin attacks from my right hand, mingling with the celestial light from my left one. It slammed into him, lifting him off his feet. I ran forwards, only to collide with a wall of lightning that raised the hairs on my arms—but didn't hurt. I'd taken in the lightning power, which must have made me immune to his own attacks.

But that meant the same applied to him. Unless one of us

found some new demonic power or I got close enough to use my celestial blade, we were at a stalemate. Either I needed to find a whole new kind of magic, or something more mundane.

I reached for a stake—one of my last ones—put the lightning power behind it, and hurled it at his chest.

He moved to dodge, so it sank into his ribs instead of hitting his heart, but blood immediately blossomed from the wound. I took my advantage and ran up to him, drawing my celestial blade, but he raised a hand and shot lightning at my feet. My hair stood on end again, and he straightened up, grinning. Regenerative powers? I'd bet my demon mark he'd stolen those from one of the demigods, too.

"Nice try," I said, drawing another stake. He summoned lightning and blasted it to pieces. The power in his hand was from a fallen Divinity. Like mine. Was it even possible for me to kill him, without knowing how to truly kill a demigod?

*He's no demigod. He's borrowing the power by proxy. There must be a way to drain it.*

My celestial blade sank into his chest, impaling him to the floor. He screeched—and disappeared through it.

*You dickhead.* He'd even stolen my demonglass power.

*"Get back here!"* I jumped through the floor with barely a conscious thought, landing in a corridor outside the hall where I'd confronted Azurial the first time around. The scent of brimstone clung to my nostrils, and several dead demons lay sprawled, some of them in pieces. Rachel, in her demon guise, stood in the centre.

"I'm sorry, Devi," she said. "There was a portal here—it already closed. I was too late."

"A portal?" I echoed. *"Where?"*

"The portal let the vampires directly into the celestial guild. They're dead."

## 22

"Shit," I said. "The vampire king—Inspector Angler—he used my ability. He didn't come here, did he?"

Rachel shook her head. "No. What do you mean, used your ability?"

"He's marked. Both of us have the same one—we can steal other demons' powers. But the guild... I can't go there. Not directly. There's no demonglass back in our realm aside from at the warlocks' place."

The guild couldn't be gone. No way. They were tougher than that. I'd wonder how the demons had transported themselves directly inside there, but I'd bet that bastard of a celestial betrayer had something to do with it.

"Then we'll go there first," Rachel said. "I'm not seeing another option here. How the hell do you kill that guy? Is he pretty much like a demigod without the weaknesses?"

"Basically. He can steal regenerative magic, too. But he'll go into our realm for sure, given the chance. He has a really strong personal grudge against the inspector. I'm surprised he hasn't done it already." My own demon mark didn't prevent me from travelling through portals—*I think.* Maybe it did, especially now I'd unlocked its true power. I'd used the demonglass to get here, not the actual portal.

I spun around at the echo of beating wings, but it was Nikolas. He landed beside me, his shadowy wings folding against his back. "I temporarily subdued Azurial, but he'll regenerate."

"The vamps are at the guild," I told him. "They used a portal. No idea where the old inspector went, but his army's in our realm. Stands to reason that's where he plans to go, too."

"Unfortunately, I think you're right," Nikolas said. "But you can't transport yourself directly there."

"Actually," I said, "I can."

For a moment, I expected him to challenge me. To say the guild's safety wasn't worth the risk. Nikolas's eyes narrowed. He knew my plan—and it depended on both of us. "The guild wants us dead."

"If they die, so does the city, and possibly the world."

"That's good enough for me," Rachel said. "I'm in."

I frowned at her. "You both weren't supposed to guess the plan."

"We know how you work by now," Rachel said. "Jump in without warning and break shit."

"Too right. Get hold of me, both of you."

They did. And we passed through the demonglass floor, falling fast. Then we emerged in the pillared corridor in the castle of Babylon. Thankfully, no ambush waited. The night sky outside was a stark contrast to the brightness of Pandemonium's gleaming pillars.

"We're on top of the guild now, right?" asked Rachel.

"Yeah, we're in the upstairs corridor," I said. "Good enough."

A second later, Nikolas's shadow magic surrounded us, to be replaced by an explosion of noise as we landed directly in the celestial guild. Nobody looked to see the three people materialise in the upper floor corridor, because nobody was here. The sounds of fighting drifted through the open window. I left the room and ran for the stairs, my heart sinking at the sight of blood on the beige wallpaper I'd hated so much.

I climbed downstairs, following the direction of the noise. The smell of burning and brimstone drifted through the corridors. I paused besides the windows looking across the quad, and gasped. The forbidden part of the guild—the tower I'd never had the chance to explore—was in ruins. Didn't take a genius to figure out where the celestial vamp had set up the portal.

"Oh, hellfire," I whispered, wrenching my gaze away from the carnage. No bodies lay outside, but smears of blood on the walls and floor indicated the dead and injured had been dragged away. Sure enough, the doors to the entrance hall were open, and two celestials carried the body of a fallen novice inside. Behind, I glimpsed more bodies lined up on the wooden floor. Including...

Mr Roth lay amongst the dead.

*They have no leader. That leaves the position wide open to...*

*The inspector.*

Horrified screams drifted in from the glass doors to the lobby. The celestials must have driven the enemy out of the building—but they'd had no warning. The demons had crept into the heart of the guild and killed their leader in cold blood.

Not demons... vampires. Black-eyed vamps tore open the neck of a young novice, and anger exploded through my nerve endings.

*I'll kill you all.*

Celestial blades sang, lighting the air. Vampires darted in and out of the chaos, fangs bared, knives and daggers in hand. So that's how they'd managed to do so much damage. Unaffected by the bright lights, they recovered swiftly from every hit, moving faster than any celestial could. But of course—the higher ranked soldiers would still be around the warehouse. Only novices had been left behind, half of whom didn't even have access to a celestial blade yet.

My stake sank into a vampire's back, and I whirled to my next opponent. Ignoring my itching demon mark, I used stakes to subdue every vamp I could. My demon mark kept up a constant burning sensation, longing to release infernal fire on all of them. If I did, though—the anti-demon wards were right there. They'd burn *me* alive.

"DEVI LAWSON!" shouted a horribly familiar voice from behind me.

I ignored the shout and withdrew my stake from another vamp's back. So the inspector *had* shown up, and actually joined in the fight at that. Blood stained his smart suit and his hair was unusually rumpled. Bad Haircut Sammy stood so close to him, I'd bet my sword he'd been hiding behind the inspector during the battle.

Both of them stared at me in horror—or more specifically, at Rachel, who still wore her demon guise and had her teeth buried in the back of a vampire's head.

"What in damnation are you doing here?" roared the inspector.

"Saving your ungrateful necks," I said in answer. "You're welcome."

"You—you brought warlocks *here?*" he spluttered.

"The vampires left the doors open," I said. "I don't have an army, so I brought these two."

Lucky Nikolas had kept his wings hidden this time around. He shot lightning at two vamps, knocking them away from a group of young celestial novices huddled against the lobby wall. Blood, glass and other debris littered the once immaculate space. As for what they'd destroyed in the tower… if it really did contain all the guild's research, they'd lost a ton of resources. Of course the former inspector didn't need to steal any information, not when he knew it all.

I needed to break the news to Inspector Deacon, but his scowl indicated he wouldn't accept any excuse from me, least of all the notion that his former partner had come back from the dead.

"Inspector Deacon," I said. "There was a portal set up in your tower by a traitor celestial soldier. That's how the vampires got in. The second portal at the warehouse was also set up by the same person. He might have more hidden throughout the city. Or even under our feet. He aims to kill all of you."

"*Who?*" he demanded.

"Damian Greenwood," I said. "But the real one calling the shots is Inspector Kenneth Angler."

He looked at me like I had three heads.

"She's telling the truth," Nikolas said.

Rachel nodded, blood dripping from her serrated teeth.

"I won't accept this lie," he said. "Never. Inspector Angler died four years ago—"

"Or so *you* told everyone," I said. "You betrayed him, just to further your own career. He did this, inspector. The blood of your own people is on your hands."

His face reddened in fury, and celestial light sprang to his palms. I'd never seen him use it before, but he'd been a legendary fighter in his day.

"I really wouldn't," I said. "Nikolas and I will have to hurt you, and that'll look awkward for your reputation. If you don't want a fire demon materialising on top of you, I'd hold your fire. Literally."

He didn't look amused. "Devi Lawson—what is that on your hand?"

Shit. Smoke had helpfully begun to pour from underneath my right sleeve. "Vampire bite. Thanks for nothing, by the way."

Nikolas stepped up behind me, and we disappeared into the shadows, landing outside Babylon's castle. Apparently, the lobby overlapped with the space just outside the castle's front doors.

I twisted away from him. "The hell was that in aid of?"

"He would have killed you, Devi," he said.

"That can't have been the end of the battle," I said. "I thought for sure Inspector Angler should have shown up in person. He must be using another portal."

"I'm inclined to let him and the inspector finish one another off."

"You and me both, but I don't want the city to be collateral damage, either." I grimaced, shaking my demon marked hand in the hope that it'd stop smoking. "What about Azurial? Because last time he planned to use celestial energy to cross realms, and there are an awful lot of pissed-off high-ranked celestials running around. Not to mention people who've been bitten."

He gave me a dark look. "If that's still his plan, we're in a lot of trouble. But I suspect Azurial has been acting as a puppet for a long time."

"Ow." My demon mark continued to pour smoke out, blazing bright. "What the hell is happening to it?"

"I can guess," he said. "You absorbed more than one kind of power, didn't you? I'd wager it's overloaded."

"So I need to use it? But—I can absorb *any* power? Even from a demigod *and* an arch-demon at the same time?"

"Only because the mark belongs to an arch-demon," he said. "If my knowledge of demon marks is accurate, your ability works on anything below that level. He's the same."

"And we have the same mark." Wait. "How much of your

magic did he steal?" Being in his own realm meant it'd regenerate, but when faced with a normal demigod, Inspector Angler could drain them dry. No wonder he had Azurial under his control.

My gaze drifted to Zadok's tower. The one place where there was a chance in hell of luring either of the enemies away. If I was prepared to face the one who owned the tower.

"Nikolas," I said. "You have an army inside that castle, right?"

"No. Absolutely not."

"They'll destroy Haven City. You know what Zadok has— it's the real deal. If we redirect the portal over there, the army will land in Babylon instead. I'm pretty sure Zadok's army of scorpion demons, not to mention the other demons living out there in the wastelands, can take those vamps to pieces with no issue. That'll leave our realm safe, and give me a shot at killing him."

His mouth pressed together. "And throw this realm into chaos, too. My brother will never make a deal with you."

"It's that or let the city burn. I'm not bargaining with your brother. I'm stealing from him." I held my demon marked hand up. "I've got this, okay? Trust me."

"I do trust you. I don't trust *him*."

"You and me both, but seriously. This has to be done. I'm going to Pandemonium to head them off, and then—"

"If they're even still there," Rachel said darkly. "But I'm in. I watched one realm fall. I won't let it happen to ours."

Nikolas's jaw tightened. "We can't stay out here anyway. We need to find more demonglass. Devi—I think this is a mistake."

"Then argue with me about it later." I took off towards the front doors, but Nikolas shook his head.

"Use the side door," he said. "We don't want to run into anyone inside the castle."

I heard *especially not my brother.* Not stopping to argue, I made for the side entrance again. Despite my unfamiliarity with the rest of the castle, I knew this section by heart, including the path to the pillared walkway. I even kept pace with Nikolas on the way there. Maybe I really was going full-on demon. The inspector had definitely seen the smoke pouring off my sleeve, and I didn't exactly have a ready-made explanation he'd believe. Add in the Grade Four's disbelief about the reason for my aura change and the idea that I'd ever be able to put this behind me seemed an impossibility. But right now, I couldn't summon up half a fuck to give. All my attention was focused on my enemy.

Pushing my sleeve up to reveal my demon mark, I pressed it to the glass pillar.

"Let's go."

I thought as hard as I could about the white-haired wannabe-demigod, picturing him in my mind's eye. Then I shoved my hand through the pillar, and we passed through into Pandemonium—

And fell into empty air. The city wheeled below, sandy roofs careening around us. I flailed, desperately kicking out to make contact with the nearest solid object—which happened to be the side of the palace. Rachel clung to my back, yelling in my ear. There was the sound of beating wings, and Nikolas's hand snagged the back of my coat, yanking me upright. We slowed, rotating on the spot. Gasping for breath, I took in the details—the castle tower we'd just fallen out of, and directly below, in the courtyard, the large outline of a pentagram. *He's portalling into our realm.*

I shouted to Nikolas, who directed his descent in that direction. Fire licked the edges of the portal, and Azurial stood in the centre. His head raised to look at us, and the flames leapt into the air, aiming at Nikolas.

He flew higher, and the flames dashed past, narrowly

missing us. Azurial's winged form rose, fast as Nikolas himself. Fire flared from his hands. It didn't burn me, but Nikolas and Rachel were vulnerable, and my smoking, burning demon mark made it impossible to concentrate enough to grab a weapon. Not to mention I'd die if I hit solid ground from this height.

"Drop me into the portal!" I yelled, my words snatched away on the breeze. Rachel whooped as we flipped upside-down to avoid the fire, and Nikolas swore, lightning arcing from his fingertips. Azurial was too fast to hit, his fire just as powerful. Worse, it was fuelling the portal below both of them. And if just one of them got through to our realm, people would die.

Nikolas flew back above a castle balcony, yelling something to Rachel. I caught the gist—we needed to let go, before Azurial knocked one of us out of the air.

Someone slammed into my back without warning. I fell several feet, catching hold of the balcony high off the ground. Righting myself, I spun to face Damian.

"Watch it," I said. "If I hadn't landed there, we'd both be dead."

"I can't die. You know... even celestial vampires are immortal." He laughed. "And I'm the first of my kind."

"Watch your ego doesn't pull us both into the inferno over there."

Risking a look over the edge, I saw the portal directly below. Nikolas and Rachel had disappeared, fighting Azurial in mid-air, leaving Inspector Angler entirely unchecked. And this dickhead was between me and shutting that damn portal off before it unleashed hell on Earth.

Grabbing a stake, I swung it at him, but he caught my hand in his, driving both of us towards the balcony's edge.

"This ends for you, Devi," Damian said. "If you're not with us, then you're our enemy."

"Glad we cleared that up." I twisted free, the inferno roaring from the portal making my hair stand on end. "You deserve to burn for what you did."

"I offered the vampires a lifeline," he said. "The guild has known for a long time about the potential for cures for vampirism in demon venom. But they hoarded that information for their own selfish gains. Isn't anything worth being able to walk in the daylight again? The vampires I've spoken to certainly seem to agree."

"Nothing's worth having a demonic parasite in your head." Fire sprang from my fingertips, narrowly missing him. He ducked, eyes widening. *So he didn't know I absorbed Azurial's power?*

"The demons will flood our realm either way, Devi," he said, his words muffled by the crackling flames. "The celestials are built to fall, like the Divinities."

"You know what happens when you're idiotic enough to jump at someone on a balcony?" Fire leapt from my fingertips, driving him backwards to the edge. His eyes widened, but an inexplicable smile curled his lips. "See you in hell, Devi."

A fresh set of flames roared from my hands, driving him over the edge and into a torrent of fire.

The portal had already opened.

## 23

Damn it all. The former inspector had disappeared behind the surging fire, and I was still stuck twenty feet above it. With no way to shut it down. I had only one option remaining. Demon mark flaring, I stepped back through the demonglass wall.

Zadok didn't flinch when I appeared in front of him on the carpeted floor of his tower. "Nice of you to drop in and visit," he said.

"Don't fuck around. Give me that device of yours."

"This?" He tossed the pentagram between his hands, deliberately out of reach. "Now, why would I do that? You already turned me down once."

Lightning spun from my fingertips. "Because things will get pretty uncomfortable for you if you don't."

He smirked. "You do have demon magic after all. Strange. It looks awfully like—"

I directed the demonic lightning at him, twin streams trapping him on either side. He glanced left and right, still grinning. "I like this from you, Devi."

"Give it over. *Now.* I'm not playing your games." Lightning struck inches from his feet. I could get used to this.

"Well, now, there's no need to be hasty. You're welcome to it. I think you could make good use of it, and I'm very much looking forward to watching the show."

The pentagram flew from his fingertips and I caught it on reflex, demonic lightning still flowing from my other hand.

"See?" he said. "I'm no enemy of yours. I don't particularly want the nether realms to flood this one, believe it or not. But you owe me for this, Devina."

"I'll be the judge of that."

I stepped back through the demonglass and emerged from the outside of the tower, landing in front of the bridge —and its customary army of scorpion demons.

"Got something for you," I said, holding up the pentagram. If it worked like any other, I knew how to activate it.

Fire shot from my hands, into the pentagram. Themedes's fire—and Azurial's. The essence of that dimension. The scorpions backed away as I threw it down, fire still surging within, raising an inferno. Within, all manner of horrors rose, demons of fire, and behind them… the shadowy outline of Inspector Angler.

I called my celestial blade and ran forward, hoping the combined power of heaven and hell was enough. We might bear the same mark, but he used his with more confidence. Had he had direct contact with the one who'd marked him? It wasn't like I could stop our battle for a friendly chat, but still. It'd be nice to know why the Divinity who'd marked me was playing for the enemy team, too.

Lightning forked from both his hands, colliding with my own. Several smaller demons and vampires emerged behind him, surging towards me. So this was the army he'd planned to unleash on Earth.

I waved a hand at the scorpion demons behind me. "Give them hell," I said.

Enemies or not, no demon would let an attack on their own territory go by without punishment. As the venos demons lumbered out to meet their foes, I raised my hands and summoned my demonic power.

Fire surged past, barely ruffling Inspector Angler's hair. Two grappling winged shapes appeared in the pentagram. *It's synced into that realm.* The others must have flown close to the portal, and now they'd been drawn here, too.

Nikolas's dark shadowy form clashed with Azurial's bright one, neither giving ground. Hoping he had the situation in hand, I renewed my attack on the former inspector. Ducking another lightning blaze, I ran out behind the scorpion demons, my hand raised high. It didn't respond to their closeness and I wasn't stupid enough to stick my hand in venom, but apparently I couldn't absorb their power. *It must only take in powerful magic, then.* Grade Three or higher. Right up to arch-demon level.

Inspector Angler faced me across the bridge, perilously close to the edge with no apparent fear of falling. Neither of us had wings, unlike the warring demigods above. And our power was entirely on loan. But the fire of an arch-demon, borrowed or not, was powerful enough to bring an army crashing to its knees.

Several larger demons leapt from the portal at me. I grabbed my celestial blade, severing heads and claws. As I did, he inched backwards, towards the portal again. *Nope. Don't you dare.*

My blade came down and I jumped high, using my boots to catch my balance before the portal. "It's no use," I shouted above the crackle of flames. "The pentagram will keep summoning you back. You can't run from me, Kenneth.

You'll never get your conflict with Inspector Deacon, but you'll sure as hell get one from me."

Lightning cloaked him on all sides, an evolution of Nikolas's ability I hadn't seen before. My attacks simply bounced off, even with a clear shot. As another bolt shot from his hands, the bridge trembled underneath. I stepped forwards, calling my demonic power again. Inspector Angler and I circled one another. Lightning speared from his hands, only to fizzle out on contact with me. I shot fire back, which he dodged. With the fire demon close by, he could keep siphoning off his powers—but so could I.

Lightning whipped from his hands, grabbing my ankles and pulling me over the edge of bridge. Below, waters surged, too deep to see what might be lurking inside. I kicked out, grasping the cold stone with my fingertips. *No. I won't fall. I can't die here.*

"Sure would help to be able to fly." I didn't think of something fast, I'd be on my way to a watery grave.

Thick, dark shadows rose to bolster me, pushing me back onto the bridge, and I found solid ground beneath my feet. *No way. That can't be—*

"You're not done, celestial," whispered Zadok's voice from inside the shadows.

Seven hells. It really was him. But why save me?

"Thanks," I said. "Any tips?"

"You're still thinking of both hands as separate. That's your issue. Even I can see it."

*Both hands?* Celestial and demon. Wait...

Of course. The Divinity had fallen... but it was the same being who'd given me both marks. Maybe I wasn't supposed to choose one over the other. They were reflections of one another. Celestial and infernal fire, one in each hand.

The shadows receded, leaving me on the bridge once

again. In front of me, the former inspector stood cloaked in lightning and fire.

I pressed the marks together.

Fire surged from one hand to the other, both stemming from the one who'd given me the mark. An arch-demon. I was channelling *his* magic, and it was far stronger than Inspector Angler's. After all, he'd entirely given up the celestial part of himself. Even if he still had it, I'd bet he hadn't touched his celestial power in ages. He'd cast them off, utterly, turning himself entirely into a demigod.

Bright flames exploded from my celestial hand and demon hand both, clashing together in a torrent of light. Crushing his lighting and fire. Lighting up his expression of sudden terror.

He fell back, screaming, as the fire burned him. With a flying leap, he jumped into the portal again. *Dammit.*

Almost immediately, he materialised with darkness pouring from his hands. *Darkness... Zadok. He stole* his *power.* But I'd bet he didn't know how to use it.

I, however, did. My ability wasn't dimension-jumping or even fire—it was the power to take on any other demonic magic I encountered. I had his fire. I also had lightning.

And thanks to Zadok, I also had the power of the shadows.

I countered the enemy's shadows with darkness of my own, pouring from my right hand, surrounding him in the terrifying manner Zadok had once done to me. The former inspector was completely covered in darkness so absolute, nobody could see through it. He yelled in surprise, his senses abruptly cut off. Doubtless he could break out if he wanted— but the bridge kept him above the ground. If he stepped too far the wrong way, he'd fall into darkness.

*Now to finish the bastard.*

Celestial light in one hand, demon light in the other, I

called a fire that was both and neither. The inferno surged between my palms, crushing the darkness—and him—beneath it.

The fiery, shadowy mass fell over the bridge, dropping into the dark.

I watched, carefully, but he never rose again.

Then I stepped back, the god's power still in my hands. Looking up, I saw Azurial grappling with Nikolas. Deliberately, I raised my hands, took aim, and fired light at Azurial's wings.

The demigod dropped out of the sky like a stone. Nikolas flew down to meet him as he crash-landed on the bridge.

Azurial lay in a crumpled heap, unmoving. Nikolas looked at my hands. "What's that?"

"The gods' touch." I grinned. "Want to let me finish him off?"

"I was more into the idea of letting him suffer for defying me, but I'm intrigued to know what you can do with that."

"Watch and see."

Azurial gave a shriek of terror and attempted to crawl along the bridge. The fire reached him first. The demigod lit up, consumed in the god's flames, until nothing remained of him but ashes. Now I knew what could kill a demigod... the righteous hand of divine fire. It didn't burn me, not at all.

The portal rotated, flames still whirling inside it. I approached the pentagram, extinguishing my demonic fire, though it still burned beneath the surface. Zadok's shadows surged from my hands, blanketing the fire, switching off the luminous lights glowing around the edges. I waited, but it didn't turn back on, and this time, Zadok's voice didn't speak from the shadows. It was Nikolas who put an arm around my shoulders, taking the pentagram from me.

I turned to Nikolas with a nod. "Let's go home."

2 4

---

While Nikolas used his shadow power to remove every trace of the demons from the bridge, I stood at the side and tried not to look at Zadok's tower. I knew I'd have to pay a price for him helping me out eventually, but I didn't have the energy to feel anything other than glad to be alive.

"That's the last of them," Nikolas said, the shadows disappearing. "I assume their leader's body fell into the river. There are enough demons in that water to strip him down to the bone."

"Lovely image," I said. "He won't come back, anyway. He's no demon, no matter how much of their magic he took." Sure would be nice to know why the arch-demon had chosen to mark him, but it was too late to ask, and I'd had quite enough of arch-demon magic for one day.

First stop: check on Pandemonium. We found Rachel in a deserted corridor, in her human form and sitting on a heap of dead vampires. "There you are," she said, picking blood off her fingernails. "I was starting to get bored."

"All taken care of," I said. "Both of our troublemakers are dead." Still, the idea that the fallen Divinity would mark anyone else at all didn't put my mind at ease. I was still for all intents and purposes a potential pawn in the war between heaven and hell.

But with the gods' fire in my hands, maybe I could overcome that.

Next stop: Fiona, and the warlocks' guild. My heart climbed into my throat when we passed easily into the demonglass room. My phone buzzed instantly, now the connection was back. Ignoring it, I walked out into the corridor.

"Fiona?" I called.

"I hid her upstairs," Javos said from the open door to the living room.

I breathed out. "Thank you."

His tone implied *you owe me for this.* He wasn't the only one. I dreaded what Zadok would think I owed him for helping us out during the fight. For whatever reason, he'd sided with me over Pandemonium. Doubtless demonic scheming was involved, but I'd deal with that later.

Nikolas walked in behind me, with Rachel at his side. "Is this realm stable?"

"As much as you'd hope," Javos said. "Looks like someone directed all the instability elsewhere." His gaze lingered on me. *Oh boy. Here goes.*

Somehow, we got through the explanation without him blowing anyone's head off. Fiona gawped at me through the entire thing, and even Rachel raised an eyebrow when I mentioned wielding the gods' magic. When I finished speaking, silence fell.

"You're a thorn in my side," said Javos.

"Thanks."

"You're a menace, a liability, too damned dangerous to be

allowed to wander off alone, and possibly the greatest asset we have in this realm."

I blinked. "Thanks for laying it all out. Is there any reason you want me on your side other than my usefulness, and the fact that you don't want the enemy getting his claws on me?"

"No," said Nikolas. "Javos thinks in terms of assets only as far as everyone else is concerned. That includes me and Rachel, and every other warlock."

"Then what incentive do I have to stay?" I asked. "I can use this power alone. I have done."

"What you get is the best backup squad in any realm," Rachel said. "Also, Javos might not like you, but I do. You're a riot, and your friend's pretty awesome too, for a human. And Niko—"

"Would like to add his own reasons at a more appropriate time," he said, in tones that sent warmth tingling down my arms. It more than made up for Javos's indifference. I didn't need his approval, or anyone else's.

Javos cleared his throat. "You'll follow our rules, except in case of an emergency like this one."

"I feel like it won't be the last," I said.

"No," said Nikolas. "Babylon in particular is a target."

I frowned. "Why? We killed them."

"We can't erase evidence of the battle," he said. "Even with the bodies gone. That there's been a link between those realms at all... it's not good for any of us."

"Precisely," said Javos. "Luckily for the both of you, that's not my problem. I intend to report on today's events to the warlock council and I expect all of you to be present when I do so. For now, you should lie low."

No kidding. More like sleep for a week. But there was work to be done, and I doubted the Grade Four celestial soldiers would be leaving town anytime soon. The inspector and I would go head to head someday, even if he hadn't guessed what I was yet, or just how close the enemy had come to destroying the guild.

———

Cleaning up took a long time, especially when we were supposed to be in hiding. Not only had the rogue vamps left chaos behind them, others had been driven to flee by the threat of being found by the celestials, who saw any unregistered new vamp as a potential threat.

One day, while the others and I were at the warlocks' guild checking potential vampire hideouts' addresses, I got a message from Alec.

*Sorry I didn't get back to you. Am on the run with the others. Our names are on the celestials' wanted lists.*

"Wanted lists?" I echoed, looking across the office at Nikolas. We'd gathered in there as we often did, working on whatever Javos needed doing. Mostly, it was to do with removing all traces of the vampires' illicit activity and checking there were no more portals. The bloodstones' power had mostly burned out. With all bloodstone trade under close watch, the warlocks would be able to get hold of anything dodgy before it caused any more damage. At least, I hoped so. Those who'd been bitten should recover, in theory, without turning into bloodthirsty killers. But for those already addicted, fully transformed, then there'd be no reprieve. The celestials would hunt them down.

"For whom?" Nikolas asked.

"Vampires," I said. "The inspector wants the names of everyone who got bitten. It doesn't sound like there's much distinction between those who fully turned and those who didn't."

"Prick," said Rachel. "Let's bring them here."

"The vampires already said no," I said. "Madame White

will hand them over to the celestials to avoid anyone else getting infected. The others don't want the celestials to target them next."

"Nor do I," Nikolas said. "We're one step away from a war with hell, and our allies are as likely to kill us as anyone else."

"No kidding," I muttered, skimming through my messages. I'd also got one from Clover.

*Where have you been?* I messaged her.

*Avoiding the celestials. Your name's on their list, Devi.*

"Great," I said. "I'm on their watch list, too. I reckon Rachel's onto something. Fiona's already here. And there *might* be a cure. You said yourself—if we don't help them, the celestials will label them as a threat and slaughter them."

"We'll discuss the matter with Javos," said Nikolas.

Rachel grinned at me. "I'll get the music ready."

As she sidled out of the room, the two of us looked at one another. We'd hardly had the chance to talk since the aftermath, since we'd been so busy, and he'd seemed to be avoiding my eyes most of the time.

"Of course he won't say yes," I said. "But we'll do it anyway."

"I knew you'd give us a run for our money," Nikolas said, not making a move in my direction. My demon mark hadn't twinged since the fight, but merely the idea of being closer to him made it spark to life. I didn't know if there was any more of his magic left inside it. Now I had an explanation as to why his lure had affected me so strongly, but using it against him would have no effect. I'd been out of my mind with lust, but the need I'd seen in his eyes had been real.

"You bet," I said. "So… are you up for it?"

"Rescuing vampires?" He raised an eyebrow. "I suppose I don't need to tell you the risks. And anyone involved with the illegal bloodstones—or demon eggs—might be plotting to re-establish the link with Pandemonium. We can't ignore your role in this any longer." The words sounded like they pained him to say aloud. "You'll have to come with me to Babylon. It's easier that way.'

"You sure?" My voice rose in surprise.

"I'm more than sure." He took a step closer to me. "If you want to give this a go, there are certain things you'll need to know about me."

"Incriminating things?" My breath caught as he leaned forward, lips brushing against the curve of my ear.

"Sinful, certainly." His lips found mine, hot and intense, and warmth tingled up from my demon mark. Drawn to him… drawn to the shadow, wanting to take his magic. *Hey. Don't do that.*

Okay, maybe we had an issue or two to work through. Or my demon mark did. But now I knew how it worked, you'd better believe I had every intention of using it. Whether the arch-demons liked it or not.

"Sinful is more than fine with me," I said. "I'm ready to learn how to be a warlock."

# ABOUT THE AUTHOR

Emma is the New York Times and USA Today Bestselling author of the Changeling Chronicles urban fantasy series.

Emma spent her childhood creating imaginary worlds to compensate for a disappointingly average reality, so it was probably inevitable that she ended up writing fantasy novels. When she's not immersed in her own fictional universes, Emma can be found with her head in a book or wandering around the world in search of adventure.

Find out more about Emma's books at
www.emmaladams.com.